The Dream
Behind The Fence

Francine Bartholomew

The Dream Behind the Fence

ISBN 978-0-615-69299-9

Dedication

For the best family in the world, my husband and best friend, Don; my beautiful and incredible daughters, Ashley and Taelor, my wonderful and exceptional sons-in-law, Greg and Adam and my amazing grandsons, Carter, Tanner and Briggs. And for my other incredible family across the ocean, Bobbie, Dirk, Tiago and Dani, who popped into my life almost twenty years ago and became a part of our family and who will be a part of our family forever. Thank you all for your never-ending love and support.

Acknowledgements

My heartfelt appreciation to Don, Ashley, Taelor, and my dear friend Terry for reading and re-reading a multitude of edited versions.

A special thank you to the Mountain Point 4th Ward Book Club in Draper, Utah, for reading and reviewing my book in one of their monthly book club meetings and for offering their most helpful editing suggestions.

A well-designed book is not just the work of the author's words but also the publishing and editing team. I'd like to express my appreciation to Kimberly Martin, Stephanie Anderson and the entire team at Jera Publishing for their many hours and numerous design choices they offered in creatively designing the presentation of *The Dream Behind the Fence.*

Francine Bartholomew was born and raised in Salt Lake City, Utah. She now resides in Draper, Utah and works full-time at a leading molecular diagnostic company as a Senior Laboratory Administrator. Prior to that, she worked at a national point-of-purchase advertising placement company as the Director of Account Management, having accounts from the East Coast to the West Coast, where her duties included meeting with clients across the nation, producing training videos and writing instruction booklets for field representatives. In her early years she worked at a major telecommunications company as an Accounting Supervisor, where she trained employees in the Intermountain West on a functional accounting system.

Francine is actively involved in her church, and when she is not at work or at church, she spends as much time as possible with her family. She has been married to her high-school sweetheart, Don, for 47 years, and he is still the love of her life. Most Saturdays, she can be found shopping, running errands and going to lunch with her two daughters, Ashley and Taelor, who all claim to be "attached at the hip." She adores both of her sons-in-law, Greg and Adam, who tease her relentlessly and who she claims are more like sons than sons-in-law. Her grandchildren are her pride and joy. Her two oldest, Carter and Tanner are avid sports players, and Francine rarely misses one of their games, whether it's baseball, soccer, basketball, lacrosse or football, sometimes going to as many as eight games a week. She is often considered the "team grandma." Her family travels together almost every year and usually tries to include a professional sports game to attend wherever they go. They are truly a sports family and even have a family fantasy football league. Her youngest grandson and newest member of the family is Briggs. He has brought incredible joy to the lives of the entire family as everyone fights over who gets to play with him and hold him. He is destined to become a family sports enthusiast.

Roberta (nick-named "Bobbie" by their family), is her *adopted* daughter. She lived with Don and Francine and their girls for a year when she was in high school and truly became a member of the family. Bobbie is originally from Brazil, but has since married and moved to Switzerland. Her husband, Dirk, is like another son-in-law. Their boys, Tiago and Dani, are like grandsons. Francine's daughters consider Bobbie to be one of their sisters. Their family has visited the United States many times in the past twenty years, and Francine and her family have visited them in Europe. They keep in touch on a weekly basis.

Francine was involved for twenty-three years with the Festival of Trees, which is a large charity event to support the local children's hospital, Primary Children's Medical Center. It is the single biggest community fund raiser for the hospital every year. She served on their Board of Directors for six years. Her hobbies include tole painting, decorating and reading. She usually has a book in every room of the house and a book on CD in her car. She belongs to a book club called "Bookmark Babes." They meet once a month to review a book that was chosen the previous month. She always had the desire to write a book, but it wasn't until her club read "Twenty Wishes" that she actually decided to make it a reality. So that goal was added to her bucket list and has now become "THE DREAM BEHIND THE FENCE."

Table of Contents

September 2002

"Seize the moment of excited curiosity on any subject to solve your doubts; for if you let it pass, the desire may never return, and you may remain in ignorance."

William Wirt

Her eyes opened ever so gradually as she caught a partial view of the crisp morning sunlight beginning to peek through the large bedroom window. Frost covered the corners of the panes and she knew immediately that today would be another chilly day. Fall had emerged! Well, not officially, but there was no denying it was in the air. Everyone had complained about the unseasonably cold weather at the party last night, but Breck actually found it invigorating and was enjoying the change from the previous two months' sweltering heat. With that being said, she still had the urge to pull the soft, creamy white, down-filled blanket up under her chin for ten more minutes. She had debated at the time whether to spend that much money on a blanket, but this morning she was certain it had been a good investment. It gave her a nice warm, cozy feeling to lie there and reflect for a few moments on the events of the previous evening and then to quickly prioritize her tasks for the day ahead.

"What specifically had happened at the party last night that made the evening so enjoyable?" Breck wondered. She really couldn't put her finger on any one thing, but something was different. She always enjoyed being in the company of this diverse group of friends, but last night left her with a lingering, somewhat pleasurable curiosity that seemed to be occupying more of her thoughts than was justified.

When she got home, she went through her nightly routine. She washed her face with her new *Kiss My Face* olive bar cleansing soap, brushed and flossed her teeth and went straight to bed. She slipped under the covers, and lay there for a few minutes wondering what it was that had preoccupied her feelings to this extent. She lay there for awhile thinking about the evening, and it was the last thought running through her head right before her eyelids closed, and she traveled on a swift journey into a deep, comfortable, contented sleep.

And now, as the first morning light slowly peeked through her window, her eyes were gradually forced to open and she was compelled to cross from that somewhat foggy space in time between a bleary sleep and total wakefulness. Her very first distinguishable thoughts once again transported her to the previous evening's party.

For the most part, it was the same usual crowd that got together on a pretty regular two-month basis and on most special occasions and holidays. Breck was thirty-one now, and it crossed her mind that many of them had been enjoying each other's friendships since college, over ten years ago. However, there were a few faces that were new to her—invited guests of Clark and Heather and an acquaintance of Scott's. She hadn't really spent too much time with any of them, so she rationalized that it couldn't be the guests that made the evening stand out. What little time she did spend with them was pleasant enough, but it was just that—a little time—so she convinced herself they weren't responsible for leaving her with this most inquisitive sensation.

It had taken just fifteen minutes to learn that Clark and Heather's friends, Adam and Celeste Montgomery, had just moved from Pembroke Pines, Florida about three weeks earlier. Boulder, Colorado would most certainly be a sharply drastic adjustment for them. The weather alone would be a shock to their systems, but they appeared to be mentally prepared to accept it. Time would tell. They had visited Boulder a year ago on a ski vacation and had fallen in love with the majestic mountains. They discussed at that time what it would be like to trade the year-round sunshine and exotic white sandy beaches of Florida for a chance to ski in the clear, fresh mountain air in the winter. When the possibility of a job transfer came up for Adam, they explained how they weighed the *palms* against the *pines* and, with a giant leap of faith, agreed on the *pines.* They seemed to be adventurous and fun and Breck thought without hesitation, "They will be a welcome addition to this group."

Then there was Scott's friend. He was an old buddy from his childhood days who was visiting, according to Scott, for about two weeks. Greg Williams was hilarious and Breck found herself laughing at just about everything he said from his description of his chaotic flight out here to the trouble he and Scott had caused their sixth-grade teacher, Miss Denture. Her name alone lent the perfect opportunity for harassment from these 11-year-old boys, especially as Greg described her missing eye tooth on the upper left side and the crooked one on the upper right side. Breck was almost certain there was some exaggeration in his storytelling in order to expound upon his humor. Nevertheless, he seemed to capture everyone's attention as he cleverly narrated tale after tale. Whether his narrative was factual or fictional didn't really matter—he was darn funny! Breck didn't spend a whole lot of time in the group that seemed to crowd around Greg. It was her custom to mingle with everyone, and she didn't want a stranger to monopolize all of her time no matter how much she was enjoying it.

"But his eyes," Breck said to herself while lying under the covers. "What was it about those eyes?" she wondered. "Was it the gorgeous blue color?" They were a deep blue, with just a tint of green, making them almost turquoise, but not quite. She had seen beautiful blue eyes before, but Greg's were piercing, and it was hard to look away once they connected with hers. They were like the blue of the ocean pulling her in with the tide. And that smile. It was almost cocky as it turned up a bit more on the right. He was incredibly good looking, and she wondered why he had made this visit alone, and whether or not he had a wife and family or a girlfriend waiting for him back home. She made a mental note to ask Scott when she saw him at work on Monday, but she would have to think about how to approach the subject without Scott thinking she had more than just a casual interest. Breck was long past the stage of infatuation at first sight, but something intrigued her about this man, and she just couldn't isolate what it was. She reminded herself that she had learned long ago to be cautious about being enamored by anyone on their first meeting.

"Well, this is ridiculous," Breck thought as she came back to reality. She hadn't even taken a few minutes to rehearse in her mind what she was going to accomplish today, as was her normal custom, and she had already been lying there twenty minutes—ten minutes longer than usual and ten minutes wasted! "Oh, well," she thought. "At least it's Saturday, and I can allow myself to be a bit more flexible just this once." Normally, she gave herself ten minutes and then energetically hopped out of bed and proceeded to go about the day's agenda she had set forth in her mind. Breck's days rarely consisted of idleness.

She sat up and pulled the covers back stretching her arms up in the air then pulling them down to her side, making an audible noise as she stretched. As she swung her legs over the side of her king-size four-poster mahogany bed, her feet magically found their way into the cozy red slippers that lay waiting on the floor next to her. She walked to the bathroom with new morning vigor and brushed her teeth. As she turned on the shower and removed the slippers and matching red and black plaid *Lauren by Ralph* pajamas, the crispness of the morning startled her senses, and she was anxious to step in and have the warm, comfortable temperature of the water clear her thoughts. "I'll plan my day while I'm in the shower," she told herself, and she immediately put the questions about last night's activities out of her head. But the second the hot steam surrounded her, she closed her eyes and memories of the previous evening once again invaded her mind. All thoughts of planning her day vanished.

CHAPTER 1

April 2001
"The New Girl" (Greg & Scott)

"I do not think that what is called Love at First Sight is so great an absurdity as it is sometimes imagined to be. We generally make up our minds beforehand to the sort of person we should like, grave or gay, black, brown, or fair; with golden tresses or raven locks; -- and when we meet with a complete example of the qualities we admire, the bargain is soon struck."

William Hazlett

———————◆———————

"Her name is Parris Roberts," Greg told his roommate and best friend, Scott Freestone. "Like in France, only with two r's ... P-A-R-R-I-S," he spelled out for Greg's benefit. "She's so hot she sizzles like bacon on a hot griddle, and she was sitting directly in front of me in my Political Science class today. I slipped into my P.I. mode, looked over her shoulder and saw her name neatly written at the top of her notebook. I'm pretty sure she didn't even notice me, but every time she moved, I got a whiff of that exotic citrus perfume, and I felt like I was in the Garden of

Eden and she was tempting me with a strawberry-kiwi concoction instead of an apple."

Scott smiled at his description. Greg always had a knack for portraying everything in an unusual, yet humorous, way. He had been doing that ever since he could remember. Greg had moved into the house across the street from Scott's when he was six years old. It didn't take long for them to discover their birthdays were only two days apart, and within a week, they had become best friends. Now here they were in college, and nothing had altered that friendship. The bond had actually grown stronger through the years. They were like brothers, and Scott would do anything for Greg and he knew Greg would do the same for him. So he listened patiently and with genuine interest while Greg went on for at least fifteen minutes talking about Parris "like in France" Roberts.

"Greg, my man," Scott said with a smile. "I think you've been smitten by this goddess, and she doesn't even know you're alive. I guess I'm going to have to check her out and see if she is worthy of all this admiration."

Greg leaned over, picked up the ragged, oversized, comfy beige pillow off the floor and tossed it on the unsightly red and green faded tartan plaid hand-me-down sofa his grandmother had given them. Then with his back arched in a pole vault type position, he took a jumping leap, soaring across the coffee table and landing perfectly on the couch. His head hit the pillow flawlessly, with his body stretching out in a reclining position and his legs quickly, almost imperceptibly, crossing neatly at the ankles as they hung over the arm rest at the opposite end, demonstrating his expertise in this exceptional move. He had obviously done it a million times before. He grinned and said softly, almost as if he were talking to himself, "Oh, she's an angel. Of that I am sure. I can feel it with every fiber of my being."

With that, Scott felt a sudden flash of concern—like little warning lights going off in his head. He didn't know why. Greg was a big boy now and could take care of himself, but what he did know was that it was totally out of character for Greg to get serious about some girl he had never even met, and he knew him well enough to recognize when he was serious and when he was joking, and this was no joke.

Greg was tall, about six feet two inches, with very dark brown hair, the color of a strong cup of coffee, just a shade away from black. He had piercing blue eyes that captivated most girls the minute theirs linked up with his. In addition to his good looks, he had an appealing dry wit that came to him naturally. The jokes seemed to roll off his tongue without any effort or contemplation. However, being the complete package in no way affected his ego. Greg was actually quite humble which added to his charm, and if all the guys weren't constantly teasing him about staying home so that they could have a chance with the girls, he would never have even considered himself handsome. He saw himself as just another ordinary guy.

While most girls ached to be the one who would impress him, he had no desire for a serious relationship. He was focused on getting his degree and, "After all," he said, "college is the time of life when you should just be concentrating on your studies, fitting in very small doses of fun somewhere in between hitting the books." He lived by that philosophy and was determined not to let any relationship interfere with his goals. It was not the time for any kind of a commitment to anyone or anything other than the books. There would be time enough for that later. Of course he enjoyed dating and having fun, but he couldn't understand why anyone would want to rush into being tied to one person, so he never took any girl's advances seriously.

He and Scott had worked together on a construction crew for about a year and a half earning some money before going off to college. This made them a little late getting started, but they had remained focused on school, working particularly hard once they got there and signing up for lots of extra hours. Now they both had only one more year until they completed their master's degrees. Greg did not want anything to alter that path. This didn't stop practically every girl who met him from trying, but he was oblivious to their attempted advances. A long-lasting relationship was just not in the cards for these starry-eyed college co-eds.

Greg closed his eyes and his thoughts drifted back to the girl in class. He let his mind wander in circles as he played a number of scenarios over and over in his head, planning an approach to meet her. There just had to be a way, but it had to be perfect. He had no intention of coming off wrong and blowing it before it got started. He closed his eyes and actually dozed off for a few minutes, but his little nap didn't last long. He was startled awake when Scott attempted to knock his flip-flop off by hitting the foot that hung over the couch.

"Let's go grab some fine Chinese cuisine at Ming Li's," Scott said. "It'll be my treat." That perked his interest. Greg was always up for some good food, especially when someone else was picking up the tab, so it didn't take much coaxing; in fact, it took no coaxing at all. He quickly jumped up, ran his hand through his hair smoothing it just a bit, and said "It's difficult to argue with my belly since it has no ears. Lead the way."

Ming Li's was more like a sit-down fast food joint. There was nothing fancy about it, but it was good food and easy on the pocketbook, so lots of the college students gravitated to it, and Ming, the owner, wisely catered to the finicky tastes of the young crowd. No Peking duck, chicken in oyster sauce or anything quite so sophisticated, but plenty of tasty fried rice, pot stickers and sweet and sour pork. And best of all, it was just a fifteen-minute walk from the Florida Atlantic University's Boca Raton campus and even closer from their apartment.

With almost no effort at all, they took the stairs two and three at a time from their third floor apartment down to the ground floor, then walked across the small patch of lawn in front of their complex and cut through the parking lot of the Winn Dixie grocery store. The purpose of cutting through wasn't to avoid the few additional steps, but any shortcut they could find got them to the food that much quicker. It wasn't even 5:00 yet, but they both had the notion they were starving.

The day had been a pleasant 82 degrees and was just barely starting a slight cool-down when the breeze from the ocean started picking up. When they first arrived in Boca Raton, the odor of the salt sea air had been a little hard to get used to. They had lived more inland in Ocala, Florida near the Ocala National Forest, and they were convinced there was no fresher air anywhere. It didn't take long, however, for this smell to become part of what they loved most about Boca Raton—the beaches, the surfing and a reminder of their independence in this college town.

As they approached Ming's, the smell of the salt sea air was replaced by a far different aroma. At least halfway down the block the enticing scent started permeating their nostrils and tantalizing their taste buds. The big Chinese antique doors transformed the look of the otherwise ordinary façade of the building. Scott knew they must have been an extravagant addition to the building, but suspected the expense of such a purchase was worth it, drawing in locals and tourists alike. Instead of the usual tinkling sound of bells that was heard when walking through most restaurant or shop doors, they heard the sharp staccato sound of the big Chinese Shueng Kwong gong that was hooked up to announce the arrival of anyone walking into the restaurant. Somehow, the gong had been rigged to be less obtrusive than the reverberating blast it was capable of, thus eliminating any possible annoyance to those who were dining, but still loud enough to announce the arrival of anyone entering or leaving. As they walked through the massive front doors, they saw Suzy at the register. She smiled and without a word, she grabbed a couple of menus and started walking them to a table.

"And a good evening to you, Suzy-Q," Greg said, as he bowed slightly. "How is the prettiest Chinese lotus blossom I know?" She grinned at him and let a demure smirk escape from her mouth, accustomed to his sweet compliments by now, but never tiring of them. "You know, you put all the other girls in here to shame with your beauty, don't you?"

The cooking was still done by Ming. He brought others in to help from time to time, but this was his place, and he didn't want anyone trying to change the tried-and-true, generations-old recipes that were on his menu. He believed these authentic family recipes and combinations of fresh ingredients were what set his place apart from all the other traditional American fast-food Chinese joints. Nevertheless, at dinner time, he was forced to bring in help or else face the wrath of hungry students not getting their food quickly enough to satisfy their growling stomachs.

As Ming heard Greg's comments, he glanced up from behind the kitchen window, peering through the hot lights that hovered above the dishes sitting on the eye-level, stainless steel countertop. Suzy was Ming's daughter-in-law, and he felt very protective of her, but he knew Greg well enough by now to know that he was a stand-up guy just making a girl feel special. Suzy knew it too, and nothing he said was ever taken out of context as she was devoted to Ming's son, Wei, and only had eyes for him.

They were seated in a corner booth. Their table, like all the others, had a white linen cloth draped over the edges with a square piece of red vinyl fabric on top for easier clean up, thus avoiding the necessity of changing the white cloths for every patron. In the middle of each table sat a wrought iron lantern resembling a miniature pagoda. Each one contained a small candle which was always non-scented so as not to compete with the delicious aromas of the food. The lanterns gave off a modest amount of light, certainly not enough to light the room when it was dark, but enough to showcase the food and make it even more appealing. There were round paper lanterns hanging all over the dining area in a variety of shapes, sizes and colors, but heavy on red. Huge posters with beautiful pictures of China adorned the walls, with descriptive Chinese characters written across the bottom, although almost no one eating there could decipher what those characters were telling them about the picture.

Scott and Greg both knew, without so much as a glimpse at the oversized laminated menu, what they would order. Scott always ordered the sweet and sour pork and pot stickers combo, while Greg always ordered fried rice and chicken chow mein. That way they would each have their own bill, but when the food came they always ate it family style, sharing a part of each other's dishes. But this time, Scott ordered everything and told the waitress, "Put it all on one ticket."

While they were waiting for their food to come, Greg started quizzing Scott for clever ideas to meet Parris without looking stupid and scaring her off. Since Greg had opened up the topic for discussion, Scott felt this might be as good a time as any to approach him with some suggestions. "Hey, Buddy." Scott said. "Are you really sure you want to start something right now? The year is about over, and then we'll be heading home for the summer. If you still want, you could look her up in the fall when we come back, and I've known you long enough to know if she's not here, it won't be difficult for you to find someone else who is new and entertaining to spend time with during your last year. We all know you're a babe magnet. You know with less than a month left and with finals flooding our lives during the next few weeks, it might be a good idea to table this idea for the time being."

"Are you kidding?" Greg almost yelled the question. "I can't let this one get away. I'll never find another one like her. If I can figure out how to get acquainted, and if I know she won't be going off somewhere, I'll stay here for the summer."

Scott had just started to take a drink of his coke and he almost choked at hearing those words come out of Greg's mouth. "Who are you, and what have you done with Greg?" Scott asked. Mentally he was observing Greg. Normally he would laugh at the ridiculousness of the situation, but since it was so out of character, all he could do was worry. "She must have done something to lead him on," Scott thought to himself. "He couldn't just fall in love without even having met this girl."

Scott knew he was going to have to figure out a way to meet her himself and see just who this Parris girl was and what she had up her sleeve. Then it hit him. "My biology class is canceled next Monday" he thought. "I just might have to make a visit to Greg's Political Science class that day." Yes, that's what he would do. He would let Greg know that he would be there to help him figure out a way to meet Parris. This would give him a chance to get acquainted and figure out if she was the real deal without telling Greg what he was up to.

The waitress was heading to the table with their food and Scott couldn't wait to satiate his appetite, while he and Greg came up with a plan. But when he glanced over at Greg, his expression had changed. It was almost as if he were in a stupor. He wasn't taking any notice of the food that was being placed before them on the table. Scott followed his eyes to see what he was looking at. It was just another girl; one he hadn't seen in here before, but he was glad to see Greg looking at someone else. This was the old Greg, pretending to see an angel, with that familiar slightly upturned lip, barely giving way to a smile. He was just waiting for Greg's quip. She was a pretty red-head, with her hair flipped up in back and one side pulled up with a bright yellow and white daisy barrette that was a perfect match to her yellow and white sundress. Yes, this was the Greg that Scott knew and loved. "H-m-m-m," Scott thought. "This could be just what his buddy needed as a distraction." Scott could see she was alone, so he said, "Wouldn't it be a friendly gesture on our part if we invited her over to sit with us?" Chuckling, he looked over at Greg, who was still staring.

"It's her," Greg said almost hypnotic-like. "It's Parris."

CHAPTER 2

January 2002

"The Valentine Encounter" (Heather & Clark)

"Constant attention by a good nurse may be just as important as a major operation by a surgeon."

Dag Hammerskjöld

———◆———

I t was 5:30 p.m. and Heather Larson Neely was on her way to work at the 24-hour Family Care Clinic. It was her second week there, and she was still trying to adjust to the night schedule. Up until two weeks ago, most of her evenings had been consumed with homework assignments and studying for tests.

She had wanted to be a nurse for as long as she could remember. When she was four years old, she encouraged every girl in the neighborhood to bring her doll over so she could check out the colds, runny noses, sore throats, earaches or any other ailments and to put Band-Aids on every pen line that had accidently been marked on the cloth bodies. She told her friends they had bad scratches that needed to be cared for. She was so convincing that her four-year old friends almost believed her. Her mom jokingly told neighbors she had to buy Band-Aids by the case so that Heather could heal every doll within a ten-mile radius of their house. If a doll had a rip in her well-worn cloth body, it was a major problem that had to be dealt with using more than just a Band-Aid. These more severe injuries were wrapped up with her mother's scarves, and she was scolded more than a few times when her mother would go to wear one only to find it missing. She knew exactly where to go to find it, and when reprimanded, Heather wasn't repentant at all. She just cried and told her mother that one of Jodi's, Bonnie's or Cynthia's dolls was hurt badly and she just had to fix it.

As she got older, bikes and games replaced the dolls, and she was the one to run to anyone who fell and got a scratched knee or a cut on the elbow. She would help get them home to their moms, or if their moms weren't home, she would take them to her home and out came the Band-Aids again. In her teen years, her friends teasingly gave her the nickname of Florence, after Florence Nightingale, but really her compassion for others endeared her to just about everyone she met.

When she graduated from high school, Heather was determined to get her nursing degree in record time, taking extra classes and focusing on nothing but studies. She had taken college courses in high school, earning dual credits and giving her a jump at the end of her senior year. She didn't take the summer off for the usual graduation trip with friends, even though she was tempted when they elected to go to fabulous Cabo San Lucas. Nor did she decide to have one last summer of pure relaxation as some of her other friends were doing. Instead, she started right in with summer classes, not wanting to waste a single minute. Prior to making her college choice, she had investigated every nursing program in the state and after a great deal of research had determined that she would attend the University of Colorado at Denver where she could continue her education after she got her baccalaureate. Most of her friends wanted to get away from home and go somewhere far away so they could have what they called the *real college-life experience*, but Heather wanted to stay close to home so she wouldn't get caught up in the party life that so many students fancied. She wanted her focus to be on finishing her education in record time. With her previous credits and her dedication to hard work, it took only two and a half years to get her BSN degree, and at the end of those two and a half years, she met all the necessary criteria and passed the HESI 2A exam with flying colors.

Now she was focused on her graduate studies where she planned to get her master's degree and become licensed as a nurse practitioner. The NP program normally took about 43-52 semester hours to complete which included 12-14 credits of clinical experience. Her work at the clinic was part of those credit hours. The school sent the clinic good students, who were extremely helpful in covering their rush-hour and late-hour shifts. These shifts were always more difficult to fill, so the clinic was willing to work around the schedules of the students. It was a win/win situation.

Heather was eager to start her graduate studies but even more excited to be working at the clinic. The long hard push for the past two and a half years and the intense high school courses hadn't diminished her enthusiasm in the least. She was driven to accomplish the goal she had set years ago and was anxious to be doing what she loved so much. She was determined not to let anything get in her way.

The one thing she hadn't calculated into her seemingly perfect equation was Clark Neely. It was only eleven months ago when she let herself be talked into going to a Valentine's Day party at one of the neighboring student housing apartment buildings. Driving to work, she reflected on how much her life had changed in those past eleven months.

That Valentine's evening had been a night to remember. Her best friend, Breck, whom she did everything with, hadn't been able to go, so she went by herself, and still couldn't believe she had done that, since it was uncharacteristic of her. It was a rare outing for her and when she arrived, she wondered why she had let herself be talked into it.

The door entrance was draped with pink tulle with red crepe paper streamers hanging playfully from the ceiling. Walking through the streamers led her to what she immediately summed up as a land of enchantment. Almost instantly she was being introduced to a number of strangers. One of her neighbors she barely knew greeted her and locked arms with her, dragging her to meet one of her buddies. "Heather, this is Clark Neely. Clark, this is Heather Larson," Jill said. Clark didn't say hello or any such familiar greeting. All he said was, "Wow!" Then he took her hand and brushed his lips softly across the top of it. Somewhere deep in the pit of her stomach she felt the fluttering of butterflies that had apparently been trapped in cocoons, but had somehow been released the moment he took her hand. Clark was about six feet tall, had sandy blonde hair and hazel eyes. "Nice to meet you," she said, pulling her hand away as casually as possible without seeming rude or unfriendly, all the time pretending not to notice his dashing good looks and charming smile. He caught her off guard, and she excused herself rather abruptly to avoid putting her shaky hand on display for everyone to see—especially him. She turned away and nonchalantly walked to the other side of the room toward the buffet table where she could catch her breath and gain her composure. Memories of that evening flashed through her mind now, all of them seeming surreal yet vivid.

Ashley, Taelor and Bobbie had done a wonderful job on the decorations, she remembered. The hallway entrance and the pathway leading to the buffet table were dusted with pink and silver glitter. "What a mess they would have to clean up after this glitter was transported through the entire apartment from the soles of everyone's shoes," Heather thought. She would have to remember to wipe her shoes off before she walked through her own apartment when she returned home.

They certainly had spared no expense making everything look festive. In lieu of an entrance fee or buffet contribution, they had required everyone entering to be dressed in Valentine's Day colors, which meant a myriad of red, white and pink. There were people in white shirts with giant red hearts and girls with pink sweaters, pink bows in their hair or pink shoes. One guy had on a bold red, pink and silver plaid shirt, which drew a lot of attention, and Heather was certain after observing him for awhile that it was getting the exact reaction he had hoped for.

The table was stunning. In the center was a tall vase with pink and white roses. The giant vase was sitting in an even larger, but shallow clear glass bowl containing floating red carnations. The effect was awesome. All the hors d'oeuvres had been cut into heart shapes, and even the breadsticks had been formed into hearts. There were large, heart-shaped bowls filled with delicious salads, and each bowl sat on a red paper heart-shaped placemat. On each end of the long table sat beautiful candelabras, with pink candles glowing in the dimly lit room. Scattered randomly across the table, surrounding the countless dishes of food, were candy hearts and Hershey kisses wrapped in red, pink and silver foil. A small cardboard cupid hung from the chandelier directly above the table, while a life-size cardboard cupid stood behind the table waiting to strike any young romantic couple directly through the heart with his bow and arrow. She knew a lot of thought must have gone into these decorations and she marveled at the time it must have taken.

There were balloons galore. Some, filled with helium, were floating in the air, reaching for the ceiling in an attempt to get away from the crowd, but unable to succeed as they were tied securely to the ends of the buffet table, the lamps and the arms of the chairs. The floor was covered with solid white ones devoid of helium. Occasionally a popping sound could be heard as someone would step on one. For the most part, however, people walked through them effortlessly, their steps triggering the slightest breeze, causing them to glide through the air for a few feet before bouncing back to the floor where they rested for a few moments until someone once again strolled through them, disturbing their sleep. It looked like big fluffy white cumulus clouds floating from room to room.

The pictures on the walls had been removed and carefully wrapped to look like presents. Some were wrapped in pink, some red, and some a combination of red and white, all with coordinating bows. They were re-hung on the walls and it looked like presents were floating everywhere in the room just waiting to be unwrapped.

The room was surrounded everywhere with lovebirds and doves. They were on the chairs, tables, lamps and some were even tacked on the walls above the word strips reading "Be Mine," "Kiss Me," "Forever Yours" just like the candied hearts.

Yes, the decorations and food alone made it a night to remember. But those are just minor memories compared to the memories that changed her life forever.

She mingled with the crowd a bit and took a small plate of food since she hadn't eaten all day. She was famished and couldn't resist. Her schedule was so busy that oftentimes she forgot to eat, not even realizing until there was food in front of her, just how hungry she actually was. She was about to pour herself some sparkling pink cider, but then glanced at the warm hot chocolate and decided on that instead. Each apartment had sliding glass doors that led to a small balcony, just large enough to put two chairs and a little table. She went outside and sat down. The chair was wrought iron, accentuating the coldness of the night. Everyone seemed to be having a great time and she was enjoying the evening, but she just wanted to relax for a few minutes and spend some time away from the normal chaos that overwhelmed her life these days. She felt a shiver run through her and could see her breath in the cold night air, but it felt good. It had been such a long time since she had allowed herself a night out—a night just to enjoy her friends and to let her thoughts drift to something other than school and studies.

Her eyes were following the winter clouds that moved through the dark night in slow motion until they skimmed lazily across the half moon, showing off its illuminated side. It was so peaceful it almost lulled her to sleep. She was totally lost in her thoughts and hadn't even noticed the sliding glass door open or sensed his presence until she felt the warmth of a coat being placed over her shoulders. "February isn't the best time to be sitting out on a deck in Colorado," Clark said. "You're going to catch pneumonia." This time there was no "Wow!" accompanying his statement, just a certain look in his eyes.

"Thanks," she said. "Would you care to have a seat and catch pneumonia with me?"

He chuckled and sat in the chair next to her and said, "For you, I'll risk it." Heather laughed and decided right off that she liked this guy. "I'm sorry for the way I reacted when Jill introduced us inside. It was hardly the way to make an impression, so I've come to make amends." Clark said. "Sometimes I speak before I think. I've been told that by a lot of people."

"Oh, so you say 'wow' to all the girls you meet, huh?" she asked.

"No, no, no," he quickly responded, almost apologetically. "That's not what I meant. I just meant sometimes I put my foot in my mouth. It's my buddies who are always telling me I do that." Heather smiled to herself as she could see he was nervously scrambling to make the right words come out this time but wasn't too successful. She had always prided herself on having good instincts. For some reason, she sensed that he was an honest guy, not some chump giving a standard pick-up line to a girl who might be an easy target because she had arrived at the party alone. She couldn't resist telling him she had heard better pick-up lines in the express line at the grocery store. As he started once more trying to explain, he stopped in mid-sentence when he looked over and saw her grinning. He smiled back and she laughed right out loud.

They talked easily for about ten minutes before he said, "It's really, really cold out here. I think I'm growing icicles where no icicles should grow. Wouldn't you like to go in and get a refill on that hot chocolate?"

"Actually, I should be getting home. I just wanted to stop by for a few minutes, and already I've stayed longer than I intended. I need to get back to my apartment and get going on my studies. I have a big test in my anatomy class in three days."

"How far do you live? Did you drive a car or did you walk? Could I drive you home?" he asked, spitting the questions out one after another without allowing enough time between each question for her to respond. She could tell he was nervous and she found it charming.

"Actually, I walked," she finally said. "I just live four buildings over. I think I would beat you home if I walked while you went and got your car and raced me over there." She said.

"Well, I was thinking maybe we could take a detour. We could get out of this crowd and go get that hot chocolate refill somewhere else and talk a little away from the noise."

That's when her whole life as she knew it began to change. They went to George and Alice's Café, and sat in a booth talking for the next three hours. Heather had not thought about homework once, and that was the first time in as long as she could remember that she had let herself do that – maybe she never had. It felt good. It felt right. Conversation came easily. She told him about her goals and he admired her fortitude. He told her he was just finishing up his BA degree in Accounting and had to quickly decide if he would continue his graduate work at the University of Colorado Denver or if he would transfer to the University of Utah where they had a Master's of Science in Finance program. There were only two such programs in the Intermountain West. It was an intensive program that he felt would add clout to his resume and expand his career options. The program could be completed in as little as nine months. He talked about a recent Wall Street Journal article he had read that said this degree was fast becoming preferred over the MBA in financial trading and investment banking, asset management, and other technical areas, and the average starting salary was usually higher. "I want to move beyond merely tracking income and assets," Clark said. "I'd possibly like to go into financial management or mergers and acquisitions."

Heather was impressed by his ambition, but felt sad to think he might be leaving the state. "This is stupid," she thought to herself. "I hardly know him." But in those three hours, she felt like she had known him for years. "You need to get a grip on yourself, girl" she told herself. "You can't afford to get involved in a relationship anyway, so it would be better if he went somewhere before this thing got started."

He took her home and walked her to her door. He asked if he could call her again. He didn't try to kiss her, which she appreciated. She wasn't in the practice of doling out kisses on the first date, but she didn't hesitate for a minute to give him her phone number. "Funny," she thought, "didn't I just tell myself not to let anything get started?"

She went inside, put on her warm, cozy flannel PJ's and hopped into bed, taking her "Anatomy and Physiology" book with her, figuring she would study for just awhile. She crawled in, pulled up the covers, and opened the book, but she couldn't concentrate. She found herself reading the same page over and over. She kept thinking about Clark leaving. Their conversation on the balcony and at the cafe kept replaying in her head like a CD that wouldn't turn off, but just kept starting over once it reached the end. She told herself she hoped he didn't call again so she could keep focused, but she liked him. She liked him a lot, and secretly she hoped deep-down that she would hear from him again very soon.

The next evening, her wishes were granted. Her phone had rung twice already and each time she jumped up to answer, hoping it would be him. The first call was Jill wondering where she had disappeared to last night. "Oh, Jill, it was a wonderful evening. I can't believe all the work you went to. The food was delicious and Ashley, Taelor and Bobbie did a terrific job as your decorating committee. I'm sorry I skipped out without saying goodbye, but I had a lot of studying I needed to do. I was going to call you tonight to let you know what a great time I had. Thanks so much for inviting me." She hardly knew Jill and was surprised to hear from her. She had meant to call earlier, but she got side-tracked and it slipped her mind so she was glad to have the opportunity to express her appreciation for all her hard work.

"Ashley said she saw you leave with a good-looking guy," Jill said. "I was just hoping our cupid actually had a good aim with that arrow of his."

Heather squirmed a little thinking that people were already gossiping about her. "Oh, if you mean Clark . . . she paused . . . Nelson, or Nielsen or whatever his last name is, we were just talking." She knew exactly what his last name was. "I actually couldn't stay long and he couldn't either so we walked out together." She didn't want rumors to get started when there was no basis to them.

The second ring was a wrong number, and she felt a twinge of disappointment. She told herself this was stupid and got out her book ready to focus on studying. By the time the phone rang the third time, she was engrossed in her studies and had put Clark out of her mind. She wasn't even thinking about him and wondered who could be calling her now. It took her off guard when she picked up the phone and heard, "Hi Heather, it's Clark, your hot chocolate buddy. I was wondering if you would be interested in a repeat of last night. Not the party part, but the hot chocolate part."

"Hi Clark," she replied. "I'm actually in the middle of studying for a test. I wonder if we could make it another time." She was not about to sound like she was desperate and couldn't wait to see him.

"Well, everyone needs a break from the books. Come on, I won't keep you out for more than an hour—I promise. You'll study even better after you have some warm liquid in you."

It didn't take much persuasion before she accepted and agreed to meet him at the same place. "Let me pick you up," he said. She declined and told him she would be there in half an hour. It was close enough for her to walk.

Once again, the conversation was easy between them. The hour turned into two and a half before she realized it. When she checked her watch, she gasped. "Where did the time go? So much for your *just one-hour* promise," she teased. "I'm sorry, Clark, but I've really got to get home."

"What can I say? Time flies when you're having fun," he said. "I insist you let me drive you home. I can't let you walk and get cold again, wasting the warmth of that hot chocolate. I don't want you to get back to the books and be colder than you were before you left them." The fact was she had her first cup of hot chocolate, but the refill had gone almost untouched. The warmth from it had long ago left her, but it had been replaced by a different kind of warm feeling. Once again, she knew she liked this guy. She had never felt so at ease with anyone of the opposite sex.

The good night at her door went a little differently this time. "I had a really great time tonight, and last night too," Clark said. Then before she could say anything, he bent down and kissed her softly on her lips. Then he kissed her again with just a little more fervor, and she let him. In fact she wanted him to.

She kept up with her school work, but from that night on, they saw each other at least four times a week until the end of the school year. After that they were almost inseparable. Within five months from the time they met, they were engaged and by August they were married. It was a whirlwind courtship by any standards. It was so impulsive for Heather and completely uncharacteristic, but she was sure of one thing. She loved Clark and she knew with all her heart that marrying him was the best decision of her life.

She came back to reality as she pulled into the parking lot at the clinic. She was happy. She had been happy since the day they met. Just thinking about Clark made her smile. And what's more, she not only loved Clark, but loved her work too. What more could a girl possibly want? She walked through the glass doors at the entrance to the clinic as they opened automatically upon her approach. She went straight to the time clock, punched in and crossed seamlessly over from her memory mode to her work mode. She felt very fortunate to have such a wonderful life. All was right with the world.

CHAPTER 3

February 2002

"The Fields of Criminal Justice" (Adam)

"How many condemnations I have witnessed more criminal than the crime!"

Michel de Montaigne

———◆———

It was dark and late and Adam just wanted to get home and crawl into his own nice comfortable bed with Celeste, his beautiful bride of three months. The night was chilly, and he knew it would take less than ten seconds of lying next to her warm body to take the chill off.

There was a crescent shaped waning moon which gave off barely enough light to cast a shadow on the building he was watching. His partner had caught some sort of stomach bug at the last minute, so he was there alone. That wasn't normally allowed, but it did happen on rare occasions when someone was sick at the last minute. Tonight, however, was expected to be just a routine parole so his superiors allowed it. If he was still sick tomorrow, he would be assigned a temporary partner. They never let them be alone on watch two nights in a row. The chances were too great that they could be spotted alone, and it was just too dangerous.

It obviously was harder to stay centered on the job at hand when he was alone. Having no one to talk to at such a late hour, especially after an already long day, could create an environment easy for drifting off, but Adam wouldn't allow that to happen—not ever. "Focus," he told himself. "Remember this is your dream job. You were lucky to get your foot in the door, so don't start getting sidetracked."

Adam had completed his degree in criminal justice in 1999 and just a year and a half later, received his master's degree. Almost a year prior to his graduation, he started sending out his resume, hoping to get a job in any of the departments under the Department of Justice's jurisdiction. He was particularly interested in working under one of the U.S. Marshals and was willing to move anywhere or do anything.

In late January, 2001, exactly one month after he completed his post-graduate work, he was hired by the Palm Beach Juvenile Correctional Facility located in West Palm Beach, Florida, an eighty-bed residential treatment facility for male offenders between the ages of thirteen and eighteen. This facility was considered a *Level 8*' or high-risk facility, and the kids sent there were assessed as high risks to public safety and required close supervision twenty-four hours a day. The average length of stay for the youth was nine to twelve months and they offered mental health and substance abuse services, medical and psychiatric services, and educational and vocational services. It was considered a top-notch facility.

This isn't where Adam wanted to be or what he wanted to do long term, but he knew it would be the kind of work that might capture the right attention on his resume. "It might be just the thing to get me in the door at the Department of Justice," he thought at the time.

It was hard work and long hours and the pay wasn't commensurate with the demands of the job, but he gradually found a kind of satisfaction working with these boys that probably no other career opportunity would ever rival. Still the job was draining, and he didn't want it to be his life-long profession.

Some of the boys at the facility were just kids. He couldn't help but wonder where things had gone wrong for them. Thirteen short years ago, a handful of them were just babies. Now they had attitudes of hardened criminals and had committed crimes that one would hope had not even crossed the minds of most thirteen-year olds. It was disheartening and at times downright depressing. Most of the older ones had committed even worse crimes, but a small number of them had finally matured a little bit and were really trying to make changes in their lives. Some of the younger ones were scared, but they put everything they had into acting like they weren't. They pretended to be tough. Reaching them and getting them to trust was difficult for most of the counselors, but Adam had the kind of personality that just naturally lent itself to forming a connection with them.

The second week Adam was there, one boy in particular caught his attention. His name was Steven Bolt and everyone called him Lightning. He was fifteen years old and commanded the respect of all the other kids, even the older ones. The first time Adam met him, he said, "Hey, Lightning, how's it going?" That was the first time any of the teachers or counselors had ever called him Lightning. They always made sure they used his given name, Steven. Adam knew the system wanted to get the kids away from these nicknames that were usually used to indicate a sign of power, but

Adam told his superiors later, "I want to get to know what makes these kids tick before I start trying to change them."

Steven was surprised by the way Adam addressed him and Adam thought he saw a quizzical look in his eyes. Steven studied this new counselor without any pretense of hiding the way he looked Adam over from top to bottom and then from bottom to top—just staring and silently studying him. Over the next two months, Steven spent a number of hours counseling with Adam over the crimes he had committed, and gradually he started opening up, talking to Adam and allowing him to see an inside view into his past. This was a considerable breakthrough as no one else had been able to reach through to him up to that point. Adam liked Steven and could see potential in him that had yet to be discovered by anyone else.

"My dad was never in the picture," Steven said during one session. "I'm not really sure if he ever knew my mom was pregnant or even if she knew who my dad was. She never told me, probably because she never talked to me much and was never really around. For whatever reason, I don't have a clue who my father is. I have had, however, a number of *substitute fathers* that my mom brought home over the years on a pretty regular basis," he said with obvious disgust.

"I remember when I was six, my brother, Tommy, was nine and a half and my little sister, Sara, was only four. I'm sure none of us had the same father, but we had each other. That's about all we had, so we clung to each other and tried to protect each other. One evening my mother went on one of her 'outings' as she called them, but she didn't come home that night. In fact, she didn't come home for a week. My brother, being the oldest, felt like he had to take care of us. In fact, it was ingrained in him. My mother was always leaving him in charge of tending us. She would tell him, 'Tommy, you're a big boy now. I need you take care of your brother and sister while I'm away.' But he was only nine years old. No nine-year old should have to have such responsibilities. He was just a kid, but Tommy never really got a chance to be a kid." Steven was visibly upset as these memories surfaced, but still he continued.

"There was never much food in the house, and this time was no different. The first three days he crushed soda crackers and put them in a bowl with a little hot water. He called it soda mush. The soda mush didn't fill us up, but at least it was something. Sara would cry because she was still hungry. I felt like crying too, but I knew I had to stay strong like Tommy, so I didn't complain. After all, I was six years old. On the third night, Sara cried so hard, I gave her half of my soda mush and Tommy didn't eat anything. He said he wasn't hungry, but I knew he had to be.

"After the third day, the crackers were gone. Tommy didn't know what to do, so late that evening, he told me to tend Sara and he went out. He waited until the sun had gone down and it had been dark for at least four hours. By then he was sure most of the neighbors would probably be in bed. We lived in an old, dirty, run-down trailer that most likely could have been condemned by the Board of Health, but we didn't have to worry about that because there simply wasn't enough state funding to hire enough inspectors. The good ones had other, more important assignments. The rest didn't have the time or inclination to inspect such housing. A few were on the take and there was nothing in it for them. They spent their time checking out pristine, expensive restaurants, where they knew they would get a free meal in exchange for a good report. People in our neighborhood wouldn't be able to pay fines, and they certainly couldn't afford improvements or upgrades to their places, so if their homes were condemned, there would be no place for them to go except the streets. It was just easier for everyone to ignore the deplorable living conditions and pretend they didn't exist. Of course the other kids in the neighborhood didn't have much either, but at least most of them had an adult taking care of them. A lot of dads weren't around, but most had moms who cared about them and did their best to put food in their mouths."

Adam could see this kid was smart. He spoke like he was well-educated, although he wasn't; not the usual poor grammar or lack of words that many of the kids there exhibited, but almost sophisticated words and descriptions. "Go on," he said.

"I remember it was really dark that night; darker than my mother's heart, and believe me, that's pretty dark, but Tommy steeled out in the ominous cold and started going through trash cans that had been left on the dirt road for the garbage trucks to empty in the morning. As quietly as he could, he ransacked them trying to find scraps of food for us. He brought home a relatively small amount of food that was edible, but we had to ration it out for two more days. Some of it tasted rancid, but we were starving and ate it anyway."

There was a long, almost painful silence. Steven looked like he was lost deep in the recesses of his mind, his eyebrows drawn together in a frown, reliving the past. It was evident from the grim look on his face that he had vivid recall of that time in his life. Adam usually avoided interrupting once Steven started talking because he didn't want anything to sidetrack him. He would just wait during the pauses and let Steven decide whether or not he wanted to continue. This time he couldn't help himself; he wanted to hear the rest of the story. After what seemed to be an eternity, Adam interrupted the quiet. "Steven," he almost whispered. But the hush was almost deafening and when his name erupted from

Adam's lips, the whisper nearly sounded like he was shouting. "What happened when that food was gone?"

Steven was looking directly at Adam, but he couldn't see him. It was almost as if he were looking through him, directly into a scene from his past. A few minutes passed. It seemed much longer than it actually was, but Adam was sure Steven must be through talking for the day. Still he waited. Suddenly the words began again. "After the food was gone," he continued very quietly, "Sara was racked with sobbing, unable to stop because of the hunger pains. Tommy was so worried about her. I felt bad for him, and I tried to stay strong, so he wouldn't have to worry about me too. When I thought everyone was asleep, I cried into my pillow, trying to muffle the sound. I couldn't help it. I was afraid and I was hungry."

Steven had been talking to Adam for almost an hour and Adam should have sent him back to his bunk, but he let him continue.

"The next two nights were like a miracle. Tommy brought us as much food as we could eat. We even had cookies, candy and soda pop. I didn't know where he got it, and I was too young to care. When I asked him, Tommy said we should just enjoy it. It was good for him to see us fill our stomachs. He smiled, and for the first time in three days, I saw Tommy eating too.

"My mother came home after a week, but we knew it wouldn't be long until she left on one of her 'outings' again. The 'outings' were getting more and more frequent, and they were lasting longer than they used to. She didn't even ask what we had been doing or what we had eaten. She simply didn't care."

Adam felt sick to his stomach hearing this story. He had asked himself a hundred times how these kids' lives could go so wrong. Why had they taken the terrible detour that led them on a path of self-destruction? Now he was beginning to have a better under-standing.

"The next time my mother left, Tommy brought food home to us on the very first night. We ate better than we ever did when my mom was there. It was three days later when some cops showed up at our door looking for Tommy. It would have been better if he would have just told them we were starving and that our mother was gone, but instead, as soon as he saw them, he ran. He wasn't old enough to reason that out. His little nine-year-old legs weren't long enough or fast enough to out-run the cops. I found out later the corner grocery store had been robbed of incidental food items three times that week. They told my mom it had been a young boy with a ragged grey hoodie pulled over his head. The last time it happened, he had been running from the store, and one of our neighbors bumped into Tommy and recognized him. My mom told the cops later that it served him right, and that she wouldn't interfere with their attempts to put him in a children's detention center. In fact she seemed to like the idea. She said it would teach him a good lesson. She said she didn't want any trouble, but I knew she was happy to have one less mouth to feed and one less crying kid to deal with. She actually thanked them for bringing it to her attention and for taking him somewhere where his actions could be controlled. She faked the tears and went on and on about how hard it was on her to take care of three children with no help.

"She left again two days later, but after that, she was only gone for a day or two at the most. She discovered she missed having Tommy around to take care of us, and didn't want to take the chance that someone would check up on us if she were gone for long periods of time. She didn't care about us, but she didn't want to end up in the slammer herself. That would certainly cramp her style."

Adam felt a chill in the room, and he had an overwhelming urge to go over to Steven and give him a hug, but he knew that would be a big mistake. He was just beginning to trust Adam, and he didn't want to do anything that would make him uncomfortable, but it was hard to process all the details of his story without aching inside for this kid. "Some mother," he was thinking to himself.

"Tommy came home after about three months. He seemed to be beaten down. He could hardly even smile at me or Sara, but the pattern started all over again with my mom being away weeks at a time. It went on for over two and a half years, and the incidents became more and more frequent. By then Tommy was twelve, and he didn't even try to cover up his hatred for our mom. He vowed he would get away from her somehow, but he was compelled to keep taking care of us. I've never loved anyone like I loved Tommy. I don't know what we would have done without him. He told me that one day he was going to have enough money to take me and Sara out of this place, and we wouldn't ever have to deal with her again. I didn't know how he was going to do that, but I believed him and I was excited about it. It gave me something to look forward to. I even dreamed about it."

Adam was stunned. He had been so loved and cared for by his own family, he just couldn't imagine a mother with absolutely no feelings for her own children. It seemed foreign to him. He ached for what this boy had gone through already in his life. So far, not one single part of his life had been influenced by a loving, compassionate adult who was there to teach him. He didn't need to wonder how Steven's life would have been different if he would have had a role model—a role model who loved him.

"What I didn't know at first, but found out later was that Tommy was out on the streets trying to make this dream, this promise, come true. He was at the ripe age for the sixteen-year old street gang members to feed him stories of bigger and better things. The lure of easy money proved to be a powerful recruiting tool. All he had to do was to go down to the west side of town and sell the little bags of white powder to the men on the streets. They pointed out what he should look for, and how he could tell who might want to buy it. He got ten percent of everything he sold, and it was adding up fast. He might have been young, but I know by then he was old enough to know what he was doing. He reasoned that they were already using, and if he wasn't delivering it to them, someone else would. He worked the streets for six months and was pretty sure he almost had enough to take us away from there. He wasn't old enough to really understand how much money it would take or to figure out how long the money would last.

Adam was thinking he needed to stop this meeting and continue another day. He was afraid that if Steven said too much in one sitting he might regret it the next day and stop talking altogether. But Steven assured him he wanted to get it all out.

"A month before he turned thirteen, the gang boss had given him more loot to sell than ever before. He thought this might make the difference in getting away. He knew this large quantity was an indication that he was now trusted by the leaders, but in reality he was still so naïve. None of the people he was working with cared about each other in spite of what they said. Unfortunately, one of the twenty-year-old suppliers had been arrested and turned state's evidence in exchange for a reduced sentence on drug trafficking charges. He sold Tommy out. The cops set up a sting operation, and my brother was in the very center of it. As the money was about to exchange hands, he found himself suddenly surrounded by ten cops with guns pointing right at him. He was petrified and once again started to run."

Adam didn't want to hear what was coming next, but still he let Steven talk. He knew his brother must have been rearrested, this time on a more serious charge, and it crossed his mind that maybe he was in another facility. Perhaps over the years he had repeated these offenses time after time and might possibly even be in prison. But he wasn't prepared for what he heard next.

"The cops told us when he started to run, they yelled for him to stop, but he didn't. He just kept running and before he was even a block away, two shots were fired by two separate cops with two separate guns. Both had a deadly aim. One hit Tommy in the back and one hit him in the back of the head. He died on the scene."

The tears were streaming down his face now as he was reliving this horrible nightmare. Adam handed him a tissue from the box on his desk, but Steven didn't take it. He just let the tears keep coming. "I'm so sorry, Lightning," Adam said. He knew he shouldn't call him that, but for some reason it seemed right at that moment. It was his way of letting him know he respected what he had been through. "I don't condone what Tommy did," Adam said. "But I do understand it."

Steven was gathering his thoughts now, and had suddenly become aware of how much he had opened up to this relatively new counselor. He didn't know why, but for some reason, he felt like Adam cared—really cared. He trusted Adam. He was the closest thing he had ever had to a friend besides Tommy and Sara. He didn't want to stop now. He may as well get it all out. It had been bottled up inside him for a long time.

"I was devastated. I loved Tommy more than anyone else in the world," he repeated. "He took care of us the only way he knew how. He didn't deserve to die. He was just trying to help us survive." He was sobbing now. "It took me months to get over it. Well, as much as anyone can get over a death like that. I stayed in the trailer for weeks. I didn't go to school, and my mom didn't care. As long as I didn't bother her and stayed in my room, she was fine with it. But eventually, I realized how much this had affected Sara, too. She no longer had Tommy to take care of her, and she couldn't talk to me because I was always holed up in my room." Tears were streaming down his face.

Now Adam was wondering what had become of Sara and sensed that Steven must be wondering this too. "Go on," he encouraged. He wanted to know how Steven had ended up here in this facility.

After another lengthy pause, Steven continued. "I was the oldest now, and it became my responsibility to take care of Sara when my mom went out. At first, it was only one-nighters. After a couple of months, it was two-nighters, then three, then a week at a time. I was nine now; the same age as Tommy when he had embarked on these lengthy 'keep the kids from starving' missions. I did what I could, but ended up following the same path as Tommy."

Adam knew he was nearing the end of his story, and was already wondering how he would be able to help this kid. He would have to think long and hard about the right approach after this session.

"It surprised me what I had learned from Tommy. I didn't even realize I had been paying such close attention, but he had become my role model, so I did what he did. I dealt drugs for quite awhile. I was caught a number of times and spent months in and out of different juvenile facilities over the next five years, but thought I was smarter than the system each time and could avoid getting caught. I couldn't get caught anymore because that left Sara alone. The thing that put me over the edge this last time was because I was not only dealing, but I was carrying a concealed weapon—actually two; a switchblade knife which was in a holder attached to my belt loop, and a compact semi-automatic Smith & Wesson in my boot that I bought cheap off the street from a junkie needing a fix. I never intended or thought I would actually use either weapon, but I also had no intention of ending up like Tommy, so I had them just in case. It gave me confidence and helped me look tough. I know it must be hard to believe, but I really didn't want to hurt anyone. When I was caught, I was considered armed and dangerous and ended up here, prompted by a concern for public safety. I've been here for about ten months now, and it's been hell, but I'm still glad I didn't use the weapons or it could have been worse."

"How are you feeling about your actions now?" Adam asked. "Are you ready to start making a change in your life and start the process of rehabilitating your life? I can see you're a smart kid, Steven. You have a good head on your shoulders and you could make something of yourself. It isn't too late."

Smart? Was he *smart?* That was actually the first time in Steven's entire life that anyone had ever called him smart or told him he could make something of his life. He knew he wasn't dumb, but smart was another matter. The few times he had gone to school, he had picked up on things quickly, even though he hadn't really attended on a steady basis since he was six. He also knew he liked being there, and he enjoyed learning, but it just hadn't been in the cards for him. He assumed it was probably too late. He had done too much damage and didn't know how he could survive out in the world. But this new kind of thinking Adam had planted in his mind, stirred a desire in him that he had never felt before. He didn't respond, but Adam could see the wheels were turning.

Adam wished he could take Steven out for a day. He had never been to a basketball game or to a fair or to the beach. He found out he had never even been to a movie theater or to a fast food joint for a milkshake. He wanted so badly to have him experience these things while he was still young. But because this was a high-risk facility, it was hardware-secured and had perimeter fencing and locking doors. The only time these youth were granted community access was for court appearances and health-related appointments. Adam knew that as these youth started to demonstrate positive behaviors and were eventually assessed to be a minimum risk to the community, the court could grant unsupervised home visits to facilitate their transition into society. But where in the world would Steven go? It was heart-wrenching. It would be hard, but it was time for Steven to start turning his life around.

They called it a day and agreed to meet again in a couple of days. When Steven reached for the handle of Adam's office door, he turned around and said, "I don't suppose you know what's happened to Sara, do you? Are there any notes in my file about her?" Adam slowly shook his head from side to side, and Steven turned and walked out. Adam instinctively knew it was his way of asking, without really asking, for a favor, and he was determined to find out. Steven still felt the need to protect her, which was admirable and it told Adam that this kid had a heart, and he did have a chance. He just hoped Sara hadn't fallen into the same trap, because if she had, he didn't know how he would ever be able to tell Steven.

The next five months saw a big change in Steven. Their talks continued and Adam was getting positive comments from the Education Department. He never missed assignments, and his academic prowess excelled that of most of the others. His grammar, his writing and his math skills were all above-average. He was learning new things and enjoying the challenges. It was like he was starving for knowledge, and he was soaking it up like a sponge. His psychiatric reports were improving daily. It was ironic, but the one thing he didn't have to overcome was an addiction to drugs. Even though he had been selling, he had been determined to stay clean for the sake of his sister so he had never succumbed to the pressure. He had seen what it had done to the people on the streets, and he knew he could never take care of Sara if he started using. He also knew from experience that it took just one time of sampling it to become addicted. He couldn't allow himself to become hooked no matter how many people told him it would make him feel better. He saw it in the lives of the people he sold to. It didn't really make them feel better. Maybe the first couple of times, but soon it became torture figuring out where the next fix would come from. That was just one more place where his intelligence came into play. He was able to reason.

Then one day it happened. In early July, Adam got a call to come in for an interview with the Department of Justice. It was what he had worked for and dreamed of as long as he could remember. The whole interview process took about a month and on Monday, August 6, he received the all-important call asking him if he could be ready to report to work on August 20. This allowed him time to give two weeks' notice at the correctional facility.

While he was elated about getting on with the Department of Justice, he was worried about telling Steven. It was a stressful time. Adam had mixed emotions. On one hand, he was well-aware he had gotten too involved emotionally with him; the very thing they had instructed him not to do; on the other hand, it was probably the perfect time. Usually it was hard to find counselors, but two months ago Trent had started working there. Adam had been training him. Prior to that, Trent had worked at the facility as a volunteer for a couple of years. The volunteers were referred to as "Friends of Juvenile Justice." He loved it so much and felt like he could make a positive impact on the lives of these kids, so he went back to school, got his degree, and since he was already familiar with a lot of the protocol, they welcomed him as a new staff member. Trent had the same philosophies as Adam regarding these kids, and soon developed similar feelings for Steven, so they got along well. Adam knew Trent was fast becoming an asset to the facility.

The day Adam broke the news to Steven was a difficult day. He hadn't slept well for the past several nights and dreaded the encounter. Adam could tell Steven was struggling with this news, not because he was worried about losing ground, but rather because he was losing a friend who had believed in him and who he felt was responsible for putting meaning into his existence. But to Adam's surprise, even though it was difficult, Steven adapted pretty well. His new-found maturity was kicking in. Time was fast approaching for Steven's release, and he owed that to Adam. He had desperately needed to be surrounded by positive influences.

"I'm really happy for you, Adam. I know this isn't a place to be bound to for the rest of your life. I feel that myself. I just want you to know it is because of you that I first began to believe in myself and to know it would be possible." Steven showed a remarkable amount of maturity.

Adam gave him a handshake, followed by a hug. "I expect you to go far, Steven. Don't let me down now, you hear?" Adam smiled, then seeing Steven's eyes water, he asked more soberly, "Are you going to be okay?"

"Are you kidding? I wouldn't dare let you catch me being anything less than okay. Besides, Trent will keep me on track until I get out of this place. I've got to get out there and make my own way in life. I want to finish high school and then go to college. And I want to find Sara."

"I'm sorry I was never able to find out what happened to her, Steven. I hope you are able to. I'll still keep trying when I can, but I don't even know when I will see you again." That was the hardest part. He didn't know where he would be sent or if he would ever know how Steven's life would turn out."

It was as if Steven read his mind. "I'll be okay. That's my promise to you. I want to be like you, Adam. Maybe someday I'll come back to this place in a different role and turn someone else's life around like you did mine." That was the best compliment Adam had ever had.

That was six months ago, and that was then and this is now. His eyes were focused on the building he was watching. It was about ten minutes before midnight, and he saw the light turn on in the apartment building. It was the second floor and he knew it was her apartment. Five minutes later, the light went off, and he saw her coming out of the building. She hesitated on the stoop for a minute, looking up and down the street as if checking to see if anyone was watching, then proceeded down the stairs. When she was out of ear-shot range, he started up the engine, leaving the lights on low beam as he slowly crept out from the curb at a snail's pace.

CHAPTER 4

December 2006

"The Tragedy" (Breck)

"We have to believe that only the briefest of human connections can heal. Other-wise, life is unbearable."

Agate Nesaule

———•———

She had to get her Christmas shopping done, but it was more than Breck could bear. It was already December 16, and she hadn't been out one single time. There was only one more Saturday to get everything done but that was too late. December 23 would be a nightmare, so unless she wanted to go out for an hour or two every night after work, she would have to utilize this Saturday and force herself to make one big push and get it all done even if it took the entire day. She dreaded it. The hardest part was trying to figure out what to buy everyone. The stores would be filled to capacity. Customers would be pushing through the crowds to get to the registers. Some would be frustrated and grumpy, while others would be smiling politely at the unfamiliar person standing next to them in line, and some would even strike up a conversation with a total stranger about the shirt or toy they were purchasing. There would be Christmas carols playing in the background in most all the stores, and people would even be caught humming to themselves, a practice you would never hear at any other time of the year.

It was all too hard to think about. It had been only five and a half months since Jeff's accident. It was July 3, and she had sent him out for some party plates and napkins for the Independence Day celebration the following day. "Do you need anything else?" he questioned.

"No, just get that and come home as quickly as you can so you can help me set up the tables."

"Okay, your wish is my command, my princess. I love you." And with a quick peck on the cheek, he was out the door.

An hour later, there was a knock at her door. A middle-age, middle-height, uniformed policeman stood at her door flashing his I.D. badge. "Mrs. Grayson?" he asked, pausing to wait for her response. She studied his face and saw the grim expression and knew immediately something was wrong. When she finally nodded he continued, "I'm Officer Pickett from the Boulder City Police Department. I'm sorry to have to tell you this, but there's been an accident."

"How could she survive without him?" she asked herself. But down deep she knew it wouldn't come to that; it couldn't and she couldn't even entertain that idea. By the time she got to the hospital, he was already in surgery. She hadn't had a chance to see him before they took him. It was urgent they get him to the operating room immediately they had told her. She waited, and waited, and waited—alone in that grief-stricken waiting room, sitting on one of those colorful, flowered chairs whose purpose it was to brighten the room, and which was duplicated in every waiting room up and down practically every hallway in the hospital. "They must buy them by the hundreds," she thought. But the bright floral upholstery certainly wasn't working to cheer up the people in this particular waiting room where almost everyone appeared to be crying. As far as she could tell, some even looked like they were in shock. "It will be okay," she told herself. There's no way he would die. We can get through anything no matter how bad it is as long as he survives."

It seemed like she waited there the whole night, but it was actually four and a half excruciatingly long hours later when the doctor came out and gave her the news. There was some swelling around the brain, but they couldn't see anything major causing it. They believed the bulge would go down in a couple of days on its own. They would watch it closely for fluid build-up and drain it if things got worse or if it didn't look like there was any improvement the following day. The injuries to his left leg, however, were more extensive and he had a collapsed left lung. They did the best they could on his leg trying desperately to save it. They would be watching it closely to make sure gangrene didn't set in. If that happened, they would have no choice but to amputate. She gasped at the thought, but told herself to be grateful he was alive; once again assuring herself they could get through anything together.

He was in a medically-induced coma, and badly needed some rest so she would be unable to talk to him, but she could see him for a few minutes they told her. She couldn't wait to go in and be there with him, but as soon as she did, she almost wished she hadn't. She wasn't prepared for what she saw. It made her sick to her stomach, and she wanted to throw up. They had warned her that he looked pretty bad, but she still wasn't primed. How could you ever be prepared to see someone you so desperately love looking like that? It seemed like there were tubes coming from everywhere and more monitors than she had ever seen. She had to look twice to make sure she was in the right room. His head was swollen up like a basketball, both eyes were black and cuts and bruises covered the entire left side of his face. His face was so distorted he was almost unrecognizable. It was hard for her to imagine that his leg was worse than his head.

Slowly she walked to his bedside, studied him for a minute and assured herself it was Jeff. Across the room she saw a turquoise chair with a taupe colored blanket draped over the arm. She pulled it up to his bedside and sat down, reaching over and resting her hand on top of his. Taped to the top of his hand was a needle, dripping some sort of clear fluid through a narrow tube and into his vein, perhaps to help with the pain or to administer an antibiotic or some other medication she supposed, but didn't really know. It made it impossible for her to actually hold his hand so she just let it rest on top of his trying to gently intertwine her fingertips with his. She glanced at the other side of the bed and could see that hand was free, but there was too much going on there. The bulk of the machines were on that side, and there were all manner of paraphernalia and monitors over there. It looked like some sort of board was strapped to his leg, covered with mountains of protective bandages and a pressure sleeve wrapped around it that made an awful noise every few minutes as it inflated. It was elevated by some sort of traction device. She didn't want to disturb any of that, but she wanted desperately to hold him in her arms and comfort him.

"I'm sure he can feel my touch," she told herself. "He'll feel better knowing I'm here. Tomorrow he'll wake up and I'll be able to talk to him and sooth him." She wished she could just take the pain away, but it was obvious this was going to be a long road. She laid her head on the side of his bed and finally let the pent-up tears fall down and wet the clean crisp white sheets. She was supposed to leave after a few minutes, but they let her stay. There was no way her being there was bothering him. The nurses knew that, so they just pretended to ignore her and let her stay by his bedside. One nurse even brought in a pillow and laid it by her. She was exhausted, so she bent over, and with her head lying on the pillow at the edge of Jeff's bed, Breck was lulled by the whirring sounds and the slow repetitive clicks of the machines and soon drifted off into a restless sleep.

Beep! Beep! Beep! At 4:00 a.m. she was awakened by piercing alarms that were going off somewhere. At first she thought it was in her dream, and it took her a minute to get her bearings and realize she was in a hospital room, with her injured husband, and these noises had something to do with him. A team of nurses and doctors rushed in and told her she would have to leave. "What's happening?" she screamed.

"You need to leave Mrs. Grayson. We'll come out just as soon as we can, but we need to have you leave so we can attend to your husband." She obediently, but reluctantly left, still trying to comprehend what had happened. Had she perhaps lain on something accidentally that caused the alarms to go off? What was going on?

Once again she was at their mercy . . . waiting. She walked over to the familiar floral sofa and sat down. It didn't take long this time, though. Not like when Jeff was in surgery. In fact it was only about twenty minutes, but it still seemed like an interminably long time. Breck leaped to her feet as soon as she saw the doctor walk out of Jeff's room, removing his gloves and tossing them into a nearby can.

He walked over to her and took her by the elbow. "Sit down," he said softly. She did as he said, and he sat down next to her. She was sure by his demeanor that things hadn't gone well and that Jeff was going to lose his leg.

"I'm sorry," he said. "We did everything we could."

"What do you mean?" she cried.

"Jeff is dead," he said.

"No, no, no! It can't be," she shouted. "Go back in there. You haven't tried long enough. I know he wouldn't leave me. You have to go back and try harder."

"Breck," he said, this time dropping the more formal 'Mrs. Grayson'. "He's gone. There's nothing more we can do." She started to cry, then she sobbed and then she sobbed some more. Her head dropped to Dr. Lindblom's shoulder and he just let her cry, knowing there were no words to comfort her right now.

"Why, Jeff?" she moaned. "Why? Why? Why?"

"I suspect he must have had a blood clot that went to his heart. It was touch and go from the time he arrived, but I had hoped we would be able to save him. I'm really so sorry. Can we call anyone for you?"

When the autopsy results came in weeks later, his suspicions were confirmed. It had been a blood clot. The funeral took place five days later, but that part was still a blur to her. She remembered flowers; lots of them. She remembered a casket, there were people crying all around her and lots and lots of food, but the rest of the details of that day were unclear.

In the following weeks, she eventually learned that she could get through this. Each day she got up and made it through the routines of work and daily errands, but her love and zest for life were gone. During the first few months, almost every single day she was riddled with guilt; guilt that she had sent him out that evening. "Paper plates," she kept thinking. "Jeff died for paper plates." She hated herself. She could have used plain old white paper plates and no one would ever have noticed. But no, she had to have special party ones for the celebration.

She finally confided her feelings of guilt to her best friend, Heather Neely. Heather and Breck had gone to high school together and become best friends, even though they were a grade apart. Both had been the studious type, and some of the activities that most of the students were interested in like clubs and cheerleading, held no interest for either of them. They were both more focused on their education, and having common goals drew them together in that rare kind of friendship that lasts a lifetime. Heather had met Clark while she was in nursing school and they had married relatively quickly, which had surprised Breck and everyone Heather knew, especially her family. Not too long after Heather graduated, they moved to Florida for Clark's job, and she had missed her best friend more than just a little—especially now. Breck had kept in close touch with them and being the good friend that Heather was, she made sure not to abandon Breck when she was facing the worst trial of her life. She made a couple of trips back to Boulder since Jeff's death, and she talked to her at least three times a week. Breck just wished they would move back. She was so glad Heather was here for another visit. She honestly didn't think she could have made it without this good friend's shoulder to cry on.

Heather was worried when Breck came clean and told her about blaming herself for Jeff's death. She knew if she didn't get past those feelings, it would be very difficult for her to move on with her life, but she also knew it hadn't been that long and expected it to take some time. She tried to imagine her own life without Clark and knew it would be devastating. She wanted to be there for her best friend and help her through this most trying time with compassion and patience.

"Breck, this was an accident; a terrible accident. In no way should you construe it as being your fault. You couldn't have kept Jeff inside every minute of every day in hopes of protecting him from the world any more than he could you. That's ludicrous. If you need to blame someone, blame the kid who ran the stop sign and t-boned him." But Breck knew the boy who ran the stop sign was also consumed with guilt and grief. He was only eighteen years old. The accident was neither drug- nor alcohol-related. He just hadn't seen the stop sign which was covered partially by a tree branch and difficult for anyone to see, especially at night. He had called her multiple times over the past five months to check on her, each time apologizing profusely and each time ending up in tears. It was impossible for her to blame him. She knew his life would never be the same either.

After about three months, Breck quit blaming herself all day, every single day. But still, when she was very lonely or very tired to the point of exhaustion from lack of sleep, the 'why questions' would creep back into her thoughts once again. Why had she sent him out that night? Would she ever be able to be happy again, she wondered? She doubted it, and now the holidays were here and she was lonelier than ever. There was nothing for her to celebrate this year; nothing at all.

She finally found a parking spot about as far away as she could get from the stores. It was packed and the mall was providing valet parking, but she chose to drive around and around until she found a spot herself, thus delaying the inevitable crowds she would have to face once she went inside. But she had done it. She was at the mall now, and she would get the task of Christmas shopping done. Hopefully it wouldn't take her all day. She had always enjoyed shopping for other people, especially at Christmas, but now it seemed like a chore, and such an unimportant chore at that. Why did the world require all this nonsense?

As she got off the escalator in Macy's department store, her eye caught the Christmas tree. Appropriately, it was called "The Giving Tree." For some reason, Breck was drawn to it. She observed a cute little blonde-haired girl about eight years old she guessed, standing next to it. She was full of questions, and inquisitively asked her mom why the tree had cards on it instead of ornaments. Her mom explained that the cards had names of kids who didn't have the nice things she did, and that people could take one of the cards and buy presents for the person on the card so they would have a nice Christmas also. The little girl asked if they could take a card and buy something for someone. Her mom told her they didn't have time this year, but perhaps next year, and they walked away with their arms full of sacks.

"How strange," Breck thought. The little girl was obviously feeling the true spirit of Christmas, and the mom missed an extraordinary opportunity to teach her daughter by example. Instead she chose to march off without a care in the world for others, arms full of packages, and probably heading to buy more. "People are interesting," Breck mused. "I've seen these trees over the years, and I've passed by them dozens of times myself, so don't be judging others for doing the same thing," she chastised herself. She wondered how these wishes from the giving trees ever got filled if everyone had the same reaction. The question in her mind intrigued her, and she reached over and picked a couple of cards off the tree and read them:

Seven-year old boy
Needs pair of pants, pajamas, warm coat (size 8,) gloves

Six-year old girl
Needs top/shirt and coat (size 7), shoes (size 12) and socks
(size medium)

"Interesting," she thought. "Humble requests; just clothes—all they really want is clothes to keep warm. No Barbie's, Leapsters, Nintendo DSi's, Wii's, iPod's or whatever else was predicted to be the *must have* item for 2007. Not a single thing kids usually ask for these days, and we go around totally unaware and uncaring of their needs. I'm as guilty as the next person."

In that instant, an idea crossed her mind. She thought it was a brilliant idea. "I could buy gifts for some of these kids and wrap some small boxes with notes inside for the people on my list, telling them that I bought a coat in their name for a six-year old girl. The people on my gift list certainly don't *need* anything. They might *want* something, but this is what they are going to get," she decided emphatically. She thought it was genius.

She counted the names on her list and picked seventeen cards off the tree. She was going to splurge. She had only been married to Jeff for one year, but he had been in the insurance business and the one thing he did immediately after they were married, was to take out a hefty policy on himself, with Breck as the beneficiary. He had made sure she would be well-taken care of if something happened. Well, something did happen, but the money had been no consolation. She hadn't spent a dime of that insurance money on herself since she received the check. She had no desire to. She didn't need anything, especially now when nothing mattered. She was going to spend some now, though. Jeff would have been proud of her for thinking of this. He was a kind and caring man, and he loved children. He was excited about the prospect of some day becoming a father. Besides it would only be a drop in the bucket compared to what she had in the bank. "Jeff," she thought. She went back to the tree and picked off one more card to add to her pile. She would do one in Jeff's name also.

For the next five hours, she went from department to department going through all the sizes and picking the warmest and most fashionable items she could find. There were lots of sales, but that wasn't the determining factor. She spared no expense to outfit these children. She even added a few extra things to each list including some dolls, trucks and toys. Every child needed a toy or two. For the first time in five months, for four and a half straight hours she didn't once think of herself and how unhappy she was, and the time flew by. She had to make several trips to her far-away parking spot to deposit things in her trunk, only to return to her shopping and load up again, but she had renewed energy, so it wasn't difficult.

As she walked out of the mall for the last time that evening, she caught herself humming to the Christmas Carols that were playing in the background. She smiled for the first time in months—a real smile.

CHAPTER 5

April 2001

"Falling in Love with a Mystery" (Greg & Parris)

"Those who are held wise among men, and who search for the reason of things, are those who bring the most sorrow upon themselves."

Euripides

———————◆———————

It had been two weeks since Greg introduced himself and his friend, Scott, to Parris at Ming Li's. He had seen her come into the restaurant alone, and as soon as he could manage to close his dropped jaw, had gone right up to her and teasingly asked her if that was her stomach growling or the gong he heard? It struck her funny because her stomach had actually been growling as she walked through the door. She let just a tiny hint of a smile emerge from her gorgeous lips. It might have been imperceptible to anyone else, but Greg saw it. Still, she looked at him suspiciously. "That's a little bit bold," she thought to herself. "I don't even know this guy." He recognized the guarded look she was wearing and quickly explained to her that he was in her Political Science class, and since he had seen her come in alone, thought she might want some company. At first she politely declined, saying she didn't want to intrude, but those gorgeous blue eyes and his fun personality tempted her.

"Aw, come on," he said, "we're just having our weekly blue-plate special, so you may as well join in, unless, of course, you are expecting someone." It was a statement, but sounded more like a question.

Just seconds prior, he and Scott had been sitting at a table designing an elaborate plan to meet this girl, but the minute Greg saw her walk in, all those plans went out the window. There was no longer a need for any kind of sophisticated plan.

It was more than obvious that Greg was attracted to her. Being a protective buddy, Scott was quietly studying her through the course of dinner to see if she might be sending any disingenuous signals, but to the contrary—she seemed very sweet and sincere, just a little on the quiet side for his tastes. Parris seemed to enjoy Greg's company also, but not to the same extent that Greg enjoyed hers. Scott had this gnawing feeling that the tables were going to turn on Greg and he might be the recipient of what he had so often dished out, albeit unintentional—a broken heart.

Almost two weeks later, to his surprise, Scott thought he might have to eat his words (or really his thoughts, since he hadn't spoken them out loud to Greg). During those two weeks, Greg had seen Parris five times. It would have been more if she would have accepted his invitations, but it was the end of the year, and he knew he couldn't push too hard during finals.

Their first official date was on Wednesday, two days after their introduction at Ming Li's. They went to a movie at the Mizner Park Sunrise Cinemas. Greg met her at the theater. He had offered to pick her up, but she said she lived some distance from campus and would be studying at the library so she would just meet him there. They saw the popular box office hit *Ocean's Eleven* which just happened to suit both their tastes. It was a remake from the 1960 hit which starred the Rat Pack. Greg had often heard his mother refer to Frank Sinatra, Dean Martin, Sammy Davis Jr., Joey Bishop and Peter Lawford as the Rat Pack. The new remake cast starred many new favorites. Greg in particular liked Julia Roberts, while Parris' tastes leaned toward the male hunks, as she called them; George Clooney, Brad Pitt and Matt Damon. It was enough of a chick flick for her and enough of a caper film for him. Midway through the movie, they were both pretty focused on the plot, when he reached over absent mindedly and held her soft hand, interlacing their fingers. Afterwards they went for a hamburger and talked for at least an hour rehashing the scenes in the movie. Their conversation was light and easy and very comfortable.

On Saturday they went bowling. It was the first time he had heard her laugh so loud, and he loved the sound. Greg was on his "A" game that night. Before she rolled her first ball he said, "Now if you can't knock all the pins down on the first ball, please *spare* me the reason." After eight frames Parris got a strike, and Greg said, "You have the potential to be a champ! Bowling is a sport that could be right down your *alley*." The one-liners rolled out all night long. As usual, Greg was having his way with words. The thing is, Greg didn't have to try. It just flowed from him effortlessly. It wasn't like some guys who tried to think up things to say to make the girls laugh. With Greg, it just came naturally. He was a quick thinker and very witty, so most things that came out of his mouth got more laughs than if someone else had said the very same thing.

On Monday, they met at Ming Li's again. He told Scott he wanted to go there for their first anniversary. "Hey, man, it's only been a week. That hardly qualifies as an anniversary."

"Yes, but it was the first day of the rest of my life," he responded, dreamily. And to him, it was. He was sure of it. He was definitely whipped.

That night, there were no lapses in conversation. It seemed like they had known each other forever. They talked easily about every class they had, the professors they liked and why they liked them, and what they were planning as career choices. Greg couldn't get over how perfect she was. Her soft copper hair was naturally streaked with blonde highlights from the sun. When the light hit it, it reminded him of silk autumn or spun gold. As he walked her to her car, he could sense that she wanted him to kiss her just as much as he wanted to, so he gently guided her body up against the car, leaned down and softly touched his lips to hers. They felt warm and inviting and she didn't resist. He put his arms around her and pulled her closer and kissed her again just as gently, but longer this time. Then one kiss ran into another as their passion grew and she wrapped her arms around his neck, responding in kind to the heat of the moment. Greg could have stayed there for another hour just getting acquainted with the sweet taste of her mouth, and he was sure by the way she countered that she felt the same way, but suddenly as if remembering something, she pulled away rather abruptly, looking up at him with a concerned look. He was surprised to see a deep sadness in her eyes when she unexpectedly said, "I should go."

"Have I done something to offend you?" he asked. Of course he hadn't. She had wanted his kisses as much as he had wanted hers, and he felt her desires, but the euphoria he felt just a few seconds before had quickly dissipated when he saw her emerald green eyes tear up. That melancholy look that crossed her face was hard to ignore.

"No," she said quickly, trying unsuccessfully to act cheerful. "I just have to get home and do some serious last minute studying. I had a great evening." He opened her door and watched her sleek, smooth, flawless legs slide onto the seat, resting about six inches under the steering wheel. "I'll call you," he said. She nodded, smiled slightly and drove off.

He thought about her all night, wondering if he had pushed too hard or too fast. It seemed like those kisses came so naturally for both of them, but he started questioning his impression of what had happened. Her body had gone limp in his arms. One thing he knew for sure was that she was special, and he wanted her to know he respected her and would never do anything that would make her feel undeserving of his admiration.

Their next two dates were both quick lunches; one on the following Saturday, and the other on Monday after class. They both appeared to enjoy each other's company, but something had changed with Parris. She wasn't laughing any more, and she didn't send Greg any signals that indicated he should kiss her again. In fact, she went out of her way to steer clear when he got too close.

Greg didn't say anything to Scott about it, and when he asked how things were going, Greg just told him it was splendid. But when he went to bed that night, he couldn't sleep. That day, for the first time, he realized there was something really wrong; not minor but major. He couldn't put his finger on it, but he was intent on finding out. He was pretty sure it wasn't him; the feelings were too strong and too obvious that night outside of Ming Li's. It was definitely something else. Her eyes were way too sad, and it didn't take a mastermind to know something was severely troubling her. He noticed she intentionally avoided having too much fun. Instead of letting it happen, she worked on making sure it didn't. Occasionally she would forget for just a moment and let her guard down and start to laugh. It was the most beautiful sound he had ever heard. But always, except for that one night, she would quickly curtail the laughter as if remembering that she wasn't supposed to do that. Getting her to relax was like coaxing a beautiful song out of a lark. It shouldn't be difficult, but it was.

Greg had never been in love before, but this was the girl he wanted to fall madly in love with and maybe be with for the rest of his life. He wasn't afraid of loving her too much, but he was absolutely terrified of losing her. He would find out what was bothering her and help her work through it, but he recognized he had to be careful. It would have to be on her terms. He would have to work his magic. He wanted her to know that he would stand by her no matter what this deep dark secret was that she was harboring.

It was a restless sleep that night, almost a series of catnaps rather than a sound sleep, waking and worrying, then finally drifting off for a short time only to wake up again. In his agitated state, he fought the urge to go back to sleep because each time he did, Greg would find himself in the middle of a black, cursed forest trying to rescue Parris who was lost somewhere in those dark forsaken woods. Somehow he knew she wanted him to find her, but her voice wouldn't work. There were strange noises everywhere, but they weren't her noises. When she tried to call out to him, no sound would come out at all. He knew she was there, but he couldn't see or hear her, yet somehow he mysteriously knew she was trying to call his name. His search exhausted him, but he just kept running and running through the dark thicket of twisted trees, calling for her over and over. The eerie stale brown fog was thick in the air, reaching its long gnarly fingers along the ground in every direction and slithering up the trunks of the trees into the night air. He had to be careful where he stepped for there were traps everywhere that could suck him into holes in the dank, musty ground.

When he could run no longer, he dropped to the clammy wet ground. It felt to him like he was giving up, and he woke up sweating profusely, his pillow soaking wet. He flipped the pillow over to the dry side and told himself it was just a dream and ordered himself to go back to sleep, but the intensity of the dream lingered in his mind, making it difficult to obey that order.

When he finally drifted off again, the dream resumed where it left off without skipping a beat. He woke up the next morning feeling drained, like he really had been running through a forest all night. He knew it was just a dream, but as sure as he possibly could be, he knew there was something from which he needed to rescue Parris, and he was bound and determined to find out what that was.

CHAPTER 6

February 2002

"Troubled Waters" (Adam & Celeste)

"A portion of your soul has been entwined with mine. A gentle kind of togetherness, while separate we stand. As two trees deeply rooted in separate plots of ground, while their topmost branches come together, forming a miracle of lace against the heavens."

Janet Miles

———•———

C eleste kept telling herself not to worry, but she didn't know how to make that happen. Adam had only been at his new job for about two and a half months, and they had already experienced several arguments about it. She told herself every single time that it wouldn't happen again, but then her frustrations would get the best of her and the quarrels started all over again.

Adam had been offered a job with the Department of Justice that past August. He knew there were several law enforcement agencies he could be assigned to; United States Marshals Service (USMS), Federal Bureau of Investigation (FBI), Federal Bureau of

Prisons (BOP), Bureau of Alcohol, Tobacco, Firearms, and Explosives (ATF), Drug Enforcement Administration (DEA) or Office of the Inspector General (OIG). He had investigated each agency thoroughly and was hoping to get into either the USMS or the DEA. His qualifications best fit the United States Marshals Service, which was his number one choice, so he was ecstatic when he got the call. He could hardly believe he had landed this job, and he couldn't have been more excited. Celeste knew this was his dream job, and so she shared in his excitement when he was hired. They had dated for quite awhile and not only were they totally and completely in love, but they were also very best friends. There was nothing they didn't share with each other, so she felt she was almost as prepared for this as he was. They had spent many long nights discussing what it entailed.

His official start date was August 20, but he was required to complete a rigorous seventeen and a half week basic training at the U.S. Marshals Service Training Academy in Glynco, Georgia. He completed the training on December 21, which was the Friday before Christmas.

It was amazing, actually miraculous, that they were able to stay on schedule, since just about three weeks into it, on September 11, the entire United States plunged into utter chaos following the al-Qaeda suicide attacks upon their country. All the agencies in the department had been flooded with extra assignments and were scrambling to put the pieces together. The entire nation was in shock wondering how this could have happened on their homeland.

Four commercial jet airliners had been hijacked by the terrorists. The first plane was flown straight into one of the Twin Towers of the World Trade Center, and it took only seconds for news reports to start filtering in. At that point everything was speculative.

Then the hijackers intentionally crashed the second plane into the other Twin Towers building and every news source in the country was trying to assess what had happened. One newscaster even suggested that possibly something may have gone terribly wrong with the national air traffic control system. One theory after another emerged before the third plane crashed into the Pentagon in Arlington, Virginia. By this time, everyone knew their country was under attack; it was happening on their very own soil.

Not long after, a fourth plane crashed into a rural field in Pennsylvania. Flight 93 had taken off from the Newark airport heading for San Francisco. The words "Mayday, Mayday, Mayday" could be heard coming from the cockpit just seconds before the hijackers had overtaken control of the plane. Suddenly the aircraft dropped 685 feet in about thirty seconds. The terrorists were redirecting the plane toward Washington, D.C. When the plane dropped, commotion set in and several passengers called their loved ones from their cell phones. They were informed about the other planes that had been crashing that morning, and they soon figured out that the very aircraft they were on was part of a larger scheme. Apparently, all passengers were forced to move to the rear of the plane, but they were still secretly reporting from their cell phones the scene that was unfolding. Small glimpses of the horror and fear were now being communicated back and forth. The terrorists most certainly were not prepared for the brave heroes on the plane that day who quickly led a revolt. They had been told there was a bomb on board and with the cell phone reports from their family members, they knew they were going to die. Several told their loved ones that they had taken a vote and decided to tackle the hijackers. It's still unclear whether the passengers actually breached the cockpit where the terrorists were or if the terrorists just thought they were close to getting in, but they later identified the voice of Todd Beamer, one of the heroes, yelling "Let's roll." It was evident they were trying to get into the cockpit and within a few minutes, the plane plowed down in an empty field, leaving a huge impact crater. They were just about twenty minutes' flying time outside of Washington, D.C. Everyone on the flight was killed, but the heroic actions of the Flight 93 passengers undoubtedly averted a fourth crash that day on a Washington, D.C. building, most believing it would have been the capitol.

When Adam was interviewing for the job, he told his intended supervisor of his impending wedding plans on December 28. He was assured those plans could proceed if he would agree to go to the training class that was scheduled to begin on August 20. That way he would be done before the wedding, and they could take a week for a honeymoon before his first assignment.

Celeste knew this meant she would have to deal with all the arrangements herself since Adam would be in Georgia in training, and she knew it was going to be difficult, but she didn't complain. Knowing they had escaped the possibility of postponing the wedding date, gave her enough stamina to handle the preparations without him. While she had hoped to get his input and have him share in the planning of this once-in-a-lifetime event, she realized her mom would actually be more help to her than Adam anyway.

They were very grateful their plans hadn't been delayed after September 11. Initially, they thought training might immediately cease and be rescheduled, but that didn't happen. Apparently the government didn't want anything disrupting the training of new agents, especially after the massive crisis, so the training class continued uninterrupted.

They were relieved when it was finally over so they could concentrate on starting their lives together. Their wedding went off without a hitch, and they both agreed it couldn't have gone any better. They went to the Bahamas for a week, where they spent most of that time in solace in their room, getting to know each other intimately, but occasionally slipping out to the white sandy beaches for some sunshine.

As soon as they got home from their honeymoon, Adam received his first assignment. The first couple of weeks on the job, Celeste tolerated his absence. She knew he had to make the best effort possible on his first assignment, and she supported him in his long hours away from home, but she missed him. She missed him terribly. They had been married such a short time, and she yearned to spend more time with him. The problem was, by the end of the first month, she hardly ever saw him. At first she would wait up until he got home, but now that he wasn't getting home until 2:00 or 3:00 in the morning, she simply couldn't wait up night after night and still function at work the next day.

Several times he was gone all night, and on a couple of occasions, even as long as two whole days. He would come home too exhausted to do anything with her. She started to worry that this would be what their whole life was going to be like. She had conflicting reactions. She longed for him more every day, but as soon as she would finally see him, she became irritable at his suggestions to just stay home or to go to bed early. She sympathized with his long days, and understood his exhaustion, but it seemed to her as though he had no energy left for her at all, even for simple conversation, and her anger would flare.

He explained to her as much as he possibly could, but the assignment was top secret, and he was unable to divulge too much information. "Celeste," he tried to explain, "this assignment won't go on forever. Please be patient and try to understand that I am needed. It's critical that I be there."

"Oh, and I don't need you?"

"That's not what I'm saying. It's not a matter of life or death if I'm not here with you as much as you or I would like for the next few months. *Your* life is not at stake, but it certainly doesn't mean that I don't love you."

Celeste gasped, and Adam knew he had already said more than he should. Trepidation had replaced the anger on her concerned face. "Life or death?" she asked, suddenly tearing up. She almost choked on the words as they stumbled out of her mouth. "Are you doing something dangerous? Please tell me what you can Adam. I won't breathe a word of it to anyone." Of course she knew he could be doing something dangerous, and she also knew he couldn't tell her. They had gone over and over the requirements of the job long before he even applied and had discussed all the possible scenarios. But of course when it was just something she read on paper, it was obscure and something that other people would actually get involved in, not her Adam. Not until that very minute did she understand that her husband could very well be harmed at any time on any assignment. The thought caused a shiver to slowly crawl up her spine, and she dropped to the sofa so her legs wouldn't give way. Now it was real.

What could he say? He knew he couldn't tell her anything more about the case. First of all, he would be severely reprimanded and almost assuredly fired if anyone knew. Second, he could be putting Patricia Reyburn's life at stake and if something happened, there could even be criminal charges brought against him for releasing top secret information. Besides that, he would never be able to live with himself if his mistake caused harm to Patricia. Third, and worst of all, if the wrong people ever found out that she knew something, Celeste's life could be in danger. That thought alone was enough incentive to insure his silence.

So, yes, it was true, he was in danger himself, but of course he wouldn't consider telling Celeste that even if he could. She didn't need one more thing to agonize over. This incredible woman that he cherished with all his heart, was being forced, as a newlywed no less, to be put on the backburner in his life. He knew her well and understood her pain and worries. They had always been so close. They shared each other's thoughts and dreams and discussed every part of their lives from the moment they met two years ago. There had never been any secrets between them; at least not until this job. This was unchartered territory for both of them, and he could see it was eating her up inside. This line of work was going to be more of an adjustment than either one of them had ever anticipated.

He knew how critical it would be if he didn't devote every possible moment to Patricia Reyburn right now. He did not want her blood on his hands. But right now, Celeste needed him. It didn't matter how tired he was, he would spend the evening doing whatever she wanted. They could go to dinner and go bowling or whatever she wanted. Hopefully she wouldn't pick a movie because he feared he would only see the insides of his eyelids at a movie, and that would frustrate her even more. He was very, very tired.

She did choose to go out to dinner. They hadn't been on a date in such a long time. She told him to pick a place so he decided on a quaint restaurant a little outside of town, but not too far from where they lived. It was their favorite spot, and they had decided long ago to reserve it for special occasions only so as not to become blasé about it. They didn't want it to ever lose the charm it held for them by becoming a routine date location, so going there less frequently, kept it their unique spot. Adam decided this was one of those special occasions; special because he needed her to know without a doubt that he loved her more than anything in the world. No other justification was needed to take her to this favorite location.

Dinner was incredible, just like they expected it to be. Some good things never change with the exception of getting better. They smiled and she laughed as she fed him an oyster in a half shell making some comment about the power of aphrodisiacs. They shared a slice of rich chocolate cheesecake that they had indulged in only twice before, but it was worth every calorie. No one was counting; not on this night, anyway. They talked about anything and everything except work, which they had unanimously agreed was off limits. It was like they had stepped back in time to just a few short months ago. Everything was good. They were both happy, and they were both in love. The night was magical.

He had almost forgotten how drop-dead gorgeous she was and her beauty was emphasized in the candlelight. She was dressed in a simple black dress, with tiny rhinestones dotting the square neckline. Her silky blond hair fell softly to her shoulders. Tonight she didn't wear the oversized chunky fashion jewelry that she generally wore on a day-to-day basis that was so in vogue these days. Instead, her neck was adorned with the simple diamond abstract-shaped heart necklace that he had given her on their wedding day. The reflection of the diamonds in the candlelight created a mirror image in Adam's eyes. She thought if she stared into them long enough it might blind her, but she could not look away. She loved those eyes.

Celeste always looked classy, but tonight her beauty was staggering, almost exquisite. No, not almost, she *was* exquisite. Adam felt so lucky. He loved this woman so much he almost felt like his heart was being crushed by the weight of that rock-solid love. It felt like a boulder on his chest. He could hardly wait to hold her in his arms again like they had on their honeymoon. "Our honeymoon should still be going on," he thought to himself. It had ended much too quickly since he had had to start on this assignment the week they got back.

He was so grateful when she told him she just wanted to go home after dinner and have him all to herself for the rest of the night. She wanted to feel the warmth of his body next to hers, and that sounded extremely agreeable to him. They made love all night long. Her touch gave him renewed energy, and it was as if they couldn't get enough of each other. When they finally drifted off to sleep, their bodies and legs were entwined like strands of hair in a tangled braid, not wanting to separate for fear this beautiful human braid they had created would completely unravel.

Adam slept better than he had for months. Once again they were complete. That night no thoughts of Patricia Reyburn disturbed his sleep.

CHAPTER 7

June 2003

"A Friend's Shoulder" (Heather & Celeste)

"We are already one. But we imagine that we are not. And what we have to recover is our original unity. What we have to be is what we are."

Thomas Merton

———◆———

C lark and Heather had been living in Riviera Beach, Florida for about three months now. In just two more months they would be celebrating their two-year anniversary, and it still seemed like they hadn't really had a chance to settle into their marriage. Their introductions at a Valentine's Day party in 2001 led to a whirlwind romance and after a six-month relationship, they tied the knot in spite of skeptical parents and friends. They were both young, but they were both smart and level-headed and were definitely mature beyond their years.

The truth is, they spent most of their six-month courtship planning their future rather than dating and having fun. Part of that plan was for Clark to go to Salt Lake City in January of 2002 to get his Master's of Science in Finance degree at the University of Utah. There was no way they both could go to Utah. Clark understood that Heather had to stay and finish her classes in Colorado, and they thought it might actually help both of them to stay more focused on their studies without the normal newlywed distractions. They also knew they couldn't live apart for nine months and survive this separation without seeing each other fairly often, so Clark came home about every third weekend, and she went to visit him twice. There was no money for flights so driving was their only option. Sometimes it was too snowy and the roads would be closed over the mountains, so he would have to skip a planned trip home at the last minute. Those weekends were pure torture for both of them. They tried to combine their Monday or Friday holidays with a trip home so they could have a little more time together. The trips were quick, not like a real weekend. It took him about seven hours to get there and the same back not leaving much time for each other, but when they were together, they buried themselves in their apartment and didn't leave each other's sides. Every time Clark had to go back to Salt Lake, he waited until the last possible minute, putting off the inevitable as long as possible. Heather worried about him every minute of every hour until she heard the phone ring with Clark's voice on the other end announcing he was there safe and sound. It was a long, tiring trip, and she knew it could be easy to doze off, so she wasn't able to rest until she got his phone call that he had arrived safely back at his one-room apartment in Salt Lake.

Those nine months were stressful, but they made the most of the situation and in the process, they grew even closer to each other, knowing that some day it would pay off. Now those pay-off days had finally come—at least to some extent. To Heather's relief, Clark finished his degree in October and moved back to Boulder,

Colorado. It was like having a second honeymoon. They loved and laughed and loved some more.

Over the next few months, when he wasn't with Heather, practically every minute of his time was spent completing lengthy applications, sending reams worth of resumes and visiting company employment websites, all the time knowing that most of his efforts would end up in a pile that would eventually be trashed and never even read.

In January, one of the nation's largest banking firms with a huge private client service division called expressing interest in his resume and an appointment was set up for the end of the following week. He expected it to be one more of those endless interviews, answering the repetitive questions and expounding on his qualifications as much as possible without bragging. It was a fine art to sing your own praises without coming across like a showoff. Secretly, however, he was hoping this would be the one, and he even revealed a little of his excitement when Heather came home from work that evening and he filled her in. Usually he tried to keep the interviews low-key because they had experienced a number of disappointments and he had learned not to express too much excitement.

"Florida!" she gasped, "but what about my job?" After her initial shocked reaction and after they had talked everything through, she was looking at the prospect of moving enthusiastically, approaching the idea like a brand new adventure for them.

"Well, don't get too excited just yet," Clark said. "I haven't even had the dreaded 'in-person' interview yet." He had ten anxious days to plan for his trip and when the time came, he was more than ready to leave for Florida and this eagerly-awaited interview. During those ten days, he read every motivational, self-help interview book he could get his hands on. Among many, there were "Winning Job Interviews" by Dr. Paul Powers, "Acing the Interview: How to Ask and Answer the Questions That Will Get You the Job" by Tony Beshara, "You're Hired! Interview Skills to Get the Job" by Lorne Epstein, and "Competency-Based Interview Style and Give Them the Answers That Will Win You the Job" by Robin Kessler. In the end, though, when he was sitting across the desk from his potential new boss, all that he had studied went right out the window, and he found himself letting go, relaxing and just being honest about his qualifications and not trying to be something that he wasn't. He decided boasting wasn't the answer. Obviously that was a good choice, as six days later they called him and offered him the job.

As soon as he hung up, he called Heather at work. "Hey, would you like to go shopping tonight for a new bathing suit—maybe even two?" She knew exactly what he was telling her, and she let out just a tiny little squeal of excitement, controlling herself so she wouldn't look too unprofessional in front of patients.

That night over a steaming bowl of homemade chowder, they discussed the details and started a list of everything that needed to be done. In her precise handwriting she listed everything she could think of, then transferred it to a spreadsheet on her computer later that night. Her list was numbered from one to forty-three, but by the end of three weeks, she found she was adding a new item to the list for every two she scratched off as complete.

The day after Clark told her the news, she went in and told Dr. Thomas she was giving her notice, and scratched *number one* off the list. Dan Thomas had been an excellent physician and a terrific boss, and she loved her job. He had taught her more than she could ever have learned from the textbooks. She regretted having to leave,

but he understood and kindly offered to write her a letter of recommendation before she could even ask. He was good to his word
when two days later he presented her with one of the most impres-
sive letters she had ever read. "You're too good to me," she commented. "I appreciate it more than you will ever know. I'm really
going to miss this place." It turned out the letter is what sealed the
deal on a job offer in Florida. By the time they loaded up their U-
Haul, they were both off to their new jobs.

On her first day at the clinic, she met Celeste Montgomery. She
was naturally pretty, wearing very little make up. She wore her silky
blonde hair in a shoulder-length bob, which suited her face well.
She had long, side-swept bangs, drawing attention down to her
light periwinkle blue eyes and away from the wider forehead that
can sometimes be the nemesis of heart-shaped faces. Her bangs hit
the outer corners of her eyes on the sides, almost grazing the
cheekbones and touched the arch of her eyebrows at the shortest
spot, keeping attention away from a slightly pointy chin. She had
just the right 'do' to flatter her good looks. She reminded Heather a
little bit of Reese Witherspoon.

The very first words from Celeste's mouth were, "I've been looking forward to meeting you since the minute they told me you were
coming," making Heather immediately feel welcome. "I was told
you were about my age and I could hardly wait to make a new
friend." Celeste's easy manner was equivalent to putting Heather in
a big, soft easy chair where she suddenly felt very, very comfortable
and right at home at this new clinic. All those unfamiliar territory
jitters vanished within the first thirty minutes.

That was the beginning of what was to become a life-long
friendship and the closeness they felt that first day had blossomed
in just three short months. It seemed like they had known each

other for years. Heather knew that one of her hardest trials in moving to Florida would be leaving her best and dearest friend, Breck, in Colorado. Breck and Heather had gone to school together and had shared their most intimate secrets for years. They often laughed about being "hooked at the hip" and she suggested to Breck, it might require surgery to separate them when she left.

Celeste was instrumental in making Heather's transition less painful, and their friendship was becoming very similar to the one she had with Breck. At work, they rarely found time for a break, but they went to lunch together almost every day, and within two weeks, they were sharing things about their lives and laughing about their experiences, as only best friends do. It didn't take long to plan a barbecue so they could introduce their husbands. Clark and Adam made a connection right off the bat, talking baseball, football and every sport they could think of. Clark talked about skiing in the beautiful mountains of Colorado, which held great appeal to Adam, and Adam talked about water skiing and wake boarding in Florida. The girls were pleased that the friendship they were experiencing was carrying over to their husbands.

Heather knew Celeste's love for Adam was as strong as hers was for Clark. When she talked about him, her eyes lit up like tiny fireflies dancing in the night sky. At first that was all Celeste displayed, but as the weeks passed, and they started sharing more and more with each other, Heather saw those tiny fireflies escaping into pools of tears more than once.

Heather had been observing Celeste all morning, and knew she was holding something in that she needed to let out. It was getting harder and harder for Celeste to hide her feelings from Heather. It had been unusually quiet in the clinic that particular morning so they took a rare break. Celeste hardly said a word and Heather knew she needed to talk, but the clinic cafeteria was not exactly the most conducive atmosphere for a heart-to-heart. Heather suggested they walk around the block at lunchtime just to get a breath of fresh air, knowing that she would open up more if she were away from the office, and her assumptions proved to be right.

"I'm so worried about him," Celeste said. "There is never a day that goes by when I feel calm and secure. Not one single day—not ever."

That was a pretty grave statement and Celeste had been so emphatic about it. It shocked Heather. "Talk to me, Celeste. Tell me what's wrong." She couldn't imagine what was going on that would lead to such a desperate statement. They had only walked a few feet from the building when a young boy came speeding past them in the opposite direction on a bike, forcing them to step toward the inside of the sidewalk. In a robot-like motion, Celeste jumped to get out of the way of the intruder and brushed up against a pyramidal-shaped Emily Bruner holly bush. She was oblivious to the long prickly spines, scratching her arm and didn't even notice the blood trickling down her arm from the scratch. Heather reached in her purse and pulled out a tissue to wipe it off.

Then she let loose. It was as though someone had shaken everything loose that had been bottled up inside of her since the beginning of their marriage, when Adam had taken the job as an agent with the U.S. Marshalls. The cap was finally being unscrewed and the contents of the secret ingredients inside were spewing out everywhere for Heather to witness. The problem was the contents were less like the fizz of some soda pop escaping, and more like a volcano spewing out molten lava from Celeste's heart causing a tremendous burning pain.

Heather went into her concerned, caring, *let's-nurse-this-person-back-to-life* mode that came so naturally to her. It was a remnant from her childhood Band-Aid days, and it was obvious that this was going to take one big Band-Aid to patch up the hurt. If Celeste had just cracked the lid and let some of the pressure out slowly, a little at a time, it would have been easier to clean the wound, but instead of the whishing sound of a venting bottle, the pressure inside had caused enough energy for the lid to propel off like an explosion, and there was clearly no forcing the eruption of feelings back inside. The tears flowed like a pot boiling over for the next twenty minutes and Celeste could hardly speak, but when it finally shifted from a rolling boil to a simmer, she was able to share what she could with Heather, and the burden she had been carrying all by herself started to ease.

"I can't tell you much because I don't know much. Even if I did know, I couldn't tell you." she said. "Much of his job is top secret, and he can't even share it with me. That's part of the problem. Before he got this job we shared everything. The communication between us was like no other, but now it doesn't exist. I know it's not because he doesn't want to tell me, but he simply can't. He would lose his job, and even worse, it could put a lot of people in danger. His hours are long and when he gets home, he's too tired to spend any time with me other than sleeping time. Most of the time, we don't even eat together. When we talk about it, it changes for a week or so, and then it starts all over again. Last Friday, you know when I took the day off, I knew he was coming home by 7:00, so I spent the whole day cooking his favorite meal. I bought some beautiful country-style spare ribs and made my specialty barbecue sauce that he loves so much and cooked them all day until they were fall-off-the-bone delicious. He got home an hour late and at 8:00 dragged in too tired to even eat."

"Thanks, Honey, but I'm so tired. Can we save them for tomorrow?" he asked. "I actually grabbed a sweet roll around 6:30 so I'm not really that hungry, anyway."

"Save them? He actually wanted me to SAVE them, after I had taken a vacation day to make sure everything would be perfect for that one night. It's not like I wouldn't understand if that happened once in awhile, but it's the story of our lives. The night we had our barbecue with you and Clark was the first night we had spent time with anyone for over three months. The first time we had actually done anything fun. I can't tell you how grateful I was that you guys were able to come over that night. It was the first night in so long that he didn't have to work late."

Heather was taken off guard for a minute, but had to ask, "Are you sure it's just his job that's taking him away?" By the way Celeste was talking, she couldn't help but wonder if there was someone else in Adam's life, but if so, she sure hadn't seen any sign of it in his body language.

Celeste finally let a smile sneak out from her lips. You could tell her thoughts were drifting back to Adam. "Yes, that's what's so hard about this situation. There are so many secrets, but the one thing I'm sure of is that he loves me and only me. You must think I'm crazy. I'm actually jealous of a woman I don't even know, but whom Adam spends more time with than he does me, and yet I know with all my heart that he doesn't have any romantic feelings for her. I'm jealous that he feels sorry for her, but I can't know why he does. I'm jealous that he doesn't feel sorry for me for having to be alone all the time. I just want some time with him. I want to have time to have fun with friends, and to go to dinner with him, and to sit at home alone and watch a TV show or have a candlelight dinner. I want him to hold me and cuddle with me on the sofa until we fall asleep in each other's arms. I want him to have enough energy to make love to me. I feel like we are growing farther and farther apart because we simply don't have time to talk. It's not the things he says, it's the things he doesn't say. "

"How long will this assignment go on?" asked Heather?

"Well, it's been his first and only assignment so far. At first he thought it would only be a couple of months. It's now been a year and a half. Every time I ask, he tells me it should end soon. I get the impression that there is a court case pending that has something to do with it, but it just keeps getting postponed. If I just knew when it would end, I know I could deal with it better. My biggest fear, though, is when this is over, what will the next assignment be? Is this what our lives will be like forever?"

Heather ached for her sweet, tender-hearted friend. "Is there anything I can do to help? How about if we come over once in awhile and spend time with you, even if Adam isn't there?"

"Thanks, Heather. I can't tell you what your friendship has meant to me. I think it has literally saved me. But no, if I see you and Clark together it would just make me miss Adam even more. Besides, I'm sure Clark has better things to do than to spend time trying to calm a hysterical woman. You're so good to offer, though. Just keep being my friend no matter how loony I get. Help me to stay in focus, and let me vent to you when I need to let it all out."

"Are you sure you are going to be okay? Will you be able to handle this situation much longer? I just don't want you to have a breakdown or anything. I'm worried about you, Celeste."

"I'll be okay. I'm better now, just having talked to you. Thanks for being my sounding board. It wouldn't hurt so much if I didn't love the guy so completely. You know, Heather, it's strange, but he's the most wrong thing in my life right now . . . but he's definitely the most right thing in my life, too."

CHAPTER 8

September 2003

"Dancing in the Moonlight" (Greg & Parris)

"There is no difficulty that enough love will not conquer, no disease that enough love will not heal, no door that enough love will not bridge, no wall that enough love will not throw down, no sin that enough love will not redeem... It makes no difference how deeply seated may be the trouble, how hopeless the outlook, how muddled the tangle, how great the mistake. A sufficient realization of love will dissolve it all. If only you could love enough, you could be the happiest and most powerful being in the world... "

Emmet Fox

G reg and Scott both got their master's degrees in April 2002, and both joined the workforce over a year ago. Scott majored in electrical engineering and was working for the State of Florida coordinating the development of a new power station.

Although Greg's major was in Political Science, it didn't mean he wanted to be a politician—in fact, he did not. But he did love being involved with the principles and the work that goes into affecting every aspect of people's lives. The knowledge and discipline he gained in dealing with the theory and practice of politics, combined with the analysis of political systems and political behavior, made him marketable for a position in State or Local Government. It didn't take long for him to land a job as Labor Relations Specialist in the Governor's office.

So both friends ended up working for the State Government but in totally unrelated fields. Scott was a methodical, hands-on, figure-out-how-it-works kind of guy and Greg was a people person, but it didn't matter how different they were, their friendship never faded.

Scott spent a lot of time dating, but the right one had not come along yet. He wasn't opposed to falling in love, but he wanted to make sure it was with the right person, and that just hadn't happened. To some extent, he was a bit methodical in his quest to find that special someone, not dissimilar to how he treated his education and his profession. It was simply his nature.

Greg, on the other hand, met Parris Roberts in 2001 and had almost immediately fallen in love with her. At first, it had seemed totally out of character, but the people-person side of him succumbed to this tantalizing beauty the instant he laid his eyes upon her. His draw to her was almost hypnotic. Their relationship had been somewhat rocky at first—not because his feelings ever waivered, but rather because Parris' moods seemed to change as often as a runway model's outfits. And with those mood changes, her affection for Greg went from passionate to subdued, from exuberant to cautious, from hot to cold.

Almost from day one, Greg had known there was something that bothered Parris. It was something that was embedded so deeply in her soul she was still unable to share. She didn't tell him anything specific that led him to this conclusion, but he felt it. He was sure, though, with enough patience, she would eventually confide in him and once that happened they could move on. She was definitely worth the wait. He thought . . . no he *knew*, even when she was in her cautious mode, that she loved him. She had never said the words, but somehow he knew it. He, on the other hand, told her he loved her every time he saw or talked to her. Her response was always, "You're so sweet, Greg" or "You're too good to me" or "I know you do" or sometimes she would just change the subject.

It took Greg three months to find out that Parris was three and a half years older than he was. At first, it surprised him since she just graduated with her bachelor's degree the same year he had graduated with his master's and he got started late.

At first, their dates mostly consisted of going to the movies, but eventually the beach became a regular. They would pack a dinner or they would stop at Super Stef's deli for a quick take-out order.

The beach was almost always crowded, but rarely did they go on the weekends because, as Greg put it, "It's über-crowded from Friday night through Sunday." And while it certainly wasn't private on the other nights, at least he could roll over on his stomach with his hands clasped under his head and his elbows outstretched without hitting the person on the blanket next to him. He couldn't do that on the weekends.

"What does über-crowded mean?" Parris asked while they were sitting on their blankets on the sand. "It's a different language and means extremely or super crowded." What language is it?" she asked. And then, in his most serious voice, responded, "It's called *'beachtalk'.*" After a few seconds a smile broke out, and then she laughed. It was the best sound ever. "You need to laugh more because you do it so well," Greg said. She pushed him softly and he fell over on his back, exaggerating the fall as though she had knocked him over with the strength of a human wrecking ball. He grabbed her and pulled her down on top of him, tickling her hard under her ribs. She laughed until she was almost sick and when he finally stopped, she just looked down at him and kissed him softly on the lips. "Yes, she loves me," he assured himself.

Sitting there on the beach that night, watching the sunset, she eventually opened up and told him her mother and father had died when she was a teenager and she had lived with her ailing grandmother, taking care of her until she died when Parris was 20. She had to work hard for the next three years to get enough money saved up for her tuition. "Sometimes," she explained, "I didn't even earn enough at my two jobs combined to pay for a full schedule, so that slowed me down some more." Greg was proud of her determination to pursue her education, even though she had had such a tough life. He was even more proud to think she had postponed her dreams to take care of her sick grandmother on her own.

He saw a teardrop escape from the corner of her eye. She had let her guard down, and he knew this was a turning point. At last she had chosen this moment to let him into this secret corner of her life. He knew there was more to come—much more. He loved her so much and wanted to fill her life with all the happy memories she had missed while growing up. There were so many things she had never experienced, and he wanted to be with her when she experienced them for the very first time.

They lay on the beach that night until the sun went down and the moon took over as king of the night. The sky at sunset, with its magnificent colors of crimson, orange and purple was breathtaking. Each color was almost a distinguishable stripe, one on top of the other, yet blending into each other so softly that it was difficult to tell where one left off and the other began. It was eventually re-placed with a multitude of twinkling stars against an almost black night sky with only the moonlight left to reflect a brilliant luminosi-ty on the waves. The light extended from the shore where the sand met the water all the way to the horizon where the light narrowed almost to a point. The water seemed calm with the shimmering light glowing on it, but it was deceptive as was evident by the sound of the waves crashing to the shore, indicative of an increasingly turbulent tide. Neither the sunset nor the moonrise was more captivating than the other, but the moon freed the heat of the day turning it to a pleasant, but cool night.

They lay there on their blanket watching the sailboats decline in numbers until all but five, then four then none could be seen. Only a few surfers remained until they too had exhausted their last bit of night vision and soon were forced to retire for the evening so they could renew their energy with a good night's sleep in order to start all over in the morning.

"It's so beautiful," Parris said as she cuddled up closer to Greg on the blanket. "I wish we could have met five years ago."

He wrapped his arm around her and pulled her close, letting her head rest on his shoulder. She was shuddering, so he held her tightly, trying to warm her. "I wouldn't have been ready for you five years ago. I was totally engrossed in studies and not mature enough for an incredible woman like you. But here we are now. It's the perfect time." He kissed the top of her head.

"But it would have been so much easier for me then, before..." She stopped suddenly as if she realized she had almost exposed a secret that was intended to be buried.

"Before, what?" he asked curiously, waiting for her to continue. But she jumped up, quickly grabbing his arm and pulling him. "Get up!" she squealed. "Let's not let this moonlight go to waste. Let's dance in the sand."

So they did. The words of an old Peabo Bryson and Roberta Flack song popped into his head and he started humming. Then the hums became words as he sang them softly in her ear. They danced, but their feet were almost standing still in the sand as they just swayed back and forth in each other's arms, as he softy sang the words.

Tonight I celebrate my love for you
It seems the natural thing to do
Tonight no one's gonna find us
We'll leave the world behind us
When I make love to you tonight

Tonight I celebrate my love for you
And hope that deep inside you feel it too
Tonight our spirits will be climbing
To the sky lit up with diamonds
When I make love to you

Tonight I celebrate my love for you
And that midnight song is gonna come shining through
Tonight there'll be no distance between us
What I want most to do
Is to get close to you, tonight

Tonight I celebrate my love for you
And soon this old world will seem brand new
Tonight we will both discover
How friends turn into lovers
When I make love to you

Tonight I celebrate my love for you
And that midnight song is gonna come shining through
Tonight there'll be no distance between us
What I want most to do
Is to get close to you

Tonight I celebrate my love for you

Tonight

And when he stopped, she whispered softly, "I didn't know you could sing."

He buried his face in her hair. The salty smell of the sea in her hair combined with her spellbinding perfume was almost more than he could stand. "Only for you, my love . . . only for you." He wanted her more than he had ever wanted her before. They walked over to the blanket and lay down. He took her in his arms and started kissing her from her head to her toes. Her body started to quiver all over. The temperature had dropped considerably in the last few minutes and he knew she was cold.

She said, "Just hold me, Greg. Please just hold me."

Once again he kept his desires in check, knowing he had to respect her. He took the oversized beach towel that was folded up next to him and wrapped it around her. Then pulling up the sides of the blanket they were lying on, he enclosed both of them tightly inside, like a cocoon, and within minutes, her trembling stopped and when he looked down at her, he saw she had fallen asleep. He watched her, studying every eyelash, her nose, her lips and every inch of her face. She was perfect. "You are such a mystery, Parris," he thought. "What is that secret you are holding onto?" Soon he also drifted off, content for the time just to hold her in his arms.

At midnight, the moon had reached the point where it was closest to the earth and the high tide had crept up and reached their blanket. It only took seconds after the water touched their feet for them to wake up. Neither wanted to be disturbed, but they knew they had to pack up before it was more than their feet that were wet. Besides, they both had to be to work in the morning.

"Let me drive you home tonight. You can leave your car in the parking lot and I'll pick you up tomorrow night, and you can get it then. I can't stand to have you drive home alone this late." As always she refused, having a ready-made reason in her growing bag of excuses. And, as always, he knew not to press it. He had tried that before and it hadn't worked out well. She always took two steps backwards when he pushed too hard.

When he got home, he went straight to bed, pulling the covers up around him with thoughts of the evening swirling around in his head. Before drifting off into a deep sleep, the last thoughts on his mind were of Parris. He assured himself once again that the time was close for her to open up and they could move on with their lives. How many nights, months, years now had he gone through this same routine, trying to convince himself? But tonight, he had gained some confidence that it was true; he was more certain than he ever had been before. He dreamed of dancing with her in the sand, then in a foggy cloud he could see a stunning bride walking down the aisle but he couldn't see her face, and he desperately wanted to so he could see how happy she was. Then suddenly the scene switched to him playing with children in the soft green grass behind a white picket fence in the front yard of a comfortable home, but he couldn't see Parris there with him and the children. Where was she?

CHAPTER 9

July 2010

"There's Healing in Service" (Breck)

"What is the essence of life? To serve others and to do good."

Aristotle (384-322 BC)

———•———

"Well, it's been four years now since Jeff died," Breck said to herself as she was getting ready for work. "Am I ever going to move on with my life or will I be stuck in limbo forever just going through the motions? I've tried. I really have tried." As she lifted the *touch-of-bronze* eye shadow from her metallic striped cosmetic bag she noticed for the first time how old and worn out that cosmetic bag was looking." She stared at herself in the mirror for a few minutes wondering what she would look like in five or ten years from now. She had turned 29 this year. In just seven months she would be 30. She checked for signs of crow's feet around her eyes, and then started to reminisce to a time five years ago when her life was so different, filled with more happiness and promise than she had ever thought possible.

It had taken Breck over two years following Jeff's death to go out on a date, and she remembered how difficult that first step had been. It had been a blind date. Her friend, Emma, from work had lined her up. The truth is she hadn't wanted to go. It was merely easier to hide everything inside and just be alone, but she knew she couldn't do that forever or she would mentally waste away. She didn't want to explain to some stranger all about what had happened and most of all she didn't want to cry around someone she didn't even know, and she knew there was a good possibility that could happen if her date started probing. It was still difficult for her to open up to anyone and talk about it, much less a stranger. But to her relief, Carter had been a perfect gentleman that evening. Emma had briefed him on Breck's situation beforehand, and he handled everything with the tact of a great politician.

"What time can I pick you up?" Carter asked. But Breck wasn't ready to give out her address, as she was sure it would be a one-date-only situation. She made an excuse about having to work late, and they agreed to meet at the ESPN Zone on 16th Street in Denver. During several telephone conversations prior to their date, they determined that sports was a topic they both enjoyed, so it seemed like a casual enough place for a blind date where they could enjoy a juicy burger and fries and talk about a ball game rather than about her.

The evening went pretty well and fortunately, there was no lack of conversation. It just so happened that the Colorado Rockies were playing the Los Angeles Dodgers that night and since Carter was originally from L.A., he was a big Dodgers fan. She was easily able to keep up with him in stats and player information, and they enjoyed bantering with each other while watching the game and eating burgers and fries. When the Dodgers lost, she mocked him relentlessly, but Carter took it pretty well. He was a really good sport about it, telling her that next time he would get even. When the evening ended, she realized she had actually had a good time with quite a few laughs here and there.

She dated Carter on and off for about three months, and although they shared a commonality in their love for sports and really enjoyed each other's company, their relationship never developed into anything more than a really special friendship. They both knew there were no romantic connections blossoming on either side, and Carter became more like the brother she had never had. With the companionship they shared, they became pretty good buddies and confidantes, and about six months after they met, Carter revealed he had met someone he was very interested in, which hadn't taken Breck by surprise in the least. She was very happy and excited for him, and she quizzed him about every detail of his new love interest to make sure she deserved this great guy friend of hers. They kept in touch for a few more "non-dates" but that quickly fizzled out, as he was spending more and more time with his new girlfriend, Terry.

Not long after they met, Carter and Terry got married and now have one child. Carter still calls Breck quite often to check in on her, and they get together occasionally. As an extension of Carter, Terry has also become a good friend and has taken up the role of matchmaker, lining Breck up with someone every chance she gets.

Since that first date with Carter, there have been several dozen dates with other guys, but in her eyes, "none of them compared to Jeff" and none of them held any real attraction for her. At first it was kind of depressing, but she tried hard not to give into those feelings. She just kept plugging away at trying to get through each day.

The one thing that had made a huge difference in her life was the first Christmas after Jeff's death, when she had shopped for everyone on her list from "The Giving Tree." It was the first thing she had done that had taken her mind off her grief. Everyone had responded so well to the gifts being given in their names that she decided to make it an annual tradition, always making sure to pick a name and include a gift from Jeff. After two years she decided to get more involved, so she investigated the possibility of doing volunteer work at the Children's Hospital at St. Joseph's.

She was amazed at how many things were being done by The Volunteer Chapters within the Association of Volunteers at the Hospital. She found a Boulder Chapter which sponsored golf tournaments, Teddy Bear Teas at the Boulderado Hotel, auctions, gift-wrapping on the first weekend in December at the Barnes and Noble bookstore and many other things. The group met the first Tuesday of every month at 7:00 p.m. at a member's home, with the exception of July and August, and Breck became one of their most faithful supporters. She loved being involved with activities to help these sweet children. They almost became *her* children, as her fondness grew into a deep love for every single one of them, old and new patients alike.

She also became involved in the Cardiac Kids Chapter, especially in July when she wasn't at the Boulder Chapter. They hold a reunion picnic every July which requires a lot of extra help. Pumpkin Patch Day in October was another favorite.

But the one she preferred the most was the Friends of the Hospital Sports Program chapter, which was developed to provide funding for children with disabilities so they could participate in the disabled ski program at Winter Park. It was almost miraculous to see how this program helped to build a sense of freedom and self-esteem through skiing. They also got the children involved in golfing and in a bike tour. This chapter met the second Wednesday of every month at The Children's Hospital with the exception of February, July and December.

There were so many chapters it could actually be a full-time job, but she had her own full-time job so she had to limit what she could do. She didn't want to take on too much and do everything only half-way. "Better to do only a few and do them well," she told herself.

Every payday she contributed books to the Gift of Gracie Chapter, where books were in much need. While she didn't have any more time to spend on another volunteer chapter, she could at least help this one through her pocket book. On occasion, when she was able, she would fill in at one of the many other chapter events, and all in all, she kept very busy, finding that she didn't miss the companionship of a male friend nearly so much when she was involved with these children. It really was a Godsend and a huge blessing in her life. It gave her a purpose in life that she had been unable to find elsewhere since Jeff's death.

For the most part, she found it was women who were involved with these volunteer chapters. Once in awhile, she would see some men participating, but the women really made up the bulk of the volunteers.

She zipped up her make-up bag and made one last check in the mirror. "How nice it would be," she thought, "if I could meet a guy who loved helping these children as much as I do." She was sure Jeff would have.

"Dream on," she said to herself. "Dream on, Breck."

CHAPTER 10

July 2003

"The Deposition" (Patricia)

"Behind every great fortune lies a great crime."

Honore de Balzac

———◆———

He arrived at the office at 5:30 a.m. He left the house before Celeste was up, and he knew she would be upset that he had gone without waking her, but he couldn't bear to disturb her from her sound sleep; it came so rarely these days. She tossed and turned and quite often in the middle of the night, he would turn over to wrap his arm across her body and instead of the warmth of her frame to curl around, he just found an empty pillow. He would open his eyes just enough to see a soft light barely creeping into the otherwise dark bedroom from under the doorway and he knew she was having a hard time sleeping again. Some nights he would wake up to sounds of muffled crying. Adam was well aware of the toll this job was taking on Celeste and their marriage. He was trying his best to hold it together and was sure the case would be over in the next couple of months, and he would make it all up to her, but they had to hold on until then. Man, he loved her and he hated seeing her so unhappy.

He would explain to her later that tonight why he left without waking her, but in his mind, he wasn't sure it would make any difference. Still, she needed the rest. He was hoping if he got an early start, he could get home early and surprise her. Maybe that would make up for it in some small way.

He swiped his card which allowed him into the lobby of the secured building. As soon as his shoes hit the highly polished white and gray swirled Italian marble floor in the atrium, the silence was broken. The normal clatter that could be heard at the 8:00 hour was absent so there was nothing to conceal the sound of his footsteps. No one was there when he arrived at 5:30 except the security guard who was sitting at the desk behind a glass enclosure in the middle of the foyer, looking at a magazine. "Graveyard shift would be a drag," thought Adam, "nothing to do and no one to talk to all night long, every single night. I wonder how he stays awake."

"In kind of early, aren't cha, Agent Montgomery?"

"Hi there, Bernie. Yes, I've got a lot of paperwork to do, and the morning hours are the best time to get anything done. Quiet time is the name of the game. How's the family?"

"They're doing great," said Bernie. "My youngest daughter is going off to college in the fall. She's a smart one, ya know, like her mom. I'm gonna miss her, but I'm glad she's doin' it. She'll make something of herself, and who knows, maybe one day she'll earn enough to take care of her old dad." He laughed heartily as though he had just told the funniest joke ever.

Adam slid his card once more and opened the bulletproof glass door adjacent to Bernie's enclosed station, walking past him to the elevator a few steps beyond. He said over his shoulder, "Hang in there, Bernie. It'll be worth it. See you later."

"Right, Agent Montgomery. Have a nice day, ya hear?"

He pushed the up button and the doors opened immediately; no one waiting for the elevator—the elevator just waiting for him. He stepped in and pushed FLR 3, feeling the Braille dots beside the number. As the doors opened on the third floor, he stepped out and walked down the newly carpeted hallway to the first door on the left. What an improvement, he thought as he looked at the carpet. The old one had been just that—OLD. You had to watch every step you took so you wouldn't catch your toe on one of the seams that had come unraveled. He hadn't realized until now how that dingy carpet could set the mood for the day. Funny how a little thing like that could make such a difference. It actually picked up his spirits. The hallway was clean and bright; not depressing and dirty-feeling. He knew it wasn't really dirty before; it was vacuumed every day by the cleaning crew, but it was so worn and dark, it just gave the impression of being dirty. Today it seemed like he was really going to an official place of business, not just a rundown old building disguised as offices. He felt like his day was starting off fresh already. He unlocked the office to face several rows of cubicles. On the way to his space, he stopped at the water cooler and grabbed a cup of water to take to his desk.

Adam sat down and rolled his grey tweed chair up to his steel-gray, L-shaped computer work station inside the small cubicle. He referred to this small space as his office. He kept his desk neat and orderly. There were rules about leaving files out. They had to be locked up before leaving, but even if there hadn't been any regulations, he would never have left things lying around. He had seen more than a few agents get lazy about the rules, leaving files lying out on their desks overnight, but he was more careful; one never knew what might turn up missing. Not that any of the agents would intrude in another's area, but he just wanted to be careful. The furniture was mostly modular and not very fancy—what could you expect from the government? Any excess budget had been spent in making the lobby presentable to the occasional rare, but distinguished visitor. But Adam was cost-conscious about government spending and felt his space was sufficient for his needs. After all, most of the agents spent the majority of time out working in the field on their cases, so they really didn't need much office space. The only thing they needed a desk for was to do the dreaded paperwork, so they avoided it as much as possible.

But today he was there to read the file—again! He couldn't begin to count how many times he had gone over the file, but he knew he had to make sure he was aware of every tiny detail in that folder. No one involved could afford to make a mistake now. They were too close.

He unlocked his drawer and pulled out the file. The label on the tab at the top of the manila folder read **PATRICIA REYBURN** in big bold letters. He opened the folder and pulled out the papers, his eyes skipping past the birth date, social security number, place of birth and other miscellaneous facts at the top of the deposition and going straight to the report.

Deposition Date: January 14, 1993
I met Johnny Castilletti when I was still in high school. I was seventeen and he was thirteen years my senior. I was working part time at Mama Maria's delicatessen in Tampa Bay, Florida. He told me that my shy, but friendly manner caught his attention, and said he appreciated my childlike beauty. He was full of the right words back then. He came into the deli for about five days straight, always ordering the

same "Italian Works" sandwich, and always making sure he waited until I was available to wait on him.

I was pretty naïve and his good looks and pleasant smile captured my heart in those first five days when he made no effort to hide his interest. I guess I responded to his flirtations by flirting back, but in a subtle manner—you know—kind of like assuring myself the whole thing was harmless. I enjoyed the attention he gave me and was flattered that a "more mature" man would even notice me. On the fifth day, he brought me a gift. I opened the box and was surprised to see a pair of beautiful diamond stud earrings, at least a carat each. I remember I almost choked when I opened the box. The earrings were gorgeous, and I had never seen anything like them before. Not real ones, anyway. I came from a pretty humble family who worked hard and went without luxuries in order to save money for my education. There were no diamonds in my household. Even my mother's wedding ring was a skinny plain gold band, without a single diamond on her finger. She never even mentioned that she would like a diamond. She just seemed content to save any extra money for my education.

Johnny told me to wear them on our date. I asked him what date. I knew my mom would never allow me to go out with someone who was thirty years old, much less accept a gift like this. He asked me if I had ever been to the horse races, and I told him no. He said, "I want to take you to the races at Tampa Bay Downs on Saturday."

I remember feeling this sudden surge of excitement, and immediately started conjuring up an excuse to give my mom—actually not an excuse but a lie. I had always been a good girl, done the right thing, and it had never even occurred to me to lie to my parents before, so this would be difficult and I wasn't even sure I could pull it off. I knew I would also have to arrange to get the day off work because I was always on the schedule for Saturdays, since no one else wanted that shift, and I really didn't care. I was enamored by this good-looking guy, whom I barely knew, but who was mature and obviously rich; unlike anyone I had ever known in high school.

That was the first date I had with Johnny Castilletti. In the following months he wined and dined me and treated me like royalty, buying me everything I wanted, and I was simply swept off my feet. Eventually my mother and father found out and from that time on, we were in constant battles with each other, which was new to all of us. We had always gotten along remarkably well. I had been an excellent student and they often told me I was a "too-good-to-be-true" kind of daughter, always making the right choices and doing the right things. I honestly never gave them any trouble and that was the role I enjoyed. But as I continued to see Johnny, confrontations with my parents began and soon became more and more frequent. When I turned eighteen and they no longer could tell me what to do, Johnny seized the opportunity to lure me into moving in with him. He told me he would take care of me, and I wouldn't have to do anything I didn't want. It sounded great to me.

Much to my parents' dismay, I moved out as soon as I graduated from high school in May of 1992. I felt guilty because I knew they were devastated, but not guilty enough to abandon the idea. It was the most reckless thing I had ever done in my life, and I will always regret it, but something had taken hold of me, and I found I just couldn't say no to him. I obviously wasn't smart enough or mature enough to see just how much pain I was causing my parents. They had saved all their lives, sacrificing to give me all the things I needed and to provide for my college education. I was pretty bright and had always excelled in school no matter what the subject. Learning came easy for me. I was an only child and my parents would do anything for me. They were certain I was going to make something of myself and have a good, productive life; that is, until Johnny Castilletti came into the picture.

After only a couple of months of living the life of luxury with Johnny in West Palm Beach, I started to get bored. He was gone a lot, and I was lonely. One day I told him I wanted to go to school. Of course I didn't have any money of my own, and I certainly couldn't ask my parents for money now, so I asked Johnny. After all, he had told me he would give me anything I wanted. At first he put me off, telling me we could talk about it after he got home from his next trip. Later, he flat out told me no. That's when he started controlling my life. I would tell him I was going somewhere, and he wouldn't let me.

Chuck was my bodyguard, and he was always close by, though he rarely talked to me. I thought it was ridiculous and wondered why I needed a bodyguard, especially since I spent most of my time in the house. Johnny told me that people with a lot of money always needed to have someone watching out for them, as there were always people in the business world looking for an easy buck, and when you didn't give it to them or when a deal didn't go as expected, they wanted revenge. I didn't understand what that had to do with me, but he told me they could get to him through me. It was for my own protection. In reality I think it was mostly because he wanted to keep an eye on me when he wasn't around.

Johnny had told me it was my sweet, quiet nature that he had been drawn to in the beginning. He liked my gentle, demure, naivety. I was aware I was almost subservient with him, which didn't agree with my nature, but which suited him fine. I don't know how I could have been so stupid. But as time went on, I started getting more inquisitive and demanding answers from him. He didn't like that one bit. He said I had gone from being diffident to almost dissident.

After just three months, I was ready to go home. I knew I had made a big mistake, and I was sure my parents would take me back and help me get through this, but he told me that was out of the question. He was furious and told me I was ungrateful and slapped me violently across the face, knocking me to the hard Italian stone floor, and for the first time, he viciously raped me. It was to become the first of many times that this scenario played out. No longer was he kind and gentle and no longer did he care how I felt. He would take me wherever and whenever he wanted. But it was strange. When he was through, he always apologized, telling me how sorry he was and that he couldn't bear to live without me, and I was sucked back into his snare. He knew just how to play me, turning the tables to make it look like it was my fault and telling me I just made him so angry when I was so selfish, thinking only about what I wanted. I would feel ashamed for being so ungrateful and would succumb to his demands once again.

Leaving me alone, waiting day after day for his return had become pretty routine by then. I was eighteen years old and had no one to talk to and nothing to do. It was no different than an animal in the wilderness suddenly being caged. The bruises on my body came and went, but no one else ever saw them. I was sure, though, that Chuck was aware of what was going on because he was always nearby, and I know he must have heard my screams when Johnny was beating me. At times I would feel Chuck's eyes on me, and when I looked at him, I could see pity, but he never said anything, just quickly looked away, as if to keep any feelings out of this business arrangement he had with

Johnny. I knew he could never betray Johnny no matter how he felt about the situation.

One day when Johnny been gone for about a week, I wandered into the library, as was my daily ritual, looking for a new book to read to help pass the time. The library had become my sanctuary. The books kept me from going crazy. The room was massive, and the walls were lined from floor to ceiling with elaborately carved bookshelves. I walked across the hardwood floor and climbed up the classic mahogany rolling track ladder that reached to the top of the twenty-foot ceilings, studying the book titles for a minute before picking up a leather-bound copy of *Judgment at Nuremburg*. I had started it a couple of times before in high school, but had never finished. I had found the movie intriguing, however, so I decided to tackle it once again since I had so much time on my hands these days.

I climbed down and walked over to my favorite oversized leather wing-back chair, sat down and propped my feet up on the matching tufted footstool. I remember I had been reading for about an hour when the dead silence in the room was broken by an odd but familiar noise. I glanced in the direction of the sound, already knowing what I was going to see. It wasn't the first time this had happened. I saw Chuck sitting right outside the doorway in his usual spot on the massive, red velvet Victorian chair. I had sat in that same chair before and had found it very uncomfortable, always feeling it must have been purchased for show and not for comfort. It had been designed in the Rococo style, as Johnny had taught me, copying the period in France when the furniture was recognizable by its intricate wood carvings and extensive scrollwork. Oftentimes, the pieces had carved flowers, but this one had animals carved in it—much more to Johnny's masculine tastes. The legs were shaped like an 'S' in a cabriole style.

I didn't understand how Chuck could be comfortable enough to fall asleep in that chair, but he must have been because he had drifted off to sleep, snoring in a rhythmic tune of his own making. This actually happened on a fairly regular basis when I went to the study to read. I didn't blame him. I assumed he must get very bored too, just sitting around all day while I read for hours on end. I never told Johnny, because I knew he would be furious and would fire Chuck on the spot. I took pity on him and figured it may as well be Chuck guarding me as someone else, so I kept it to myself. I understood boredom and could not see any harm in his taking a little nap. I also knew that Chuck's internal alarm would have awakened him quickly to respond to any unusual noise because his brain was geared for listening to the slightest sounds, even in his sleep.

As I turned my head back to my book, my eyes stopped at the desk—Johnny's desk. There were so many things I thought were strange; so many rules and instructions from Johnny. For instance, he never allowed me to call him at work and wouldn't even tell me what his company's name was. He told me it was for my own security. The unanswered questions just made me curious. I stood up and quietly wandered over and sat down at the massive solid Honduran mahogany hand-carved judge's desk, rubbing my hands across the intricate carvings on the edge. Instinctively, I started opening the drawers and thumbing through papers. I didn't even know what I was looking for or what I would do if I found something, but I was intrigued to say the least, even though I knew my curiosity could get me into a lot of trouble. I worked my way through the drawers, finding nothing unusual—pads of paper, rubber bands, paper clips, pencils—the usual things you would find in a desk. None of these things would ever be allowed on the top of the desk in traditional desk caddies as they would distract from the beauty of the desk itself, and it was all about projecting a perfect image for any invited business guests. When I tugged at the middle drawer on the left, my fingernail caught the handle and snapped off at the quick as I wasn't expecting the drawer to be locked. I made another attempt, this time more carefully, to make sure it wasn't just stuck. I moved on to the drawer below and found it was also locked. My curiosity peeked and I wondered just what secrets these two drawers held. That was the day I made up mind that I was going to find out. I didn't know how, but somehow I would; I just had to think about it for awhile.

Suddenly the silence made me aware that the snoring had stopped, and I stood up abruptly, quietly tip-toeing back to the chair, sitting down and opening my book barely in time to look like I hadn't stirred from that spot. Chuck stood up, rubbed his eyes and walked into the room. As he approached my chair, my eyes were focused on the pages. I looked over the arm of the chair, glanced at the floor, and saw his feet next to me, catching sight of his black patent leather shoes and the same red socks he always wore peeking out from the bottom of his trousers. That was too close for comfort. I looked up casually and smiled at him, acknowledging his presence.

The deposition was hundreds of pages long so he couldn't read it all this morning. But for now, he was satisfied. He had gleaned one more detail. "Red socks!" Adam said to himself. Why hadn't he noticed that before? He had read the report at least fifty times and had glanced right over that. "That's why I need to read it again and again," he mumbled to himself. Now he had one more thing to add to his list of things to watch out for . . . she said he always wore RED SOCKS!

CHAPTER 11

August 2003
"The Drawer of Secrets" (Patricia)

"Everything secret degenerates, even the administration of justice; nothing is safe that does not show how it can bear discussion and publicity."

Lord Acton

———◆———

T he word finally came down that the trial was scheduled to start on Wednesday, November 12, 2003, the day after the Veteran's Day holiday and two weeks before Thanksgiving. Patricia wasn't confident that this date would stick since it had been postponed so many times before. She had no idea they could drag it on so long, and she was tired of it. The defense kept filing for an extension so they could gather all the information and be better prepared. In actuality she was sure their money had bought the delays. The attorneys assured her this was it, at long last, and there would be no more extensions.

Although she was petrified, she wanted it over, and she wanted to move on with her life, if that were even a possibility. Frankly, she doubted it. In fact, she doubted they could really win against the Castilletti mob. She was scared. In fact, she was sick to her stomach most of the time. She missed her mom and dad and wished she could tell them one more time how sorry she was. "How did I get mixed up in this mess?" she wondered. "One day I was an exceptional student, happy with my family and getting ready for college, and the next thing I knew, I had made one wrong decision and messed up my whole life."

It was only a few short months after she met Johnny when she started to suspect that being a control freak was the least of his vices. After the day when she discovered the locked desk drawers, she started plotting how she could find out what was in them. From that day on, she went into that library every single day, picked a book, sat in her chair then listened for Chuck. The moment Chuck would drift off to sleep, she would sneak over to the desk and try to open it. She opened up a paper clip and tried to maneuver it in the lock, but it didn't work. She tried a letter opener—no luck. She tried an ice pick that she hid up the sleeve of her sweater. She tried a hairpin. Nothing seemed to work. It always looked so easy in the movies, but this wasn't the movies, and she was not trained to be an intruder. Then one day, she walked over and as she was studying the lock, she tugged at the handle and the drawer opened. Just like that! He had left it open. A gasp involuntarily slipped from her lips, and she quickly looked at the doorway to see if Chuck heard her, but luckily he was still lost in what must be an incredibly interesting dream world.

Her heart was pulsating so fast, she thought it must be visible to the naked eye. She wondered if Chuck woke up, would he be able to hear it pounding like a drum from where he sat outside the doorway. It crossed her mind that Johnny might have left the drawer open on purpose to trap her, but how would he know she had been trying to open it? She studied it carefully and found no telltale evidence of her previous attempts to jimmy the locks and dismissed the thought that it had been left open intentionally. She took a deep breath and slowly, very quietly pulled the drawer all the way open. She stared down at a neatly organized and efficiently labeled set of files, pulling out the first black Pendaflex hanging folder and replacing it with a sticky note to carefully mark the space from where she had removed it. Her hands were shaking as she carefully opened the folder. She concentrated hard on keeping the papers in the exact order so as not to be discovered. It was evident that the files had been placed in the drawer in an orderly manner, probably to expose any tampering. They had even been placed a certain distance apart, with almost painstaking precision.

After carefully examining the documents in the first folder, nothing really jumped out as being suspicious. It looked like regular business notes and correspondence. She placed it back in the exact position, removing the sticky post-it she had used to mark the spot. Before pulling out another folder, she studied the tabs across the tops to see if any of the labels triggered suspicion. She noticed that a small number of the folders were red and had been placed intermittently throughout the black ones. It seemed out of sync with the rest of the system. Everything else about this drawer was extremely well-organized. "Why would these red ones not be all together in one section, and why were there red ones at all? Could the color have any significance and were they placed randomly so as to reveal any possible tampering?" she wondered. It took only moments after she pulled out the first red file to establish that she was on the right track with the color-coding theory.

Opening the file, she found a massive fifty-two page spreadsheet with column headings at the top of each page; *Date Acquired, Place Acquired, Description, Value, Disposition, Profit.* Under the *Description* heading there were pages and pages of jewelry items—rings, necklaces, earrings, bracelets, and brooches. She wondered how he had accumulated such a large wealth of jewelry in his short lifetime. "There must be hundreds of thousands of dollars worth of jewelry—maybe millions," she thought. Then she went to the last page and looked at the total under the *Value* column. She took a second look to be sure she hadn't made a mistake. "$16,117,393.43," she said out loud.

"What are you doing?" Chuck roared loudly, as he slammed his fist down on the desk.

The roar of his voice startled her, and she jerked backwards, slamming her knee hard against the open drawer and almost falling off the large leather rolling chair. She caught the folder as it almost slipped off her lap. She intuitively knew if she even wrinkled a page, Johnny would know. But what difference did it make, anyway? She was caught, and she knew Chuck's loyalties were with Johnny.

The pounding of her heart before couldn't compare with what it was doing now. It seemed as loud now as an African Djembe drum, beating a primeval war cry. The pounding was brutal and relentless, and she could hardly catch her breath. She felt like she was about to pass out.

Chuck must have seen the color fade from her cheeks and grabbed her arm to steady her. "What the hell are you doing, lady? Are you trying to get us both killed?"

She didn't say anything for a minute. She couldn't. She couldn't speak. All the words that normally flowed easily from her mouth, were now caught in her throat . . . choking her . . . strangling her, and she couldn't get them out. She didn't move for what seemed like an hour, but was, in fact, only seconds. She sat there silently, until finally tears started rolling down her cheeks, and she was at last able to catch her breath.

She didn't expect Chuck to have a soft side. She had never seen it before. In fact, she had hardly ever heard him talk. But he did. He felt bad for her and told her it would be okay. Softly he said, "Let's just put things back and forget this ever happened, okay? We don't want Mr. Castilletti coming in here and finding out what you've done, Patricia."

Then it struck her. Her brain was finally working again, and she realized that Chuck couldn't tell Johnny even if he wanted to because it would implicate him. If Johnny found out he had been sleeping on the job it could be disastrous for him.

It wasn't until later, when she had gone through all the files, that she realized just *how* disastrous.

CHAPTER 12

November 2003
"Unloading Burdens" (Greg & Scott)

"Friends are as companions on a journey, who ought to aid each other to persevere in the road to a happier life."

Pythagoras

———◆———

H e was worried about her. It had been two months since that amazing night they spent on the beach, when Parris opened up a little about her life before they met and then slept quietly in the crook of Greg's arm. That night he had been sure it was the beginning of a more open relationship; one that would bring them closer together and one that would fashion a new direction for her love, guiding her to the end of the fork in the road, where their two trails would meet and they could walk together as one, rather than parallel on different pathways. They had created a bond that night that would link them together not just physically, but with ties of secrets she had been keeping about her past, but that were now shared confidences. She hadn't made any attempts to hide the tears that flowed and glistened under the moonlight, and as he had wiped them from her cheeks with his thumbs and kissed them with his lips, those tears instantly transformed into a kind of glue that had bonded his spirit to hers.

He knew there was much more to tell. He wasn't so naïve as to believe that was the whole story. He knew there was still something much greater troubling her, but he was positive she would now be ready to communicate on a higher level with him, sharing her most intimate secrets; the ones causing her to be so troubled.

But he was wrong. Since that night, she had once again cooled. She was withdrawn—maybe more than before. There was no more letting him in on the clandestine life that was buried so deep inside her. He didn't understand how it could happen, but time and time again, it did. On each occasion when he was certain things were changing and it would be different this time, he ended up being fooled by her days later when she reverted back to her old self. He was dumbfounded as to why he convinced himself over and over again that this time would be different.

He needed to talk to Scott about it, even though he knew Scott thought their whole relationship was crazy. Scott had never been able to get close to Parris, which wasn't surprising since she didn't seem to let anyone into her own little world. She usually found excuses whenever Scott asked the two of them to join him on a double date. Scott worried a lot about Greg and was convinced that Parris was stringing him along.

They sat in a corner booth at Shirley's Burgers, and Scott allowed Greg to blather on about the whole situation for over an hour, like only a best friend would have the patience to do. For the most part, he didn't speak, just listened. He didn't break in as Greg described the same concerns he had recounted a dozen times before. He didn't interrupt unless Greg specifically asked him for his opinion, and when he did, he was wise enough to soften his words to avoid hurting Greg any more than he already was. He knew Greg well enough to know what he really needed was someone to talk to and a place to unload his woes, and he also knew, as always, he would be that guy. He had been there for him a lot during the past couple of years, but it seemed like these "What am I going to do?" sessions were becoming more and more frequent.

He studied Greg as he talked, watching him pull one napkin after another out of the restaurant-style chrome dispenser, shredding them one at a time into little bits of confetti, creating a small landscape of white mountains on the red and black speckled Formica table without being remotely aware of what he was doing. "Greg is totally unaware of the mess he is creating," Scott thought to himself, "either on the table or in his life."

He wished he could help more, but he knew he couldn't. He had made previous attempts, but Greg's heart was so invested in this relationship he couldn't allow his ears to listen or his brain to comprehend. So Scott just lent his support by listening and worrying about him.

Where had his fun-loving, happy friend gone? He rarely heard any of the comical quips coming out of him anymore. They used to roll off his tongue during every conversation, but they were few and far between now. It was as though his vocabulary was now limited to basically two words—Parris Roberts! It wasn't hard to figure out why he no longer laughed or created that once fun-loving environment everyone was drawn to. Greg was deeply and desperately in love, but he wasn't happy. The love he so badly wanted to give, but which was not being returned by Parris, was turning out to be a lethal combination. Greg was insistent that she loved him, but he admitted that she never actually said it and as far as Scott could tell, she never showed it. It was obvious that she brought him down. As he watched his best friend's heart being ripped apart by this woman, he became angrier by the minute, but wisely held his tongue. He didn't want to say anything that would damage their friendship, especially since he knew Greg really needed a friend right now.

Greg was grateful for Scott's friendship. He knew he could always count on him to be there for him. That's the kind of friendship they had formed over the years. He was well aware of how hard it was for Scott to keep his thoughts to himself, but he appreciated the fact that most of the time he did. He remembered many of their early conversations in the past two years when Scott had tried to tell him to dump her. He knew Scott thought he was crazy and sometimes, like right now, he was sure he was probably right. He was foolish to keep investing so much of himself without getting anything in return. It was affecting every part of his life. But even though his head told him how foolish it was, his heart wouldn't allow him to stop trying.

"I know how you feel, Scott, and I appreciate your listening. I'm grateful I can talk to you. I really can't explain it other than to tell you I know with every fiber of my being, that she needs me, and I can't abandon her now."

"It's okay, Greg. I'm glad I can be here for you, even if I don't totally understand. I want you to know that any time you need an ear, mine is here waiting for you."

"I know. You're a great friend. You've been there for me ever since Miss Denture," and he smiled with a purposefully contorted grin that only Greg could pull off. Scott was glad to see a rare glimpse of the old humor from his good pal. They both laughed and stood up as Scott clapped him on the back and picked up the tab.

"It's on me," he said. "I'd pay anything to see your Miss Denture grin. Sometimes memories become elusive with time, but I can always count on you to bring them vividly back to life again."

As they walked out of the diner, they went their separate ways, promising to get together more often. Scott took about ten steps and turned his head back, glancing over his shoulder at Greg's back, still able to see his head hanging down. Scott ached for his good buddy.

Greg momentarily felt better and was determined to talk to Parris about making plans for a dinner and movie with Scott in the near future. Scott was too good a friend to lose, and every time he was around him, he realized how much he missed that friendship. "It would be really good for Parris to socialize with more people," he thought. "It would help her feel more comfortable once she got over her shyness." But in all honesty he wasn't really sure it was in any way related to shyness. For some reason she enveloped herself in a shell she had created, and although she poked her head out every once in awhile, she most often retracted back inside that shell where she felt safe, like a turtle sensing danger. He would insist on making the plans for their next date and those plans would include Scott. He suddenly caught himself avoiding the large crack in the sidewalk, and laughed at himself. Of course he wasn't superstitious and in no way would stepping on the crack break his mother's back or cause any bad luck. Still he didn't need any bad luck and as stupid as it seemed, he continued to walk around the long crack.

Scott turned his head back around, while walking in the opposite direction, reminding himself that a long time ago, he had mulled over the idea of doing a background check on Parris, but had decided Greg might consider that a betrayal if he ever found out. "It's time for me to re-visit that idea," he decided. He couldn't get Greg out of his mind. He missed his old friend and wished desperately that he could get him back; not so much for his sake but for Greg's. He also found himself feeling grateful that he wasn't in a serious relationship. He didn't need this kind of drama in his life right now. Greg walked away, totally unaware that his relationship with Parris was having an effect on Scott, but Scott was well aware of it.

CHAPTER 13

November 2003

"Friendship Remedies" (Heather & Celeste)

"There is no wilderness like a life without friends; friendship multiplies blessings and minimizes misfortunes; it is a unique remedy against adversity, and it soothes the soul."

Baltasar Gracian

——————◆——————

Heather and Celeste had a rare day off together and decided they needed a girls' day out. Nothing could be more relaxing than a day at the beach, and Celeste had been looking forward to it all week long.

Before catching some rays in the sun, they decided to pick up some Mexican food from one of the Yucatan taco stands on the boardwalk that everyone was raving about. Their tacos, with handmade corn tortillas, were not the normal fast food fare, and there was a buzz around town about their delicious menu. They both agreed this was not a day for their typical boring salad lunch, and planned to spice up their day a bit by indulging in something less sensible, and agreeing they would eat without the slightest bit of guilt.

The day was perfect. The sand was warm and soft, scrunching up in between their bare toes as they walked across the tiny creamy-white granules. Since it was a weekday, the beach was not all that crowded, and the thought of enjoying the beach while everyone else was at work was liberating.

They laid their blankets out and Celeste plopped the cooler full of water and diet drinks right between them. She was glad she had remembered. It was already apparent it was going to be an exceptionally warm and humid day for November. That often happened in Florida, and they both knew by now to be prepared. After stripping their Levi's and tops off, they settled down on the blankets in their swimming suits to soak up some sun. Heather opened the sack of tacos and passed one over to Celeste, who dived right in. She had missed dinner the night before and was famished. Somehow, everything tasted better on the beach, no matter what it was. "I'm so hungry, I could probably have just eaten some seaweed and been satisfied," she laughed.

"I could always have rounded you up a couple of sand crabs," laughed Heather. She was hungry too, and they each devoured two tacos in no time flat. They were as delicious as all the praises hinted.

Celeste brushed the few crumbs off the blanket while Heather was saturating her body with sunscreen. She was ever the nurse, telling everyone how important it was to protect their skin from the UV rays. Then they both lay down, feeling the warmth of the sand beneath them filtering up through the blanket. They automatically closed their eyes to block out the sun as they listened to the waves hitting the shore. It was peaceful and calming; something they both needed. The mesmerizing sounds of the ocean had almost lulled Heather to sleep when Celeste said, "Thanks for being there for me these past months, Heather. I don't know how I could have made it through these difficult times without you."

Without opening her eyes, Heather said, "That's what friends are for, isn't it?"

"Yes, but I'm so glad you made being your friend so easy. It's hard to believe we've only known each other a few months. It seems like we've been best friends forever. I don't think I could ever have opened up to anyone else the way I have with you, and believe me that has helped more than I can tell you. I just want you to know how much it's meant to me, Heather."

"Things seem a little better now," Heather said, sounding like a cross between a statement and a question.

"They are. We have a long way to go, but I think things are getting better, and I'm sure the case will soon be over. I've always known how much Adam loves me. Deep down I'm absolutely sure of it, so I don't understand why I've allowed this gloom to enter our home and our lives. I'm constantly trying to figure it out. It will be so nice to have Adam at home more and really be able to start our life together as a normal husband and wife. I see how happy you and Clark are, and I have to admit it makes me jealous. It's not that I'm not happy for you; it's just that I want that same kind of contentment from our relationship. You are such a great example of what a good marriage should be.

For a moment, there was no response from Heather. After what seemed to be a long silence, she emitted a long sigh and said, "I love Clark so much, I just wish I could fulfill his lifelong dream."

"What do you mean? You are so perfect, what more could he possibly want from a wife?"

"Well, it's the one thing I haven't been able to give him so far . . . a child. We both want to be parents more than I can tell you, but it's just not happening. You can't imagine how inadequate it makes me feel as a wife."

"How long have you been trying? Is Clark angry about it?"

"No, no, no. Clark is much more level-headed about it than I am. He would never say anything that would hurt my feelings, but I can sense his disappointment and concern when each month rolls around and once more there's no need to open the pregnancy test waiting in my medicine cabinet. We've been trying for eight months. I know we're still young, and have lots of time before I need to start worrying, but I ache to have a child and to be able to give Clark a son or daughter.

"I'm so sorry, Heather. Have you had any tests done?"

"No, not yet. I figured we should give it another six months since there really is no urgency. But you know how we women can put a guilt trip on ourselves, thinking we're never good enough."

"I'm so sorry I've been burdening you with all my troubles when you've been carrying this around. I haven't ever even asked you how things were because you always appeared to be so complete as a couple. You deserve a better friend."

Celeste started to laugh. "See what I mean about putting a guilt trip on ourselves? I just mention my concern and you figure out a way to feel guilty about it." They both laughed.

"Seriously, though, Celeste, I want to be there for you, too. If you ever want to just talk about it, I'm here. I hope you feel as comfortable sharing your problems with me as I do with you. I'm really going to make an effort to be a better friend. "

"No worries! I know you'll be there if I really need you. It's really no big deal. I guess I need a lesson in patience. It will happen, just maybe not as soon as we had hoped. You'll be the first to know if it does."

Then they were silent for a few minutes and almost simultaneously, both reached over and grabbed a handful of sand. With their hands cupped around the tiny warm grains, they opened their fists slightly, letting the sand release as if though a sifter. With their eyes closed, they were completely unaware that the other was doing the same thing. Their thoughts were similar also, thinking how their lives were like these little grains of sand, passing through this sieve – a day at a time, a grain at a time, almost too slowly to notice, yet fast enough to be gone before they had time to realize it. Celeste wanted to stop the days from passing before it was too late to fix her situation, so she dug down in the sand and got another full fist, this time holding it in her hand tightly and feeling the warmth it was sending through her whole body. Heather opened her fist suddenly, letting every tiny morsel go, knowing there was a lot more where that came from and recognizing it didn't help to hold onto it so tightly.

Both felt better having shared this day with each other. They were more than good friends, they were soul mates.

CHAPTER 14

November 2003

"Caught in the Act" (Patricia)

"Repudiating the virtues of your world, criminals hopelessly agree to organize a forbidden universe. They agree to live in it. The air there is nauseating: they can breathe it."

Jean Genet

———◆———

The trial date was approaching, and Patricia was spending more and more time with the FBI going over her testimony, reciting the same thing day after day, week after week. She had spent countless hours with Agent Gaines and had come to feel comfortable with him, but often asked herself why he had to keep reviewing everything over and over. She was tired of repeating the same stories, giving them the same information, answering the same questions and constantly rehashing her terrible life. The monotony of it all was getting to her. She didn't want to keep reliving her horrific past; she wanted to move on. Every time she repeated it, however, it felt like it was still happening right now in the present. Nothing about it seemed like it was in the past. It simply was not possible for her to move on. She felt like she had a one-way ticket to nowhere.

With each passing day, she longed for the trial to be over more than she had the day before. It was just about ten days away now, so she told herself to buck up and handle it a few more days. She was exhausted from worry. It had been eleven years since she met Johnny and her life had spiraled out of control.

But she knew way deep down inside that all the rehashing was necessary. It would be essential for everything to remain fresh in her memory when she was on the stand, and she had to keep reminding herself of that. The FBI wanted the conviction of Johnny Castilletti, and they wanted the conviction to stand. They wanted a sentence that would shut him down and put him away permanently, so they couldn't afford to make any mistakes during the trial. And that's why she was here again, going over every detail to make sure they hadn't missed anything. Today, they started once more on how she had discovered the drawer and how Johnny eventually found out.

"Chuck was instrumental in the weeks that followed my initial discovery of the files in the desk drawer. When he first discovered me going through the files, he agreed not to tell Johnny, knowing it wouldn't behoove him for Johnny to know he had let it happen while he was taking a little catnap. He was wiser to keep silent.

"He insisted that when Johnny went to the drawer again and found it open, he would never believe he had left it open himself, even though that was the case. He knew that Johnny kept a key on the underside of the desk top. There was a small square knob that just looked like a piece of the desk. It just blended in and really had no purpose and there would be no reason for anyone to look under there or feel where it was, anyway. But when Chuck slid the knob to the right, it opened a tiny compartment containing the key. He had observed Johnny reaching for the key a number of times, even though Johnny hadn't noticed his watchful eyes.

"When Chuck caught me snooping that first day, he told me we had better lock it up because Johnny would assume someone had fiddled with the drawer. After all, he couldn't have done something so irresponsible as to leave it open. He had an ego the size of the Taj Mahal, and never accepted the blame for anything that went wrong. Chuck knew, like I did, that Johnny really believed he was above ever making a mistake."

Patricia took a sip from the glass of water in front of her and continued, "Chuck told me about the first time he saw Johnny getting into the secret compartment. He had been sitting across from me in one of the two wing-back chairs. I was actually in the room but was engrossed in reading, and he was keeping his usual eye on me. Johnny came in the library and sat down at his desk rummaging through some papers for a few minutes. The chairs Chuck and I were sitting in faced the opposite direction of Johnny's. We were facing the fireplace, with our backs toward him, so it wasn't likely that we would be looking at what he was doing. I guess I hadn't stirred for some time, other than turning a page now and then, and Chuck's curiosity got the best of him, wondering what book had me so captivated. He leaned over the arm of his chair just slightly enough not to be noticed but enough to see the spine of the book clearly. "Interesting," he thought to himself. *A Tale of Two Cities*, by Charles Dickens. Later, he recounted to me how he had been impressed by my fondness for the classics.

"It was when he leaned back in his chair," she told Agent Gaines, "that his eyes caught the movement behind him, quite by accident, and he glanced over his shoulder just in time to see Johnny reaching under the desk. He wasn't sure what he was doing, but as his arm slid back on top of the desk, he saw a key in Johnny's hand and then he watched as Johnny inserted it into the drawer.

"After that evening, he was intrigued by the key and unobtrusively observed the process repeated a number of times, knowing Johnny would probably fire him if he ever caught him studying this routine."

Patricia cleared her throat and asked for a refill on her water. She got nervous and her mouth went dry every time she played things over in her head. He brought the water back, she took another sip and continued. "After I found the documents, I was determined to repeat my investigation. I was drawn to them, and I knew I couldn't stay away. I studied the documents a number of times during the following two weeks, carefully removing the key and returning it to its hiding spot when I was done. Chuck tried to talk me out of it, but I refused to let him, and although he didn't condone it, he knew he was helpless to stop it. If he wanted to keep his job and possibly his life, his hands were tied, so he continued to ignore it, but never failed to caution me about being careful.

"My discovery gave me a new perspective on what I had actually gotten myself into. How could I have been so stupid? Within a few days, I realized Johnny wasn't a successful entrepreneur at all; he was a crook. But he wasn't just any ordinary crook; he and his brothers were part of a long-time mob family, and Johnny was the leader of the cartel. His father was the boss before he died and his grandfather before that."

"How did you come to that conclusion?" asked Agent Gaines, studying her face.

"The first clue I found was on the spreadsheet, where the information caught my eye. I saw the entry of the diamond earrings he had given me before our first date, with my name next to the description under the *"Disposition"* column and the *"Profit"* column had been zeroed out. As I studied the pages in more detail over the next weeks, I was able to put two and two together. The *Description* and the *Place Acquired* columns gave me all the information I needed to form a conclusion. They had all been stolen. I had recognized the places as businesses that had been in the newspaper over the past months – not for their advertising, but in the headlines, *"Another Store Robbed," "Thieves Get Away with $300,000 Worth of Jewelry," "Latest Robbery Believed to be Linked to a Chain of Jewelry Store Thefts."* Then I studied the description and easily recognized some of the jewelry items. The papers had reported on the rare twelve-karat estate sapphire and diamond ring, and the triple canary diamond pendant with emerald baguettes. Some of those items just stuck in my head, and I easily figured out that Johnny was connected to the robberies in some way."

She paused and stared into space as if reliving it in her mind. Her expression was one of hatred. Agent Gaines needed her to continue, so he interrupted the silence, "So what did you do next?"

Patricia closed her eyes as though she could remove the image from her mind at will. Her eyelids were like shutters, that she could close, causing darkness to cover the movie playing inside her head. But it didn't ever work that way. "Nothing can remove the picture," she thought sadly. Then she slowly opened them, bringing her back to where she was here and now and after a brief pause, continued with her story.

"One day I took a miniature camera disguised as a car key fob to the desk and took snapshots of the spreadsheets. I didn't know why, but I felt compelled to do so. It's funny, but I had seen the little camera when I was in high school and was fascinated by its uniqueness. I couldn't afford it at the time, and I knew it was a foolish thing on which to spend my limited income, but it was so unusual, like nothing I had ever seen. Every time I walked into the store, I was drawn to it like a magnet. I eventually justified buying it by telling myself that one day it might come in handy. Johnny had seen it before on my key ring, but had never suspected a disguisable camera, and I had never thought to tell him what it really was. I really had never used it, nor did I ever think about it anymore. Just like a teenager, within a few months the intrigue it initially held had dissipated, and it just became another key fob to me. But when I found the papers in the desk, its purpose became as clear as if I were staring through a large picture window. I was grateful I had it, and believed the time might have arrived for it to prove its worth. I didn't know how or when I would use the pictures, but I knew they might come in handy. I knew I had to get pictures quickly because it seemed so stupid on his part to keep paper copies around. I was sure one day I would look and they would be gone. I concluded there must be a reason he had printed materials in his desk, and I was sure that it was a temporary situation."

"So how did Johnny find out that you knew?"

"One night I was checking some more of the folders. It was the middle of the night and I couldn't sleep. Chuck had gone to bed since he had seen me go to my room hours earlier and had naturally assumed I was asleep. After tossing and turning for hours, I got up, slipped on my robe and slippers and crept quietly down the stairs to the library. Johnny was out of town and wasn't supposed to be back until the next day.

"I was so engrossed in the new documentation I had found about some drug deals that I didn't even hear the library doors open or his footsteps coming toward the desk."

"What the hell do you think you are doing?"

"He screamed it so loudly, that I in turn let out a scream of my own in response. In that split second, I automatically contemplated reaching for the gun in the bottom drawer for self-defense, but dismissed the thought almost as soon as it came to me because I knew I couldn't pull the trigger as quickly as he could grab it and turn it on me."

Agent Gaines looked up, startled. They had gone over the details in formal depositions and informal reviews like this one over three dozen times, and she had never mentioned a gun. When they did a sweep of the house, they had not found a gun in that desk. He made a note that he would have to check it out. "That's why we do this over and over," he thought. He didn't want the defense to trip her up by twisting the story and leading her into a pressured confession about hating him and wanting to kill him. When they were done, he would go back to this and instruct her how to respond. They must be prepared! But for now, he let her go on.

"Chuck heard the noise and rushed down to see what the commotion was. He was surprised to see me there and even more surprised to see Johnny home. A quick glance at his eyes told me he was afraid; not just for himself, but also for me." Patricia said.

"Johnny saw the papers strewn all over the desk and asked me how I got in there. 'It was open,' I said without so much as a sidelong glance at Chuck."

"It was NOT open," he screamed. "I would never leave it open."

"Everything that Chuck had told me Johnny would say, he did, but I stuck to my story. There was no need to involve Chuck.

Johnny amazingly enough didn't seem angry or surprised that Chuck wasn't there watching me. I'm sure it was because it was the middle of the night; perhaps it was because the scene he walked in on took precedence over thinking about the why's and where's of Chuck. When Johnny looked down at the papers, I had a chance to glance quickly at Chuck again and caught his grateful look."

"Then what?"

"I spent the next week and a half nursing my dislocated jaw and trying to hide the bruises all over my face, arms and body. He told me if I was so curious to know everything that was going on, he was going to make me a part of the next *event*. He grabbed my hair in his fist and dragged me to the floor and said, 'do you hear me – huh?'

"I told him I wanted to leave and he told me that wasn't going to happen. I knew right then and there that I was in too deep. I knew way too much. He wasn't going to let me leave – not EVER – not alive anyway."

CHAPTER 15

November 2003

"Preparations for a Robbery" (Patricia & Johnny)

"It is not power that corrupts but fear. Fear of losing power corrupts those who wield it and fear of the scourge of power corrupts those who are subject to it."

Aung San Suu Kyi, Freedom from Fear

————— • —————

O nce again Patricia couldn't sleep. It was bad enough living day-to-day as though everything were normal, but every time she spent substantial time with Agent Gaines rehashing the events, she became extra nervous. As the court day loomed near, she spent more time in the bathroom, her head over the toilet. She always felt sick to her stomach these days but continued to move forward telling herself it would be over soon.

After tossing and turning in bed until 2:00 a.m., she tried to recall the good times she had had with her loving and supportive parents before Johnny came into the picture. She convinced herself that if she concentrated on something pleasant, she would fall asleep with those calm thoughts carrying over into her dreams. She closed her eyes once more and after about twenty minutes of splendid family memories running through her mind, she finally drifted off to sleep.

Her dreams were anything but peaceful, however. She floated off into a world right where she left off with Agent Gaines. It was so accurate in every detail it was like watching an instant replay of her life. She was transported right back to August 1993. It was just one week after Johnny had discovered her rummaging through his desk. She was still aching from the abuse Johnny had inflicted on her. She was lying in bed and had no desire to crawl out of it, when suddenly the large mahogany double doors flew open. She didn't want to see him. She shuddered inside with terror, but didn't want him to see her fear. She knew that would only give him more power. He always felt dominant over anyone he thought he could control, and he took for granted that her fear put him in command.

As he walked toward her, she trembled under the covers, pulling them up under her chin to avoid his seeing her quaking body. He picked up the soft blue robe that was draped at the foot of her bed and threw it at her. "Get up!" he shouted. "Make yourself presentable; we're going for a ride."

She didn't question him, but asked if she could have a half hour to take a quick shower. "Make it snappy. I'll be waiting downstairs." He walked out slamming the doors behind him. She glanced at her watch and knew he would be timing her. She slipped the robe on and got out of bed slowly—very slowly. Her whole body still throbbed when she moved, but she knew she had to be as quick as possible or he would see to it that she experienced more pain. The hot water felt good on her bruised and aching body. She wished she could have stayed in until the water ran cold, or even better, a nice slow soak in a hot tub. That was out of the question right now; maybe when they got home from wherever it was he taking her.

She blew her hair as dry as possible in five minutes' time. She could still feel the cold on her scalp when the air hit it, validating that it was still wet, but it would have to do for now. A few minutes in the fresh air, and it would dry on its own. A quick glance in the mirror, told her she had better do something to cover some of the bruises. Johnny would not like either of them to be making up excuses for why her face looked the way it did. He knew lying wasn't her strong suit, so that would leave him to do the scrambling, and although he could lie well, he wouldn't want to in this situation. A quick touch of liquid make-up and some face powder did a pretty good job, but not good enough. On the second try, she caked it on pretty thick, and although it wasn't her usual clean, fresh preference, she thought she did a pretty good job masking the truth. She slipped on a pair of plain black slacks and a high-neck, long sleeve pin-striped blouse that covered the bruises nicely. The first pair of shoes she tried on was painful. When he was through beating her and she was on the floor, he had pulled her by the arm and her foot caught under the sofa, twisting it sideways before she could get it loose from the grips of the sofa leg. It was swollen and she knew it was sprained the first time she tried to stand on it. She tried on another pair and another until finally the fourth pair, some black Gucci flats, proved to be roomy enough to at least allow her to walk without too much of a limp. When she was ready, she walked down the stairs to find him waiting at the bottom.

"What took you so long? You sure didn't spend the time making yourself look pretty, so what were you doing?" She glanced at her watch and noted it had been twenty-seven minutes—a record for her. She didn't respond, but she made sure he saw her checking her watch.

The minute she walked out the front door and took a deep breath, she felt grateful for the fresh air. Just being outside gave her a sense of freedom that was nonexistent for her inside the mansion. As soon as he grabbed her by the arm, the pain returned, and she almost let out a moan, but remembered in time to keep her outbursts in check. She understood immediately that the fleeting sense of freedom was just an illusion.

The car pulled up the red concrete-paved circular driveway stopping near the front door. Chet, their driver, got out, walked around the rear of the car and opened the door for them. She took one more deep breath and walked down the two short steps, holding onto one of the Corinthian-style stone columns for balance. She climbed in the rear passenger side as Johnny walked around to the other side, stopping to inspect a pinpoint speck of dirt on the rear bumper and giving Chet a look that let him know he had missed a spot when he washed it that morning. Chet opened the rear driver side door and Johnny climbed in next to Patricia. The minute the car started to pull away, Johnny pushed the button that closed the sound-proof glass window between them and the driver. "Where are we going?" she ventured to ask. "You'll see, soon enough," he answered harshly.

They drove downtown and stopped at Brilliance, an exclusive gold and diamond jewelry store in the elite area of West Palm Beach. He took her by the hand and led her into the store, where everyone seemed to know him, and he introduced Patricia with instructions to the staff to "treat her well." He was kind to the employees but she could see he demanded their respect, and it was obvious they wished to please him, an indication that he had shopped there many times in the past. Within minutes, Patricia wondered if he was trying to make up to her. He was showing incredible patience, as he showed her all the extraordinary rings, bracelets, necklaces and brooches, describing in detail the stones and what to look for in quality, clarity and size. He elaborated on the mining locations of the various stones and explained why some gems garnered higher price tags than others. She was surprised at his knowledge. It was obvious he loved the jewelry. Maybe that love was prompted by the money it produced for him. When she was spying on his ledgers, she had already concluded that he wanted only the best, but she had mistakenly assumed someone else had appraised the pieces and told him what had real value. She had no idea he was also the brains behind the jewelry facts.

His mood seemed light and she was relieved not to be facing his wrath, if only for an afternoon. He asked her what she liked, she pointed out three items, and he picked one . . . a two-carat emerald and diamond ring and said, "Wrap it up." He looked at her with his most handsome grin and said, "If you're a good girl, I might surprise you with the others some day." All the store personnel had their eyes on the couple and looked at each other approvingly, trying to contain their delight at the prospect of future visits from this generous gentleman. After some elaborate and what she knew were disingenuous farewells with the gemologists, he took her arm and walked her back out to the waiting car. Upon Johnny's instructions, Chet drove south to the corner, made a right turn, and in a few feet another right turn, until they were in a private parking area behind the store. Once again the button was pushed and the window went up, separating them from Chet and allowing for private conversation. "How did you like that?" Johnny asked and he noted a slight smile on her face which he realized he hadn't seen in a very long time.

"The jewelry was gorgeous. The settings were so unique and unlike anything I have ever seen. It was interesting to learn about everything, and I was impressed by what you knew."

"I wanted you to see one small part of my dealings so you could understand why I love this business so much," he said.

There were a few minutes of silence when she started to realize there was something more he wanted to tell her. "What are we doing around back here?" she asked, her suspicions starting to surface again. "Is there something else you want to show me?"

He pointed to a narrow alley between Brilliance and another high-end boutique clothing store. "Right there in that alleyway is where you will be parked tomorrow night. You wanted to know what was going on, so I'm going to enlighten you. You are going to be the getaway driver."

She felt her heart skip several beats and almost thought it would stop altogether. She slumped in her seat and this time was unable to cover her fear. The aches and pains returned in full vengeance, but she would rather have that pain any day than the anguish of knowing she was about to become a criminal. This was a punishment of a magnitude she could not handle.

She woke up from this terrible real-life nightmare to words that sounded almost strangled. It took her a few minutes to recognize the voice. The words were coming from her own mouth. "Oh, Mom and Dad, I'm so sorry. I'm so sorry! I love you so much and I'm so sorry." The tears were streaming down her face.

She was sweating profusely, as she always did when she awoke from her nightmares. That was ten years ago, and the memories never seemed to fade; not even a little. She ran to the bathroom and threw up again. When she was through, she just sat on the floor for a few minutes; her face still moist from the tears. She felt so sick she didn't see how she could even get herself back to her bed. "Mama, oh, mama, I need you."

CHAPTER 16

November 2003
"The Getaway Deposition" (Patricia)

*"Hope begins in the dark, the stubborn hope that if you just show up and try to **do the right thing**, the dawn will come. You wait and watch and work: you don't give up."*

Ann Lamott

———•———

After Patricia composed herself, she took a nice hot bath and got ready for another briefing with Agent Gaines. She was always escorted these days, not just merely followed. Her safety must be ensured this close to the trial. She was their star witness and they had to do everything possible to protect her. Adam was on duty and along with two other agents, they picked her up and drove her to Agent Gaines' office. When she arrived, he greeted her warmly and asked if she wanted something to drink. She declined with a slight shake of her head, and they went into his office. "Let's go over the jewelry store robbery again." She nodded and closed her eyes as if that would help her see it more clearly in her mind. It had been a long time ago. Then she began.

It was Tuesday, August 3, 1993. I remember the date because it's my Dad's birthday, and I recall thinking what a horrible birthday present this would be. It was 2:00 a.m. and I was sitting at my dressing table in black sweats with a black stocking cap on my head. I had been trying all day to finagle a way to remove myself from the role as an accomplice to a robbery. Maybe I could claim to be sick or I could tell them I couldn't maneuver the getaway van since I wasn't used to driving a large vehicle, which was true. But I knew Johnny wouldn't listen to excuses and it would make him angry. Down deep I was sure if I backed out for any reason, it would mean losing my life. For a minute I thought maybe that's what I should do. After all, my life wasn't much worth living anyway. But I wasn't really ready to die just yet. I didn't have the guts. Plus I wanted Johnny stopped from hurting any more people. I sat in front of the mirror at my vanity and stared at the reflection looking back at me. I saw a face I hardly recognized. I licked my lips and tasted the saltiness of the tears that had escaped my tear ducts and made their way down my cheeks until they found my lips which were waiting to catch them and keep them from rolling further and dropping onto my lap.

I knew I was just minutes away from walking down the stairs and on my way to doing the worst thing I had ever done in my life. I knew by the time I got home that night, I would be an accomplice to a crime—a criminal! How could my life have come to this? I told myself to take a deep breath, but when I tried, it was shallow and quivery. I did what I hadn't done since I met Johnny. I walked to my bedside, knelt down and prayed. It was hard. I didn't know how to ask God for help when I was about to commit a crime. It didn't seem right, but somehow I knew I had to do it. "Help me Father. I don't know what to do or how to get out of this mess I've gotten myself into. I don't ask for myself, but I must beg for protection for any innocent person who might possibly be in the area tonight. I know it will be the middle of the night and it's not likely anyone will be around, but if by chance someone is on the streets, I plead for your help. I'm certain Johnny would not hesitate to shoot anyone who interfered with his objective and neither would his mob crew. He wouldn't allow any witness to survive. Please, Father, don't let any guiltless person come into harm's way tonight. I couldn't bear it if I thought I contributed to someone being left without a father or mother or spouse. I pray that the streets will be vacant of people; not so that we can accomplish this burglary without incidence and make a clean getaway, I don't care about that, but only to safeguard anyone who might be in the wrong place at the wrong time. That's all I pray for, Father. Oh, and one more thing . . . if we should get caught, please bless and protect my parents for I fear it will kill them to know what I have done."

As I stood, I heard footsteps coming up the stairs. I quickly wiped away the tears, knowing the time had come. I was not ready. I would never be ready. But Johnny couldn't wait for me to prepare myself, for that would never happen.

We drove to the location. Johnny made me drive so that I could get the feel of the van. He wanted no mishaps in getting away. He was pumped. I could see the sick excitement in his eyes as it spread through his whole being. I had learned that he rarely joined his men on these jobs any more, but he had wanted me to see him in action. He actually seemed proud of himself. When he talked to me, he acted like I should be excited too. He was oblivious to the pain and fear I was feeling. This was so routine for him that I think he forgot for the time being that I wasn't really a part of this.

He sat next to me in the front seat repeating the instructions over and over. When we arrived in the parking lot behind Brilliance, the van doors opened quickly, and everyone leaped into action. The two men in the back seat opened the doors almost before I came to a complete stop. The rear doors opened and four more men hopped out. Then they started removing their equipment. You could tell they all had an assignment and knew what it was. It was evident they had been doing this a long time. I felt like I was glued to my seat. I glanced nervously in the rearview mirror, but quickly glanced away, as I knew I would throw up if I watched. I purposely hadn't eaten all day because I figured I would be less likely to vomit if my stomach was empty.

Their plan was to get to the roof and drill through the ceiling right above the vault. Then they would blast through the top of the vault, where they would drop down in and hoist the jewelry straight up without ever opening the vault doors, thus avoiding cameras and door alarms. But there would be alarms in the crawl space between the vault and the ceiling, so one of the first things they did was go to the alarm box and rather than taking time to cut any wires which would risk setting it off, one of the guys opened the box and sprayed it with liquid spray Styrofoam which hardened almost immediately, immobilizing any movement of the bell device inside, thus, disabling the sound. After they cut through the roof, they drilled holes through the top of the safe then set explosives in the holes. They were cleverly muffled, but it seemed to me like the blasts must have been heard in the next county. They quickly dropped their ladder down the hole directly into the vault which was about twelve feet high. They used a lightweight flexible-sided ladder, the type that are normally used to get in and out of confined spaces, like rescue access for firefighters, mine access or event and stage rigging. They just unrolled it and dropped it down through the narrow opening, securing it independently to an anchor on the roof for safety. They also rigged a wench that they used to hoist up the jewelry boxes, which were designed like safety deposit boxes, each with its own lock. The hoist allowed them to lift the boxes up to the roof more rapidly where one of the guys was waiting. He, in turn, hoisted it down to another man on the ground. This was more efficient than climbing up and down the flexible ladder. Johnny was point man and once inside the vault, took the time to open each box with some special lock picks. He quickly inspected the contents for the highest quality gold and gem pieces. This actually took less time and was more fruitful than hoisting up every box or randomly picking boxes. The time was short and they didn't want to be stuck with a mediocre stash. They left the boxes behind that contained run-of-the-mill jewelry. He was an expert. They were all experts in what they did. They worked quickly and efficiently. They adhered to a strict timeframe to complete the job and when that time was up they left. Johnny told me later that sometimes they left millions of dollars worth of valuable stuff behind. It was part of their strategy. They could always get more the next time, but they didn't want to stay too long and risk getting caught or there wouldn't be a next time. They knew that greediness could be their undoing, so they made the best of their allotted time and just took what they could. There would always be future robberies where they could get more.

When they were done, they loaded everything in the van with precision. When everyone was in and the doors were closed, Johnny shouted, "Go!" I hit the gas pedal and screeched out of the alley, exactly what he told me *not* to do it. Any of them could have been the driver, but they always left someone in the van in case they had to abort their mission and leave early. Johnny wanted me to have an inside view of what they were doing. He wanted to be able to implicate me.

I was so upset for the next week, I couldn't eat or sleep. Chuck looked at me with a knowing eye, and I withdrew into my own self-made shell, ashamed to look at anyone. Even though sometimes I thought he looked sympathetic, I knew I couldn't ask him for help. He would never cross Johnny. No one would cross Johnny if they wanted to live.

Two weeks after that event, I asked Johnny why he bothered to buy me the ring that day, when he knew he could steal it the next day. He told me it was because he was smart. Who would ever expect a wealthy good-paying customer to be the robber? It was all part of the plan.

He didn't insist I go with him again until about a month later. This time the plan was to hit a bank. I was in a panic. It was September and the plan was to aim for October; just a month away. I knew I couldn't do it, but could not think straight enough to know what I should do. I was a wreck. I knew if I ran, he would catch me. I couldn't go to my parents or he would kill them. I had no money, other than what he gave me, and even though he was generous when I wanted something, I always had to account for what I was going to do with any cash he gave me.

A week before the planned heist, he dropped the bomb on me. "Guess what we are doing in two days?" he asked. Before I had a chance to answer, he said, "I'm going to make you Mrs. Castilletti." I gasped at his words. How could things possibly get any worse? Why would he want to marry me? He used and abused me, but he could do that without marrying me. He told me it was for insurance. Husbands and wives can't testify against each other he told me, so marriage would be sort of an insurance policy.

That night, as I lay in bed, the fear gripped me hard. The tears ran in a steady stream down my face the whole night through, and I was completely absorbed in my own terror, I barely heard the torrential rain pelting against the window. I was still awake when the sun cast its first rays through my window trying its hardest to cheer me up, but incapable of such a difficult task. I wished it would just stay dark, so I could attempt to get some of the sleep that eluded me. I wished I would fall into a deep sleep and would never wake up. As I turned my head to the side, I felt my pillow cold and wet under my head—my tears had saturated the pillow case. I felt the back of my neck and could feel the profuse sweat that drenched my neckline and soaked my hair, causing it to curl along my neckline. There was no way to deny the fear that was griping me. I got out of bed and knew exactly what I had to do. I had no choice.

I showered and dressed, plotting how I would accomplish it. Looking in the mirror, I could see I looked more like I was thirty years old than nineteen. Less than one year of life with Johnny had really taken a toll on me. I forced the brightest smile I could muster and asked Johnny if I could go shopping for something special to wear for our wedding. He had no objections and actually seemed relieved not to be getting any resistance from me about the marriage. I knew Chuck would be within ear shot the whole time I was shopping, but I would have to take the chance.

I went from one store to another trying on clothes until at the sixth store, a small exclusive boutique, I spotted what I was looking for—an easily accessible back door. I took several outfits into the dressing room, making sure Chuck would see I had an armload and would realize I would be awhile. After trying on the first two and coming out of the room to ask the sales clerk what she thought, I could see Chuck was losing his interest and was looking around. I didn't try any more on, but instead peeked out and asked for a change of size. Chuck paid no attention. The next time I looked, Chuck was staring at a glamorous looking woman modeling a rather revealing dress, and both store clerks were helping her, so I made my move. I left everything in the dressing room and sneaked out the back door, all the while holding my breath and praying.

I ran down the alley and out onto the main street away from the store. I got a taxi and that, Agent Gaines, was the day I met you for the very first time.

CHAPTER 17

October 2003
"The Memories of Romance" (Greg & Parris)

"O for the gentleness of old Romance, the simple planning of a minstrel's song!"

John Keats

———•———

After their date on the beach last month, things had cooled off, but once again, the bond between them was warming up. Greg and Parris had spent uncountable hours together in the past couple of weeks, and with every date their relationship had been growing until once again he was feeling certain she was having the same thoughts and feelings for him as he had had for her for quite some time now. He knew he had told this story to himself a hundred times before, but he was sure this time Parris was letting her walls down and was letting Greg into her life. This past month had been the best month of Greg's life.

He wanted to make sure that Parris saw everything there was to see in the nearby vicinity. He labored over the internet searching for things for them to do, that would provide lasting memories for both of them and secure their connection to each other.

They went to the Gumbo Limbo Nature Center where he discovered Parris' love for nature. This 20-acre coastal preserve was the perfect spot. They walked through the hardwood hammock, which Parris had no idea existed. It's like a closed canopy forest and Greg explained that tropical hammocks provide important habitat for a fairly extensive species of wildlife and they are also critical for many trees and shrubs. She listened to Greg with an intense interest as he explained how these hammocks have been severely impacted by outright destruction and conversion to other things, but when he saw how genuinely sad that made her, he assured her there was significant work being done to restore existing hardwood hammocks that have been disturbed. "I hope they always keep this one thriving," she said. "It's one of the most beautiful places I've ever seen." He could see in her eyes that she meant it and she felt the beauty of nature that surrounded them.

"Follow me and I'll show you how beautiful it really is," he said. He took her to a forty-foot tower, which they climbed, Parris going first with Greg following right behind. Once at the top, they had a spectacular panoramic view of the forest. There were no words to describe it; it was gorgeous. They didn't talk much, just stood and looked out, taking in the scenery and the animal and plant life below. They stayed up there for quite some time embraced by the beauty of it all. She made no effort to leave and Greg sensed in addition to the splendor of it all, she felt safe from the world; perhaps, secluded from the world. He wanted to let her have as much time as she needed, but he had more to show her, so after about thirty-five minutes, he nudged her softly, telling her there was much more to see. She took a deep breath and turned her head slowly from side to side before climbing down. The camera inside her head was taking mental picture memories. They went to watch the sea turtles and sharks swimming in the seawater tanks, and then visited the Sea Turtle Rehabilitation Center where they observed the sea turtle patients being cared for, and once again she was touched. She watched with compassion to what they were doing and said she envied their jobs, helping these animals. They wrapped up their visit with a stroll through the butterfly garden, where there was unmatched beauty and color flying about everywhere they looked. This was a happy place for her and she enjoyed exploring every nook and corner of the garden trails.

Before leaving, they stopped at the nature-themed sea turtle shop where he saw her eyeing a pendant. When she wasn't looking, he purchased the fourteen-karat gold pendant. It was a sea turtle hatching out of a glass egg with three diamonds at the bale. It cost him a small fortune, but she was worth every penny. As they were walking to his car, he stopped and turned her around so he could clasp the pendant around her neck from behind. "This is for you to remember this day," he said.

She looked down at the beautiful necklace and said, "It's beautiful, Greg. I will treasure it always as I will treasure the memory of this day. She turned around to face him and reached up and kissed him gently on his lips. At that moment he felt total love enveloping his soul.

The following week, they went to the Boca Raton Museum of Art, slowly browsing the collection of international classic, modern, and pre-Columbian art. Greg was thrilled at her enthusiasm for the art and was surprised at her extensive knowledge. She surpassed his comprehension by a long shot and provided him with facts and data about the pieces and the artists that amazed and impressed him. It was another beautiful date with the woman he loved.

The day they visited the Daggerwing Nature Center, they gathered around the alligator tank and listened to a short talk by a caretaker about their new baby gator and watched while he was being fed. Greg was sure the whole room lit up from the smile on Parris' face as she watched that little baby alligator. He was the luckiest man alive.

On one date, they found themselves laughing almost the entire day long as they went down the 220-foot water slides at Coconut Cove Water Park and the 986-foot river ride was a blast. Parris was game for anything, and she was just as beautiful with her hair soaking wet and no make-up as she was when her copper-red hair fell in soft curls down the nape of her neck. But with all the fun and laughter they enjoyed at the water park, it was still the natural sound of the waves roaring in from the ocean and lying on the sandy beaches that they preferred most of the time.

They tried their hand at tennis a number of times, but neither had mastered the sport yet. They were improving, though, and while they laughed at their many misses, they vowed to keep trying until they got it right.

They spent many days and evenings at Mizner Park. It was a great place in a beautiful setting. Sometimes they just strolled through the shops. Sometimes they went to the museum. Twice they went to a concert, but more often than not, they caught a movie. There were plenty of places to relax and eat at Mizner Park – everything from Starbuck's to fine dining and they tried just about all of them.

One night, on the spur of the moment, they decided to go to *Coral Gables* which was across from the University of Miami. It was the first time either of them had been karaoke participants. It was usually the younger university-age crowds, but they didn't care, and the throng of people didn't seem to notice the age difference. Greg was the first to try it and he expected her to laugh, but she, along with the rest of the crowd, applauded and shouted, *"More, More!"* Parris insisted she just wanted to watch, but as the night wore on everyone else was getting up there, so with just a little coaxing, she loosened up and gave it a try. Greg was stunned when he heard her beautiful voice. She never ceased to amaze him. Most of the time, they just watched other people take their turns and applauded loudly for the ones with obvious talent as well as the ones that made them laugh hysterically, which seemed to be the majority of them. What a fun night it had been.

After all the wonderful days and evenings they had spent together the past month, he knew the evening he had planned for this night was going to be one of the most special. Parris had admitted she had never been to a ballet and Greg could hardly wait to see her reaction. He was sure she would love it. He told her to dress up and he would pick her up at 6:30. As always, she told him it would be easier to meet him since she had some shopping to do ahead of time and some errands to run, so it would work better if she came to his apartment. One day soon, he was sure she would agree to let him pick her up, but he wouldn't argue the point this time. He wanted everything to be perfect and didn't want to insist on it, taking the chance of spoiling their evening, so he agreed to let her come to his apartment.

He didn't tell her where they were going—it would be a surprise. He sported his brand new black Armani suit with a crisp white shirt and plain black tie. When the doorbell rang and he opened the door, he was speechless. If he thought she was gorgeous before, he couldn't believe what he was seeing now. She stood there in front of him looking absolutely regal. She was in a soft satin Champaign-colored dress, simple but elegant, with a matching shawl draped around her shoulders. Around her neck, she wore a beautiful strand of pearls that were the identical color of the dress. Her hair was pulled up on top of her head, with matching pearl pins holding the coif in place, and a couple of stray curls mischievously lining the nape of her neck. Her eyes looked like glittering emeralds. They were the only jewels upstaging the pearls. He noticed the blush rising on her cheeks as he took her all in with no attempt whatsoever to hide his appreciation for her beauty. With a slight stutter, he caught his breath and said, "You're . . . you're exquisite."

She smiled—slightly at first, then with a broad grin she said, "You're not so bad yourself." He offered his arm and she took it as they walked to his car. As he opened the door and she slid in, he watched her long, slim legs nestle into place as he had many times before. She kept asking him where they were going, but he didn't tell her. He wanted it to be a surprise. Her curiosity was getting the better of her on the long twenty-five mile drive, when they finally reached Ft. Lauderdale and pulled into the parking lot at the Ft. Lauderdale Ballet Classique. He glanced at her just in time to see her eyes light up as she read the marquee. *"Giselle,"* she said softly.

The night was everything Greg thought it would be. They had the best seats in the house and Parris was mesmerized by the haunting blend of ethereal beauty and vibrant emotional intensity of *Giselle.* He couldn't seem to take his eyes off her most of the night. He watched her more than he watched the ballet, and as he studied her, he could see she was captured by the interplay of love and the supernatural. It was almost as if she related to this peasant girl and her ghost. A time or two he saw a tear slide down her cheek, but she was too unaware of it to wipe it away.

As the curtains closed, she was still in the world of the ballet. They were in the dead center so the people on both sides, turned and walked to the aisles, leaving them sitting alone in their row. When she was finally aware of the people standing and getting in and out of the rows behind her, she glanced at him and stared for just a moment, then smiled softly. She mouthed the words, "thank you."

They made their way to the parking lot in silence, just holding hands. They waited their turn as the cars pulled into the street. By the time they got onto the highway, she still hadn't said anything. Finally he asked her if she liked it, already knowing the answer, but anxious for her to express her feelings to him. "It was the most beautiful thing I have ever seen, Greg. You are the most special man I have ever known in my whole life. I don't know how you have put up with me, but I'm so glad you have." Everything was right in the world. He had known this was going to be a very special night and he wasn't mistaken.

Looking back it was definitely the best night of Greg's life, full of enormous and complete joy. But now it was the complete opposite— the worst night of his life. He still couldn't make any sense of it. He didn't understand any of it – how that exuberant joy he had experienced had been reduced to complete irrelevance, but it had . . . for that was the last time he ever saw Parris.

CHAPTER 18

September 2012

"Getting Acquainted" (Greg & Breck)

"We must become acquainted with our emotional household: we must see our feelings as they actually are, not as we assume they are. This breaks their hypnotic and damaging hold on us."

Vernon Howard

———◆———

I t was supposed to be quite a pleasant day, just a little on the chilly side, so Breck grabbed her brand new Anne Kleine lightweight, double-breasted swing coat from her closet. It was perfect for this fall weather. She slipped the burnt orange coat on over her long-sleeved, brown-linen sheath dress. With the dress sleeves peeking out from the cuffed sleeves of the coat, she did up the large circle snap closures, glanced approvingly in the entryway mirror and headed out the door to church.

Yesterday had been quite a bit colder, and she knew walking weather in the next few weeks would be limited. Temperatures in the autumn were always unpredictable and right on the horizon was the transition to winter so she wanted take advantage of as many remaining autumn days as possible. It was less than half a mile to the church, which was just far enough to enjoy a crisp stroll and get in a little exercise. Besides, she wanted to check out the phenomenal blend of reds, purples and yellows that decorated the trees. Although she loved all the seasons, this was probably her favorite time of year.

About half way into her walk, her thoughts wandered to the Friday night party, and once again she thought about Greg Williams. She chastised herself wondering why she kept drifting there.

She had spent most of Saturday doing errands; washing clothes, grocery shopping, picking out a birthday present for her friend at work, and cleaning house. She thought about how quickly the weekend had flown by, and then chuckled to herself as she realized that was the same comment she heard around the office every single Monday morning. "Didn't the weekend fly by?" they would say week after week as though that was something unique and no one had ever said it before. Then the following Monday, the same thing could be heard around the office once again. "We're such funny creatures," she mused as the image of the Monday morning office chatter played through her mind.

But it wasn't Monday quite yet, and she loved Sunday mornings when she could go and mingle with her friends at church and tune out the rest of the world for a couple of hours. It was her quiet time . . . her relaxing time. The reverence was a welcome relief from the chaos of the other days. It was where she had turned to find peace and comfort when Jeff died. This was where she sought answers and where she had finally been able to come to terms with her life. The minute she walked through the doors of this old, but lovely-renovated and well-kept chapel, all thoughts of the party disappeared. It was calming and inviting and this is where she found direction in her life. She was safe here. She was centered here. She could get her bearings and find herself here. She had grown to love the peacefulness of this little church.

As she walked into the foyer, her eyes gravitated to the familiar framed prints hanging on the wall. She never tired of seeing the print of "The Hands," Michaelangelo's depiction of the creation of Adam, which represented to her, the breaking away from the world and getting in touch with a Higher Power. On the opposite wall was a picture of "The Family" and as Breck looked at it, she wondered as she did every week, if she would ever have a family of her own.

The music was playing as she walked down the aisle and took a seat on the left side of the chapel near the middle of the room. She loved the music and for a time had joined the choir. When she sang, her heart was engaged spiritually.

Blues and purples and greens dominated the multitude of colors in the stained-glass windows. The church was small so the windows, of course, were not like the massive windows seen in the cathedrals and churches in Europe which were often so large, they were formed into murals. Nevertheless, they were exquisite pictorial representations of biblical characters and narratives of times past, and Breck found the architectural details to be absolutely beautiful. The one of Mary, Joseph and the Christ child was her personal favorite, but she also loved the representation of the Tree of Life which was patterned after Louis Comfort Tiffany's famous design with the dark brown tree and plum-pink flowers and summer green leaves. She was told it was made with 416 pieces of stained glass. What was not to love about that one? Some of the smaller floral windows with climbing wisteria and white lilies displayed the beauty of the world and were breathtaking.

The chapel doors were no longer open, and her eyes were closed, her head down in calm repose as she listened to the music and waited in deep thought for the services to begin. Her own private reverie was disturbed as she heard the doors open once again and caught sight of a latecomer walking quickly down the aisle. He took a seat on the opposite side of the chapel a couple of rows in front of hers. He looked vaguely familiar, yet she was sure he wasn't a Sunday regular. Breck was looking across the opposite side of the room still trying to figure out where she knew him from, but couldn't get a good look at his face from where she was sitting. The music stopped, and as it did, he looked across the room and their eyes caught. It was Scott's friend, Greg. She flushed and tried to look away so it didn't appear as though she had been staring at him, but that slightly upturned somewhat cocky-looking smile and those turquoise blue eyes caught hers, and she was unable to look away.

"Get a grip on yourself, girl," she thought. The voice from the microphone startled her back to reality as the sermon began. She turned her face from him, and looked squarely up front, but her concentration was lost. It was as though she felt him staring at her, but was he? She told herself several times that it was her imagination. Her curiosity finally got the best of her as she turned her head slightly in his direction and saw him looking directly at the minister, but it appeared as though she got the tail end of his head swiftly moving that direction. What was wrong with her? He wasn't looking at her. She was acting like a silly school girl. She turned back focusing on the sermon, but after about a half hour, the hymn started and like sign language, the chorister's hands indicated for everyone to stand up. She glanced again across the room. This time she caught him. He was staring directly at her and once again he smiled, and mouthed "hello." She nodded, smiled and turned back to her hymn book.

The next twenty minutes passed quickly, and when the service was over, she walked out and saw the sun shining more brightly than it had for the past week and a half. She thought it would be impolite to leave without a quick greeting to Scott's good buddy, even though she found herself feeling a little nervous, but not exactly sure quite why. She glanced around, but didn't see Greg, so she figured he must have walked out without feeling inclined to say hello or maybe he was just in a hurry. Maybe he didn't even re- member who she was, but why then did he mouth *hello* from across the room? She hung around for a few minutes and said her good- byes to her friends, but still didn't see Greg, so she shrugged her shoulders and walked down the path heading for home.

"Hey, Breck!"

She turned around and saw Greg hurrying toward her. "He re- membered my name," she thought. She waited for him to catch up.

"Sorry, but I got tied up in the church with all those friendly people asking me who I was and offering their welcomes. I was hoping I hadn't missed you." She felt warm, almost hot and won- dered if her cheeks were as crimson as they felt.

"Hello, Greg. I looked around for you, but didn't see you, so I figured you hurried on out. It's good to see you. What are you doing out this way?"

"Well, I asked in town if there were any nice quiet little church- es nearby and most of the suggestions led me to this one. I didn't expect to run into you, though. Do you come here often?"

"Every week," she said. "I like the intimacy of this place, plus I'm lucky enough to be within walking distance on good days. Scott mentioned you would be here for a couple of weeks, but I didn't expect to run into you again, especially not at church."

"I never miss church unless I absolutely can't go for some reason, and Scott had some plans he was discussing with Samantha, so I thought I would get out of their hair for awhile. They invited me to stay, but I sensed they needed some private time, if you know what I mean. I actually think they were in the middle of some pretty serious discussions."

"So you'll be sticking around for awhile?" she asked hoping she didn't sound too anxious.

"Well, right now I'm not certain how long I'll be here. It might be two weeks and it might be longer, but either way, I'll be coming back. I really like it out here. I've taken a leave of absence from my job and Scott has invited me to stay with him for a time. Hey, are you in a hurry or would you like to go get some lunch with me? I think it's entirely too soon for me to make my reappearance at Scott's."

"Well, I don't like to eat out on Sundays, but I have some soup simmering away in the crockpot at home. You're welcome to join me if you're not too afraid to try my cooking. It seemed like soup weather when I was planning what to fix today, but now it's turned into a surprisingly warm day."

"It sounds great to me, actually better than great, but I didn't mean to intrude on your free time. If you'd rather be alone or if you have something else to do, I completely understand. Please don't feel obligated." Then without a taking a breath he said, "What kind of soup is it?"

She laughed at his obvious eagerness. "I have nothing else planned and would love the company. I should warn you, though. It's just plain old-fashioned chicken noodle soup--nothing fancy. I don't want you to be disappointed."

"Are you kidding? I would never be disappointed. My mother's menu usually consisted of two choices: take it or leave it," Greg said. Breck laughed. "And I know it has to be better than Scott's cooking or the same old take-out we've been depositing in our bellies. Seriously, though, chicken noodle really is my favorite. It reminds me of my Mom. I will gladly accept your offer, even though I feel like I kind of forced my company on you."

They walked and talked all the way to Breck's house. He was easy to talk to and funny, but not in a showy way. As they rounded a bend near her house, a jogger ran out around them with the tiniest little dog Breck had ever seen attached to a leash. The collar was about as big around as a coke can. The Yorkshire Terrier was only about eight inches tall and couldn't have weighed more than four or five pounds at the most. His little legs were scrambling as fast as they could go to keep up with his owner, who was forced to slow down a bit to avoid dragging the poor dog by the leash. "Oh, what a cute little dog," Breck said.

"Dog? Are you kidding me? That doesn't even qualify as a dog. It's more like a rodent." They both laughed as their eyes followed the *rodent dog* trying to keep up. She enjoyed his quick wit.

They were so engrossed in conversation that the four blocks between the church and her house passed in no time. It seemed like only a couple of minutes until they arrived at her house. She unlocked her front door and he followed her in. "Welcome to my humble abode," she said.

He glanced around slowly and then said, "It's nice, Breck. Really nice."

She could tell he was sincere. She had put a lot of effort into making her house a home, and she was proud of it. "Thanks, Greg. It's comfortable for me.

Then he sniffed and sniffed again. "Wow, that soup smells delicious. I didn't realize I was so hungry."

"Well, it's ready. I take it you are ready to eat?"

"Show me the way!"

Breck put the plain white china soup bowls on the purple placemats, with white cloth napkins on the left side of the bowls and a butter knife and soup spoon on the right. Some clear purple glasses were placed above the utensils. "Do you prefer milk or water?" "Milk," he said, and she poured milk in both their glasses. She put some fresh rolls in a bread basket and sat them in the middle of the table alongside a bowl of creamy homemade honey butter. The handle on the ladle exited a hole on the edge of the lid of the solid white tureen and as soon as she removed the lid, the steam was released into the air. The aroma of piping hot soup filled the room. It was simple, but nice. Greg took one look and was amazed. It was funny, but no one he knew who was his age actually cooked. He was impressed. And with one spoonful, he knew it was more than nice, it was delicious. With her encouragement, he downed three bowls before he finally patted his stomach and declared he was stuffed. He said, "You know, I've heard it said that a good cook is like a sorceress who dispenses happiness. It looks like I'm going to have to agree. I'm a happy man right now," and he rubbed his stomach approvingly.

He helped her clean up and they went into the family room. It had started to get cool again, so she put some logs and kindling in the fireplace and lit a match. He noticed she was experienced at this, as the flames took flight almost immediately. She tossed some oversized pillows on the floor where they sat facing the fire. She hadn't met anyone since Jeff that she could talk to so easily. One conversation led to another. He had apparently spotted the picture of Jeff on the mantle and asked who it was. It seemed easy and natural to tell him a little bit about Jeff, which was unlike her to do so with such a new acquaintance. But then, it was unlike her to invite someone to her home without really knowing them. It had seemed right, though, possibly because she knew Scott, and she knew that Scott thought Greg was as good as they come. He wanted to know everything about Jeff and seemed genuinely interested and sympathetic. "It sounds like Jeff was a great guy. I'm sorry for all you've been through, Breck."

"It took me a long time to get over his death, but I'll never forget him, and sometimes, I still revert back to feeling sorry for myself. I didn't go out on a date for over two years following his death. That first date was a blind date. My friend who lined us up had filled him in on my situation, so it wasn't a surprise to him. It was good for me because he was patient and easy to be with and helped me get through the *"dating again nerves"* and better yet, he turned into a really good friend. He's married now, and I'm still really close to him and his wife. Now I just try to keep myself busy, so I don't think about it constantly like I did at first. For the most part, I do a pretty good job of it, and I count my blessings for having such good friends. I'm so fortunate to be surrounded by them. What about you? Have you ever been married?"

Greg glanced at his watch. It was 9:00 p.m. They had spent the whole day talking and in between he had even helped himself to more soup, complimenting her all over again about how wonderful it was. He couldn't believe where the day had gone and neither could she. "Look at me...I've taken up your whole Sunday. I'm sure you want some time to prepare for your workday tomorrow, and I'm sure Scott must be wondering where I disappeared to. He may be thinking I'm lost. I hope he hasn't called the cops yet." They both chuckled. "My story can wait for another time. I'd better get going." He thanked her again, expressing his appreciation for the delicious dinner and for keeping him company.

She didn't really need time to prepare for tomorrow; she would rather spend time with Greg today, chatting and learning more about him. She sensed, however, that he was ready to go so she didn't push it. She couldn't help but wonder, though . . . would there be another time?

CHAPTER 19

July 1993
"Back into Danger" (Patricia)

"He who does not prevent a crime when he can, encourages it."

Lucius Annaeus Seneca

———————◆———————

" I want you to go back."

"What?" she cried. "Agent Gaines, I came here in good faith. I need your protection. If I go back, he'll kill me. I'll do anything, but I can't go back."

"Look," he said. "Your boyfriend is well-known by the FBI." The word boyfriend put a nasty taste in her mouth, but she didn't interrupt. "He heads a notorious crime family. We've been following Johnny Castilletti and his dynasty for years. We've worked hard for years to get enough evidence to convict not only him, but his whole family, so we could put all of them away for a long time. We're not interested in taking one of his mob leaders down for a simple gambling crime. We want to take down the whole mob family, including the mob boss, and that means Johnny, but it has to be something big that will hold up in a court against his high-paid corrupt lawyers. We arrested his brother once for petty theft, but he was out on bond before we could do the paperwork. That's not the kind of evidence we need.

"We know for a fact that they have committed horrific, sadistic murders, but there are never any real witnesses or any physical evidence tying him or his mob to the crimes. They are hardened criminals and as long as they keep committing these crimes and getting away with them, they'll keep doing what they are doing. They consider every crime a victory against the law. We need to stop them because they will not stop on their own. It's a big job, and I know we are asking a lot of you, but think about it; do you have any choice?" His voice had risen with obvious fervor and he was almost shouting.

"I can't do it. If I go back, they'll kill me and you know it. Isn't it enough that I gave you pictures of the spreadsheets and told you about the jewelry store heist?"

"Look, Miss Reynolds . . . "

"Patricia," she interrupted. "Call me Patricia."

"Okay, Patricia. Here's the thing. Now the tone of his voice softened a bit. "We know it's going to take more than a single jewelry store robbery to lock them all up. Even several robberies won't do it. If we arrest a few of them, the rest will take over temporarily. They are professional criminals and it's a family affair. They learned from their fathers and grandfathers and uncles and cousins, and they are now teaching the younger generation. We need a strategy that will take down the entire organization. We need to try all of them as a whole if we possibly can so that we can get the entire organization off the streets. Just arresting one or two individuals for a single crime is not going to do it."

She looked weak and tired and he hated to do this to her, but he had to put the pressure on her. Every time they got close, the trail grew cold. He was ecstatic when she walked in and laid out her story to him in a quick 45 minutes. They had tried before, on two separate occasions, to use an informant and it hadn't worked out. The first time, it was Grace Donovan. She was Vince's girlfriend. Vince was Johnny's cousin. When they started including her in their illegal dealings, she became frightened and went to the cops who involved the FBI. She agreed to help them, if they would provide her with protection. She was a good witness and had obtained very specific information. They were finally ready to take the case to court. But the mob knew exactly how to use the Freedom of Information act to their benefit, and it actually aided them in obtaining court documents that outlined who the witnesses were going to be. They manipulated the system and found everything they needed to know about who was going to testify. They targeted Miss Donovan as a key witness and not only did that end her relationship with Vince, but it ended her life. Just four days before the trial, her body was found behind some warehouses in an alley used strictly by delivery people. She had been beaten to death. The severity of the beating was so shocking that it sickened even the most seasoned police officers. With this turn of events, the whole case unraveled.

The second time, the informant was Jim Conroy. He came forward when his son, Dave Conroy, had been the victim of a shooting during a bank robbery. Jim Conroy was located out of state, but after his son was killed he wanted to see justice done. Dave Conroy had been a customer, just making a simple deposit. Unfortunately he was in the bank at the wrong time and it cost him his life. He was shot and killed when another customer tried to reach in her purse for her cell phone. One of the robbers caught her out of the corner of his eye. Dave had his eye on him, and saw the guy turning his gun toward the woman. Instinctively, he lunged forward to push her out of the line of fire and caught the bullet right through his heart.

The FBI was dependent on confidential sources to lead them in the right direction, but Jim had no training so they were hesitant about sending him in to gather information. But he was persistent and against their better judgment, he eventually won out. They set him up with a new identity and trained him for several months on the detailed aspects of being a hardened criminal. They went over and over his identity and practiced innumerable scenarios. He was sharp and was a quick learner. He insisted he was ready, and they decided to make their move. He posed as a career criminal from the East Coast. He worked his way into their organization and was making progress, but it had only been a few months, which wasn't nearly enough time. The mob still considered him an outsider and they were cautious, so the information they passed on to him was limited. He knew he would have to work his way into their trust, but he was ready for it. He would do anything to avenge his son's death. The initial evidence he obtained pointed toward Johnny Castilletti. The majority of career criminals are very paranoid and Johnny was no different. They trust very few people, and he wasn't sure he could trust this new member of their gang since he wasn't family. It took a long time for an outsider to gain Johnny's trust. The FBI had set up moles in the organization before, but Johnny had an uncanny ability to recognize decoys and usually not much had been gained.

Every effort was made to protect Jim. There were always two or three agents watching his every move. They discovered that Davey Crockett's bar was a front for the organization and one day when

Jim Conroy went in with them for a meeting, he didn't come out with the others. They waited and waited. Finally, they made the decision to storm the bar. They figured he was in trouble. They searched everywhere, but the owner, David Johnson, alias Davey Crockett, said he hadn't seen anyone matching his description come into his establishment. The search had come up empty. Davey was definitely part of the organization; he was their cover. There was an escape route somewhere in that bar, but they weren't able to find it until months later on another visit.

Jim was gone. They needed to find him before it was too late. They had very few leads to go on and struggled with the investigation for quite some time, but had a hard time pinning his disappearance on Johnny Castilletti. After a couple of weeks, they were certain Jim was dead. The investigation quickly changed from a search and rescue to a recovery of the body. Without a body there was no real evidence that a crime had even been committed.

About a month later, a body was found in the trunk of a car at the city dumps. An emergency dispatcher had dispensed a unit to the scene. The victim had been shot in the head. It was another brutal homicide. There were no prints or evidence left behind to send to the crime lab, but it had all the earmarks of a contract murder. The body was taken in for identification. As suspected, it was identified as Jim Conroy. He did not deserve to die. He had been willing to do anything to even the score for the death of his son, but instead, he joined him in death. It was clear . . . talking to the authorities was a death sentence. Agent Gaines wanted nothing more than to get closure for the Conroy family. He wanted Johnny Castilletti and his family out of the picture for a very long time. It was almost an obsession with him.

His thoughts returned to the present. "Please Patricia, we need your help. We're asking for one day. If you can photo as many of his files as possible it might help. But more importantly, we'll show you how to download his whole computer drive to us. You can do it in seconds. Then you can leave and we'll protect you." He knew getting people to testify was a hard sale. Her reluctance to be more involved was understandable. Like everyone else who had an association with the mob, she was afraid to even be seen with investigators. It was too dangerous to cross them. Witnesses were not only intimidated, they were killed. That had already happened with the previous informants, but he wasn't about to tell her about them. They thought they were careful before, but they hadn't been careful enough. They had learned from their mistakes, and he knew they would have to be even more vigilant this time.

"But they know I've slipped away from them. They'll grill me and Johnny will torture me until he knows where I went. He won't let it go."

"It's only been an hour. Your watchdog should be searching for you right now. He won't want to tell your boyfriend until he absolutely has to because he knows he'll be punished for it too. We'll get you back to the shopping area and stay near you until we find him. Then we'll lead you to a place where he will be able to easily find you. If we make him think he found you, he'll be less suspicious. You can tell him you just wanted some freedom to shop on your own, so you slipped away when he wasn't watching. He won't give up your secret. He'll be relieved not to have to confess that he lost you."

She knew she had no choice. She needed their protection and besides, they would prosecute her for her part in the bank robbery if she didn't, and she knew Johnny would see to it that she never made it to trial. Something deep down inside told her she had to do it. She thought of her mom and dad and her integrity prevailed, and she agreed to turn informant—not just with the pictures of his documents she had already provided, but a far-reaching informant. She wanted out of this life and she knew getting them off the streets was the only way that was ever going to happen.

They did some quick planning and gave her instructions on the computer while they were driving the short distance to the shopping center. It didn't take long to spot Chuck as they pulled around a corner. He didn't see them. They circled the block and pulled up out of his sight and let her out. They surrounded her so she appeared to be just another person in a crowd, not really visible, slowly channeling her into a store behind where Chuck was standing until she got inside. She positioned herself near the front window so that when he turned around, he would see her. Within 30 seconds, he set eyes on her. He marched into the store and grabbed her arm roughly. She was nervous, but tried not to show it. "What the hell are you doing?"

She looked down at his tight grip on her arm and said, "I should be asking you the same thing." He didn't want to draw attention, so he guided her rather forcibly outside the store, and started in with the questions. She repeated the story the way she had been instructed. She was shaking, but Chuck assumed he had just frightened her. He accepted her story and told her they better get home. "But I'm not through shopping."

"Yes you are Patricia." He snapped his fingers and a car pulled up. He didn't wait for the driver to get out and open the door. He just opened it and pushed her into the back seat with a gentle shove, letting her know he was back in charge. He walked around to the other side, opening the door and getting in next to her. If she felt afraid before, it was nothing compared to what she was experiencing now. She was going home to do the job, and she was well aware that what she would be attempting could put her life in jeopardy. She shook all over from the inside out. Chuck caught a glimpse of her shivering and assumed he had frightened her badly. He liked her and was sorry he had to scare her, but it's what he had to do. He knew if he messed up, it would mean serious consequences for both of them. She had to learn.

The FBI was watching everything from inside their vehicle. They also had people nearby listening to the whole conversation just in case it didn't go the way they expected. They pulled out and followed the car at a safe distance to avoid being detected. So far, so good.

They knew going against the mob could be deadly for her, but she had entered the world of dangerous criminals and nothing about that was easy. They had to do whatever they could to keep Johnny from knowing she was a witness. Agent Gaines wondered for a brief moment if they had done the right thing. He felt guilty for putting her through this. She was now a source and her life could be threatened. They didn't want to lose another one.

CHAPTER 20

July 1993
"Conclusive Evidence" (Patricia)

"The only medicine for suffering, crime, and all other woes of mankind, is wisdom.
Teach a man to read and write, and you have put into his hands the great keys of
the wisdom box. But it is quite another thing to open the box."

Thomas Huxley

———•———

She crept into the library and froze when she saw his desk in the shadows of the room. She was terrified. She had one day and one day only to do this. Johnny was planning on marrying her tomorrow, so she had to be gone before that happened. She had been sick all night worrying about what she needed to do and had thrown up several times. She was worn out from lack of sleep night after night and knew her exhaustion could lead to slip ups. She couldn't afford any mistakes at this point.

The previous evening, Johnny told her he would be joining her the following day to finish their last minute wedding preparations. With him by her side, it would allow her no time at all to sneak to his computer. He was rarely home during the day and this turn of events unnerved her. She had no idea what she was going to do, but trembled at the thought of abandoning the plan and going ahead with the marriage. But around 11:00 p.m. she caught a break. His cell phone rang and almost immediately after he answered it, his voice changed to a low whisper as he got up and walked out of the room. When he hung up, he informed her almost apologetically, that he had some business that had to be taken care of, and he would have to take a quick trip out of town. "It's just a one-day trip, so don't hold up any plans. You can handle it and I'll be back in time for our wedding."

She immediately wondered if someone had found out and this was a cover to follow her. She told herself not to be paranoid and not to think about it. She needed to be grateful things had fallen into place. Now her biggest concern was Chuck. She just hoped he would take his usual nap outside the door, while she was doing her thing. She went downstairs very early. Johnny had left at midnight, so she was hoping to scout things out before Chuck woke up. It was 4:00 a.m. and pitch-black as she felt her way to the library, hoping she wouldn't stumble and cause anyone to wake up. She walked through the massive doors and turned on a small Tiffany light that was sitting on a table near the chair where she always sat to read. She hoped it would give her enough light to do the job without turning on the large Italian Cavallo chandelier. It put out so much light, it was sure to creep like fog under the door of Chuck's room and alert him. He was geared to hear and see everything. Closing the library doors wasn't an option because she had to keep an eye out for him. It wouldn't pay to have him walk through the doors with no warning. If he caught her downloading information off the computer, she knew it would be the last straw and he wouldn't give her another break.

She chose a book from the fourth shelf, just within reaching distance when she stood on her toes. She opened it up and laid it on the table by her chair. In case she heard Chuck coming, she would be able to slip quickly over to the chair, pick up the book and appear to be reading it. She selected "Gone with the Wind" which she had read twice. If he asked her any questions about the book, which he often did these days, she wanted to make sure she could answer them so it wouldn't cast any suspicion. It had to be a book with which she was familiar. It wasn't likely he would ask about this one, but if there was a remote chance, she wanted to be prepared just in case.

She pulled out the chair and sat down at the desk. She had to get to the computer first. If she had time after, she would try to get more pictures of the files, but what was on the computer took priority. It was the most important thing to get done and would provide the most incriminating evidence. She turned it on and put in Johnny's user name and password. She held her breath, hoping the password he had foolishly and uncharacteristically written down in one of the folders she had copied previously had not been changed. Within seconds the screen opened up. Another break! She breathed a sigh of relief. She searched for a minute for the right port to insert the device Agent Gaines had given her. When she found it, she plugged it in and opened the email, typed in the code email address they had given her, which automatically sent the information to an offsite computer, and carefully followed the steps exactly as they had instructed. She checked her watch and checked it again three times. It took just a few minutes, but it seemed like hours. She was sure she was going to get caught half way through. When it was at about 97% complete, she heard Chuck's footsteps coming down the steps. As soon as he reached the bottom, she knew he would be moving toward the library. Her heart was leaping and she was praying that the final 3% would hurry. She was sure she was going to be sick again, but forced herself to hold it down. He was at the bottom of the stairs heading toward the library when 100% complete popped up on the screen. She almost cried, but quickly and efficiently shut down the computer, jumped up and ran to the chair, grabbing the book just as he was walking through the doors. She didn't get any pictures of files, but she accomplished the most important thing and was relieved. She took a deep breath trying hard not to shake so visibly.

"What the heck are you doing up so early?" He was grumpy and she didn't blame him. His assignment to watch her was probably giving him an ulcer in addition to lack of sleep. It was enough to make anyone irritable.

"Good morning, Chuck. I'm sorry if I woke you. I wasn't feeling well and couldn't sleep, so I thought I would come down and read for awhile." He glanced down at the book in her hands. She waited for him to say something about it, but he didn't. She instinctively glanced toward the desk. Everything looked in place until she remembered . . . to her horror, she realized she had left the device plugged into the computer. She absolutely had to get that removed. She wanted to cry. She wanted to just give up. Why did she think she could pull this off? But once again her reasoning took over and she reminded herself that she had no choice.

Chuck walked over to the fireplace and started a fire. "It's cold in here. You shouldn't be sitting here in the cold." He walked over and picked up an afghan from the other chair and laid it across her legs. She had grown to like Chuck. He didn't seem to fit in with the rest and she wondered how he had ever gotten involved with them.

"Thanks, Chuck," she said. He gave her an almost imperceptible smile, not wanting to show too much of his caring side. She knew he felt like he had to appear tough. There was no way he could let her think he was soft. But she knew better. "Have you ever been married?" she asked.

He looked at her for a minute, studying her face for something, but she wasn't sure what. "No," he finally responded, "but I came close once."

"What happened, if you don't mind my asking?"

Again he paused. He was sitting in the chair next to her now, his hands in his lap, his thumbs rotating around and around each other like cogs on a wheel; forward and backward, then backward and forward, around and around they went. She wasn't expecting him to answer, but then he started to talk, "She was the love of my life. I knew I wasn't in her class, but for some reason she seemed to like me from the first time I ran into her—literally. We were both running for a taxi and I almost knocked her over—you know, just like in the movies—it really happened that way. I grabbed her arm, catching her before she fell. I took one look into her eyes and was smitten. I apologized profusely making a fool of myself. I stuttered and stammered through my apologies for way too long, and when I finally quit talking, we looked up and were both surprised to see the taxi pulling away without either of us. We both laughed and I called for another taxi. I told her she could have it, but she said we may as well share it. From that time on we became exclusive. It wasn't until three months later, when I was already head-over-heels in love with her that I found out she worked for Johnny Castilletti. I had heard of him before and knew it might be trouble, but I didn't know the extent of it. I tried to convince her to leave—told her we would move far away and start a new life together. I knew she wanted to, but she said I didn't understand. That wasn't possible. Once you were involved with Johnny you never got away."

A chill ran up Patricia's back. She knew how true that was. "Where is she now and why haven't I ever met her?"

"After she convinced me of the danger, I couldn't bear the thought of giving her up so I figured I would join her. As the song says, I thought it would be easier to live in her world than live without her in mine, and at least that way I could be close enough to protect her." He paused again, his head still down.

"And . . ?" Patricia asked questioningly, in a way that encouraged him to go on.

"She hated that she had pulled me into this. She decided I had been right and we should try to get away. She said we could figure something out, but she needed time to think about it. By this time, I knew Johnny better and wasn't so sure anymore that we could pull it off. One day, without my knowing, she went to the police. She came home and told me what she had done, and I was immediately frightened. By this time, I had been around long enough to know we had to act fast. We hadn't made any plans, and I knew it wouldn't take long for Johnny to find out what she had done. He has insiders everywhere, including in law enforcement. They don't make much on the force and he pays well, so it's easy to convert them with a little extra cash thrown their way. It took less than an hour for him to know she had stooled on him. Can you imagine that . . . less than an hour.

The next day she was found dead in her bedroom. Natural causes they said, but I knew differently. Johnny had a nice long talk with me, and I understood that if I didn't want to meet the same fate, I would be loyal to him for the rest of my life. He had a close eye on me from then on." Chuck looked up and stared into Patricia's eyes. "It's too late for me now," he said in a soft voice. "I lost the only woman I ever loved and for all intents and purposes, from that point on, I gave up my life." Silence hung over them and she felt the ache in his heart.

"What was her name, Chuck?"

"Angela," he said. "I called her Angel because that's what she was. She got sucked into this world unintentionally, just like you did." Then, with deep compassion he said, "Be careful, Patricia. Don't do anything stupid." Without another word, he stood up and walked out, taking his usual seat on the chair outside the door.

She wanted to go to him and give him a hug; to let him know she understood and to tell him she was sorry. But she knew she couldn't. His job was to remain tough. She knew he had already said more than he should have, and it had taken a toll on him just to relive it. She forced her thoughts back to the present and the peril she was facing. She needed to focus on the job. After only a few minutes, she heard his snoring and knew he had fallen asleep in the chair. "Rest, Chuck," she thought. "Just rest for awhile." She got up quietly and went to the desk. She didn't pull the chair out or sit down. She held her breath, reached down and pulled out the device, slipping it into her pocket. There was no way she could risk getting into the desk drawers to take any more pictures. This would have to do. What she had already done would have to be enough.

Before noon, she was dressed and ready to go out for last minute wedding shopping. She had to have a new pair of shoes to go with her dress she had told Chuck. But Chuck was sick, an extremely rare thing for him he had told her. He had a fever and had been unable to do much all morning, so Joey, one of the other goons, was assigned to take his place as Patricia's bodyguard on the shopping trip. She thanked the Lord for his illness. She didn't want him to get into trouble if their plan succeeded. She didn't care about any of the rest of them.

Miraculously they pulled it off. Agent Gaines and his team had been waiting patiently for her for over two hours at the assigned store. They were relieved when they saw her getting out of the limo. Once inside the store, they proceeded with the plan. An agent right outside the window stuck his foot out and tripped another one who walked in front of him. The scene was well-done, as if they were professional actors. The first man reached down to help the man up, apologizing, but the man on the ground started screaming obscenities, loud enough to attract attention all around, including inside the store. He stood up and took a swing and the fight ensued. Joey couldn't resist and stood up to get a better view along with all the sales clerks. In that split second, an agent grabbed Patricia's arm and they slipped out the back door into the waiting vehicle.

As it turned out, the information they got off his computer was more than enough. They had accomplished the task and they would start compiling their case against the mobsters.

CHAPTER 21

October 2012
"A Nascent Relationship" (Greg & Breck)

"Love received and love given, comprise the best form of therapy."

Gordon William Allport

———•———

It had been almost two weeks since Breck had run into Greg at church and invited him to her house for homemade soup. It seemed like she had known him forever. He was easy to talk to and he had a knack for drawing out personal information from her that she was unlikely to share with her closest friends. It wasn't that he was nosy; in fact far from it. He just seemed genuinely interested in her. Not once did she feel like he was being intrusive.

The following Monday he had called and asked if he could return the favor by taking her out to dinner. "No matter where we go," he warned, "it won't be as good as your soup; I can guarantee that, but I'll do my best to get a good recommendation from Scott." She didn't even try to act coy. She immediately responded, "I'd love to Greg. What time?"

He took her to Flagstaff House on Flagstaff Road in Boulder. It was the first time she had ever eaten there, but had heard rave reviews about it being one of Colorado's finest restaurants, and she soon learned the accolades were right on target. While it wasn't the kind of place the average person would frequent often, it was definitely where you would spend a night celebrating something special. Most everything on the menu contained something she had never even heard of before, but she loved trying new things and apparently he did too. The cost of the appetizers was more than she usually paid for a main course dinner. She took one look and politely declined a precursor to the main meal. He insisted that they try something, seemingly unfazed by the prices. "If you won't pick something, then I will, and I'll tell you right now, I expect you to help me send an empty plate back to the kitchen," he said. She laughed and told him to select something and she would do her best to help him. His choice was:

PERIGORD BLACK TRUFFLE, RUSSETT POTATO GNOCCHI, HEDGEHOG MUSHROOMS AGED CAPRICIOUS GOAT CHEESE

It was the most expensive first course on the menu and after one bite, she could see why. It was delicious—unlike anything she had ever tasted. She knew black truffles came primarily from France and the earthy taste of the oak trees from where they grow dominated the dish. The tooth-like projections on the lower cap of the hedgehog mushrooms were barely visible but added a bit of whimsy to the presentation. The potato gnocchi were cooked to perfection, and the savory flavor of the capricious cheese that topped the dish traveled divinely across her palate. The mixture of ingredients complemented each other flawlessly. When she commented on how delicious it was, Greg agreed and patted himself on the back for a "wise and excellent choice." It was the perfect start to the absolutely wonderful dinner that followed.

They sat in the enclosed patio where they had one of the most awe-inspiring views of Boulder from the side of Flagstaff Mountain. Greg had done his research and explained to her that the Executive Chef, Mark Monette, had fresh fish flown in every single day, generating a daily menu change. "I read that he grows some of his own herbs for his cuisine, and enjoys creating a lot of unique organic dishes, and he is also noted for all of his exquisite combinations of ingredients and clever presentations."

It was hard for Breck to decide. Everything on the menu looked so intriguing, but after Greg's explanation of the fresh fish, she went in that direction. The dish that caught her attention was:

FLORIDA GENUINE RED SNAPPER, PROSCIUTTO WRAPPED, LUMP CRAB
TREE OYSTER MUSHROOMS, CAULIFLOWER, SEA BEANS, SUNDRIED TOMATOES,
CAPER VINAIGRETTE

She could almost taste it just from reading the exotic ingredients. Greg went all out and ordered:

JAPANESE WAGYU RIBEYE CAP
TWICE BAKED POTATO, ASPARAGUS, BLACK TRUFFLE SAUCE

She nearly choked when she saw the price on the menu; $32 per ounce with a four-ounce minimum. He ordered six ounces.

They sampled each other's dishes as if it were the most natural thing to do. They both claimed to be stuffed and declined dessert.

"Can you cook like this, Greg?" she quipped.

"Are you kidding me? I can't cook a thing. Cooking is something I've never tried to master. I don't even butter my bread, because I consider that cooking. I'm just going to have to rely on you to supply me with my favorite soup from time to time. I'm sure I can count on you to take pity on a poor starving soul. Do you have more specialties?"

They both laughed and she told him he would just have to stick around and see. He looked straight into her eyes and it felt like he was seeing right into her brain and reading her thoughts. His smiled waned, and he said softly and more seriously, "I just might have to do that." She could feel her cheeks redden and hoped he hadn't noticed.

After leaving the restaurant, they drove to Boulder Creek Path, where they parked the car and started to go on a scenic stroll. The path actually stretched for seven miles, but not far into their walk, they stopped at a bench and sat down. The night was very chilly and sent shivers up her spine. She pulled her jacket more tightly around her. Greg took immediate notice and put his arm around her shoulders. It felt good to be cared for again, and she didn't voice any objections. They started talking about anything and everything and before they knew it, over two hours had passed. She told him about some of the volunteer work she was involved in and he listened intently. He asked her all kinds of questions. He thought it would be the kind of thing that could give meaning to his life also, and doing it with Breck would be an additional plus. He wanted all the details. She couldn't remember anyone taking such an interest in the work, and it excited her to think that Greg did, so it made it easy for her to talk about every element.

Then Greg told her about growing up with Scott and the fun they had as children. He talked about how Scott had been a terrific friend, not just during the early years, but also as they got older. He was there for him through thick and thin.

"So what was the *thick and thin*?" she asked boldly. There was silence and he sat there for what seemed a very long time. "I didn't mean to pry, Greg. I'm sorry." She immediately regretted that she had asked.

"You're not prying, Breck. You've talked to me a lot about your life. You've told me about your husband and shared what it was like to lose him. You've told me about what kept you going, and what still keeps you going. You've told me about your work and your hobbies. You've been open and honest with me, yet I've avoided answering any of your questions. I know you're not meddling or snooping, Breck. It's just hard for me because I haven't talked to anyone about it except Scott. But now, I find myself wanting to talk to you and tell you everything. I don't know why, but I do. It may come slowly at first, but it will come, Breck."

"I'm here when you're ready, Greg, but don't force it. I've just enjoyed spending time with you and wanted to know more about you. I realize we barely met, but for some reason, it seems like I've known you for much longer than I actually have. You've made me comfortable sharing personal things, and I hoped I could help you feel at ease with me also."

For the next half hour, Greg talked a little about Parris and their relationship. He told her how they met and how, up until that time, he had never wanted to have a relationship until he was out of college, but he had been captivated by her from the moment he met her. By the end of the night Breck still sensed he was holding back and she was okay with that. After all, they hadn't known each other long enough to expect him to tell her everything, just because she had opened up so much to him. This was the time for her to practice patience. What she did learn was that it had been a very complicated relationship between the two of them. He gradually drifted back from talking about Parris to talking about his relationship with Scott.

"In May of 2006, Scott told me he had a job offer in Colorado. He was worried about me and was apprehensive about taking the job, even though it was what he always wanted. He agonized over the decision. I honestly think he would have turned the job down if I would have asked him to. That's the kind of friend he was . . . and is . . . and always will be.

"I lost sleep over the confusion and turmoil I had brought into Scott's life. I had messed up my life enough; I didn't need to mess up his too. That's when things finally clicked in my thick skull. I knew it was about time for me to step up to the plate and get on with my life. I vowed from that day forward I was done living in the past, and I would begin a new life; a life that concentrated on my future. Scott spent a lot of time with me that next month before he left, and when he did leave, I finally felt like I was no longer a burden hanging around his neck. Not that he ever said I was, and knowing the top-notch guy he is, I'm sure that thought probably never entered his mind, but deep inside I felt like I had been. It felt good to get that monkey off my back. He wanted to make sure I was making progress. And I was. Work started to go better for me. I didn't spend my evenings sulking in my room every night or dining on TV dinners or sometimes eating nothing at all. I started to go out again. Scott lined me up a few times, and I found I actually enjoyed myself. I started to remember what life was like before Parris. And from that time on, I never tried finding her again. I had put way too much effort into it, and finally accepted the fact that it was a lost cause."

"So what are you running from now, then, Greg?"

He looked startled. "I know it must seem that way, Breck, but I'm really not running any more. I just think it's time for me to get away and start fresh. I've accepted what happened those many years ago, and I want to make new things happen in my life now. So here I am, back to where Scott is, but this time, I have no intention of leaning on him. I just like being around him, and I thought he could show me the city so I could see if I want to settle down here for awhile. He raves about it here, you know."

Breck shivered as she suddenly became aware once again of how cold the evening had become. She saw the bare branches swaying back and forth with the gentle breeze, creating an eerie whistle and knew a storm was brewing. She glanced down and noticed her hand was cradled on top of his. She didn't know when she had put it there, but must have felt some need to comfort him while he was reliving his past. She went to move it away, but he turned his hand over and interlaced his fingers with hers. He stood up, pulling her up from the bench with him, and without saying a word walked slowly back to the car. They drove in silence most of the way. She had no idea what he was thinking. The atmosphere was peaceful, and both were deep in thought, but the silence wasn't uncomfortable. When they got to her house, she invited him in, assuming incorrectly that he would decline. To her surprise, although it was getting late, he accepted, and she was glad. As soon as they walked in, she headed for the kitchen asking if he wanted a cup of hot chocolate, which had become a late-night habit of theirs the past couple of weeks. He slipped his sport coat off and tossed it on the couch and said, "I'd love anything you'd make me, Breck." They sipped from their steaming mugs and watched an old episode of *Friends* on TV, laughing together over some of the silly scenes. They sat on the loveseat and talked a bit more, but not a lot, eventually moving down to the floor in front of the fireplace with their backs resting up against the couch. He slipped his arm around her and she nuzzled up under his arm, feeling right at home there. She already felt the inklings of comfort, the feelings you get when you are a child snuggling up with your nice soft security blanket. It felt good, but it also scared her. These feelings hadn't been awakened in her since Jeff, and she knew it was way too soon to form such a strong connection with Greg. She was also worried that in spite of what he told her, Greg was probably not ready for a new relationship.

She had almost drifted off when his arm stirred under her head. He lifted her chin up with his thumb and forefinger, and looking directly into her eyes, told her he had better be getting home before they both fell asleep. It was apparent that neither of them wanted the evening to end, but they both knew it should. He stood up and reached his arms down to pull her up. As he did, he pulled her close, their noses just inches apart. Her heart was beating loud and after what seemed like a very long time looking at each other with unspoken thoughts, he bent down and softly kissed her lips. Her knees were weak, almost fragile, and she wasn't sure if she could move without them crumbling. He walked toward the front door, still holding one of her hands. He pulled her into his arms and kissed her again, longer and harder this time. She had no power to refuse, nor did she want to.

"It's pure kismet that we met, Breck."

He turned and walked out the door. Her eyes followed him down the steps and into the car parked in her driveway. She heard the engine start and then saw the windshield wipers begin to move back and forth like two upside-down pendulums swinging simultaneously. In spite of the few flecks of snow that had started coming down, she felt warm all over. After he pulled away, she finally turned back into the house, shutting and locking the doors behind her. She leaned with her back against the door and closed her eyes, her thoughts carrying her back to the conversations of the evening. She wanted this wonderful feeling that she had almost forgotten existed to last forever.

"Kismet, huh, Greg? Is that what this is or am I just stirring up memories of Parris that you want to rekindle?" She certainly hoped not.

CHAPTER 22

November 2003
"The Death of an Ally" (Patricia)

"Fear! It was happening all over again. That sickly helpless feeling that spread with its icy fingers, slowly eating up all faith and hope."

Gennita Low, Facing Fear

———————◆———————

t was 8:15 in the evening and Adam was sitting across the street from Patricia's apartment in the unmarked jet black Ford Taurus. His new partner, Trent, was sitting shotgun, holding a cup of coffee, the benefit of which was twofold; it helped keep him awake and it warmed him up. While the weather was almost always pleasant during the day, it could get nippy at night and this was an unusually cold night.

Trent was new at this and Adam knew he was still adjusting to the complicated ever-changing time schedules. It was much easier in the summer when daylight hung around longer. But as soon as the sun went down, the dark night sky seemed to encourage lethargy and could lull the average person to sleep in a very short time. It didn't matter whether there was a full moon or no moon; either way, the night was simply the night and the majority of people's internal alarm clocks were set to sleep mode when it got dark outside. Adam had become accustomed to it, but he could see that Trent was still fighting the urge to doze off most nights. Silence didn't help the situation, so Adam usually attempted to stimulate a friendly conversation. It not only helped to keep Trent alert but also helped pass the time. They talked about anything and everything; family, hobbies, previous jobs—whatever they could think of.

At 8:45 Patricia emerged from her apartment. Her eyes automatically darted to the right and then to the left, quickly scoping out the surroundings as was her habit every time she walked out of her place. She took what seemed an intensively deep breath as though the air outside would permeate her with some sort of strength if she could just capture its cool freshness into her lungs. With each week that passed, she looked more tired than the week before. Adam was well aware of the stress this job had put on him, and knew that it was ten-fold for her; she must be like a walking zombie at this point. He felt sorry for her, and was glad it would soon be over. It was obvious that it had taken quite a toll on her both mentally and physically. Her weight loss was astonishing, and she didn't really have anything to lose from the start. But one thing was for sure, she had been tough through the whole process.

With darkness falling, the ghostlike silhouette of a shadow crept along the sidewalk as if it were crawling out from the corner preceding the man walking behind it. The boxwoods that lined the perimeter of the corner house looked black in the dusk with no hint of their rich green velvet daytime color visible. The hedges blocked the person for a few seconds before the figure materialized and a man joined his shadow from behind the hedge and turned the corner heading in their direction. Adam reached over and nudged Trent's shoulder to get his attention, nodding his head toward the man. It wasn't an unusual occurrence since this was a pretty standard suburban community with people coming in and out of the neighborhood all the time. Adam had seen it a thousand times before, and it had proven to be uneventful every time. But they were trained well and knew that even if it happened a thousand times before, the thousand and first time could be different, and they couldn't afford to let their guard down now. They watched carefully as the stranger continued around the bend, walking up the street and stopping when he reached the bottom of her stairs. Their interest peeked and Trent picked up a pair of night vision binoculars lying on the seat next to him. They knew he might be going into the apartment above or below hers, so they just quietly watched and waited.

The stranger looked up at Patricia as he gripped the handrail and started climbing the stairs toward her. The moonlight cast a dark shadow around him, so they couldn't see him clearly, but the collar on his russet brown trench coat was pulled up around his neck creating a suspicious appearance. He had on a hat with the brim pulled down low over his eyes. It was an unusual look for Florida, even in the late fall. He stopped when he reached her on the stoop. She made no attempt to walk down the stairs past him, but instead focused her eyes on his face. Patricia talked to him quietly for a couple of minutes as the exchange between them seemed friendly enough. While Adam and Trent were cautious, they were comfortable for the moment that it must be an acquaintance in the apartment. Still, Adam had a nagging feeling of uneasiness. He had been watching her for a long time and had studied all the profiles of the tenants and had never before seen anyone who looked remotely close to this mysteriously-dressed man. He seemed to Adam to be a stranger. A number of scenarios crossed his mind in a few split seconds. He could be visiting someone in the apartments and simply stopped to ask her a question. Possibly he was inquiring about a vacancy, but Adam knew of no vacancy and was supposed to be alerted if there was one. He was cussing under his breath at the possibility of something this simple slipping through the cracks.

It would be much easier if they could hear the conversation, but for now they had to keep a low profile, keying in on the body language for any clues before making a move. They couldn't risk bringing unwanted attention to her if nothing was wrong. That could be a big mistake.

Adam thought the dialogue between them was taking too long and his apprehension was increasing, when suddenly what appeared to be a calm friendly chat turned into something entirely different. By this time it was obvious she knew him. Although he wasn't making any attempt to touch her, Patricia put her hands over her eyes and began to cry. Without warning, her appearance changed from tears to hysteria.

Instinct and training told Adam and Trent they needed to get closer. They opened the car door quietly and stepped out, moving toward the steps. Just as they approached, they saw the stranger reaching out for her wrists in an effort to keep her from beating him on the chest, but she was wild and he couldn't get them. She was screaming and sobbing, and the shouting between them grew louder and louder as horror and panic filled her cries. He reached for her again, grabbing her wrists and catching them this time to stop her flailing fists. As the moon moved from behind the cloud, Adam could see the man's whole figure more clearly now. He glanced at the stranger from head to toe, quickly taking in every detail just as his training had taught him to do. His eyes abruptly stopped when they came to his feet. Red socks! He had red socks on. He remembered the red socks comment on her deposition.

"He's one of them!" he shouted to Trent. They both pulled out their guns and Adam yelled, "Let her go!" Neither Patricia nor the stranger heard him through the screaming. She pulled free of his grasp and once again started pounding his chest, crying "No, No!" and he yelled, "You have to come with me!" The weeping and hollering was escalating and they could hear the fear in Patricia's voice. Then he reached for her shoulders and started shaking her violently. "Listen to me," he shouted. "I'm taking you where they can't find you." Adam rushed up the stairs, and the stranger finally heard him. He turned, facing Adam and held his arm out as if to stop him. In that split second before Adam got to the top, he heard the sharp cracking sound of a bullet whizzing past his head, and almost immediately the stranger dropped down on his back.

Patricia screamed and instantly dropped to her knees. It was obvious that was the first time she was aware of their presence, as she looked at Adam and Trent and then at the man lying at her feet. She was stunned. Her eyes met Adam's and the look said it all, "What have you done?" She didn't say anything, but crouched over him, sobbing. "I'm sorry, Chuck. I'm so sorry."

He opened his eyes slowly and looked at her. "Don't worry about me, Honey" he whispered. I knew it would be dangerous, but I had to tell you."

"But I never meant for this to happen to you. It's all my fault." She kept repeating how sorry she was over and over, tears stinging her cheeks.

"Patricia, I knew you were being watched. They wouldn't just let their key witness be out on her own. I knew the Fed's would be here, and that it could be dangerous for me. My eyes were wide open when I made the decision to come here, and I also knew if the Feds didn't get me, Johnny would, so it's best this way. Just get out of here quickly."

"I won't leave you. We'll get you help and you'll be alright. They will protect you." Her tears ran down her face and fell on his, as she rocked back and forth, whimpering. "Please, Chuck, you have to fight."

His eyes fluttered open and shut and it was difficult to hear his shallow voice, which was almost a whisper now, but what he said was said with urgency. "Leave, Patricia. Now! If you don't, my efforts will be for naught. I'm so ready for this to be over. You've helped me to see I don't want to live in Johnny Castilletti's world any more. I'm at peace now because of you. I'm ready to go. Now maybe I can be with Angel. It's what I've wanted, but until now I haven't had the courage and haven't known how to make it happen. Don't worry about me, Patricia. I'm happier now than I have been for a long, long time. Promise me you will leave now—quickly. There is no time. They are coming."

She looked at him and knew he meant it. He was ready to go, and she knew he was just waiting for her to promise him that she was leaving. "Thanks, Chuck. You make sure you let Angel know what a hero you were, you hear? I'm leaving now, but I'll never forget you." She leaned over him and kissed his forehead, slipping his head out from her arm and laying it gently on the cement stair. As soon as she did that, his eyes closed for the last time and he was gone.

"What's going on?" Adam asked. "What was he doing here and what was this all about?"

"He came to warn me," she said through the tears. "They know where I am."

It took no time at all for those words to sink in. Adam reached down and grabbed her by the arm and said, "Come on, we've got to get you out of here."

"I need to get my purse and a change of clothes."

"There's no time, we'll get you new ones."

The urgency in his voice brought her back to reality, and a picture of a brutal, unforgiving Johnny flashed across her mind. She struggled to pull herself up, stumbling over the body. She was so weak, she almost couldn't walk. She let Adam lead her down the stairs, but they were moving so fast, she tripped where a section of the sidewalk had lifted over time from a huge tree root that had crawled under the cement. That flaw was embedded in her subconscious and normally she stepped over it automatically without even thinking. This time, however, she looked right at it and still stumbled, falling forward, but Adam had a tight hold on her arm and kept her from going to the ground.

Trent got to the car ahead of them and had the back door open. When they got to it, he almost shoved her in the back seat as he got in the front. Adam ran around to the other side, got in and put the key in the ignition. Just as he was turning it on, Trent said, "Get down, Patricia." She quickly slumped and lay across the seat without having to be told twice. Adam looked over and saw a black Mercedes screeching up in front of her apartment, with four men in black suits getting out and running up the stairs, taking two at a time. He pulled out slowly so as not to draw any attention.

Trent was already on the phone calling headquarters to fill them in. "Bring her in . . . NOW!" the voice ordered. By the time you get here, we'll have a new safe house for her." Then just as he was about to disconnect, he heard "Damn! We're just two days away from trial," coming from the other end of the line.

"Headquarters," Trent said to Adam.

Adam signaled and turned left onto the highway leading to the headquarters location about nine miles away. He felt sick thinking about just how close they had come.

CHAPTER 23

November 2003
"The Trial" (Patricia)

"I consider trial by jury as the only anchor ever yet imagined by man, by which a government can be held to the principles of its constitution."

Thomas Jefferson

————◆◆————

They had moved her to a new safe house immediately after the incident. This time, however, she was not only guarded from outside the new location twenty-four hours a day, but one of them was living inside the house with her and was by her side every minute of every day. She had completely lost any privacy, but then that was the least of her worries. She was actually glad to have someone nearby. She didn't leave the place for anything during those two days and probably wouldn't until the trial was over. Any food or supplies she needed were brought into her, but her needs were minimal.

Two days later, the trial started with the jury selection process. Patricia wasn't required to be present in court for that part. It was a

Federal Government's case against Johnny Castilletti and his gang, not Patricia Reyburn's case. She wasn't filing the charges; she was just the FBI's star witness. They knew the less she was exposed, the better it would be. Any risks they could eliminate, they did. It took almost two weeks to select a jury because no one really wanted to be selected. Most people knew of Johnny's reputation and when questioned by the defense and prosecuting attorneys, they circumvented the system to get out of serving. It was obvious they knew how to answer the questions. One by one, potential jurors were eliminated.

Questions were asked: "Have you heard or read anything about this case that would cause prejudices one way or the other?" "Yes, I've read about it and I think he's guilty" was the response most of the time. "Dismissed," came the sharp reply.

"Are you in favor of capital punishment?" "Yes, absolutely; I believe in an eye for an eye." "Dismissed," said the defense attorney.

Same question: "Are you in favor of capital punishment?"

"No, it's not our responsibility to place such a sentence on someone. That's up to the Lord." "Dismissed," said the prosecuting attorney.

She was briefed every day on what had taken place, and she started to wonder if they would ever be able to come up with twelve jurors and alternates. On and on it went until the day had finally come. A full jury was seated with alternates close by, and she couldn't help but wonder if Johnny had been able to buy any of them.

Patricia was so afraid to be in the same room with Johnny, that she shook uncontrollably every time she thought about it. Her gut told her he would get her for this no matter what happened in court. She didn't sleep even for one minute the night before the actual trial began.

While she wasn't required to sit in the courtroom until the day they called her to testify; it was her decision to be there every day anyway. She didn't want to, but she felt she had to. In light of her decision, her guards were instructed to have her at the courthouse at 8:15 for some last minute briefings. She was scared to death, but she sat in the back of the room surrounded by bodyguards and listened intently to every word because she thought it would give her an advantage when it was her turn. Seeing how the witnesses were being handled by both sides could help her be better prepared.

Sitting in the back, however, didn't ensure that Johnny wouldn't see her. He spotted her the very first day as he walked into the room in an orange jumpsuit. His feet were chained and he sported some serious handcuffs. He was bordered on each side by guards. The jumpsuit was a far cry from his Italian custom-designed suits, and it seemed strange to see him dressed like that. It almost made him unrecognizable.

His eyes scanned the room studying every attorney in their own high-priced Armani suits, the frumpy middle-aged court reporter, the stout bald-headed bailiff and finally the stiff guards standing attentively at the doors with their guns clearly visible. Then slowly, he scanned every person on every bench. She followed his eyes and knew they would eventually spot her. His eyes reached the back bench and started at the opposite end. She was so afraid, she couldn't catch her breath. She wanted to crawl under the seat, to somehow hide from his gaze, but she couldn't move; she was frozen in the moment. Fear took over and she started to tremble uncontrollably. The bodyguard to her left sensed her shuddering and reached down and grasped her leg just above her knee, letting her know he was there to protect her and wouldn't let anything happen. She was grateful for his instincts, and took a deep breath. But then it happened, his eyes reached hers and they didn't move. They were locked on her, and in that split second, she saw the most incredibly wicked look of hatred on his face that she had ever seen. The fury and rage behind his gaze was undeniable as he mouthed, "You're going to be sorry. You'll pay for this." He didn't seem to care who saw it, just so long as she did. He mouthed it clearly and slowly enough to make sure she could read his lips. It caused the trembling to start again, but it was so strong now she didn't recognize it as coming from her own body. She thought there must be an earthquake shaking the whole bench. She was going to be sick and grabbed for her purse realizing she had nothing else to throw up into. But just then, the bodyguard leaned forward putting his body in front of Patricia, blocking Johnny's view. It was only then that she was able to take a breath, look away, and try to calm herself. She put her head down between her knees and started taking long, deep breaths.

In the days that followed, she learned not ever to look his way. Most of the time she wasn't aware of him looking at her, but occasionally her peripheral vision caught his head turning around toward the back of the room, but she never ever looked directly at him again. She knew if she did, she would never be able to concentrate on the events of the trial and her purpose for being there would be in vain. She also knew, without a doubt, that whether Johnny was convicted or not, he would make sure that she was killed, and since she was convinced that she would die, she may as well do her best to make the case against him.

Every day brought new surprises. She wasn't sure why the details shocked her so much, but they did. She just couldn't believe she hadn't been able to recognize sooner how depraved this man was. His crimes were heinous, and she was stunned that anyone could be so evil. The things she had personally witnessed were nothing compared to some of the other things he had done to construct his empire. He truly was a monster.

They used violence in every part of their operations to rule their empire. They were not only into jewelry store thefts, but committed bank robberies on a regular basis, with different M.O.'s and in different cities so as not to tie them to each other. Drug rings were commonplace in a number of locations. They made millions of dollars for just a few minutes of work. The buyers made the dealers rich, and Johnny ran the dealers, taking the biggest part of the profits. He was smart, though, and paid the dealers a hefty profit making them rich too, which kept them loyal to him and kept their business thriving. Gambling and loan sharking drew in a number of suckers and when they didn't pay up, it wasn't out of the ordinary to see double and triple homicides within the gambling community. Extortion rackets were the name of their game and bloodshed was a common occurrence. Victims were beyond count. The details were nauseating.

Patricia wondered how they had gotten away with so many different crimes and why they hadn't been caught before now, but as the facts unfolded, it was easier for her to understand. They were good at what they did – so good, they never left any evidence behind. Sometimes they left bodies behind in order to get away, but no evidence on the bodies. They always used stolen cars. She had wondered why she had never seen the van they had forced her to drive, but now she knew. She learned that whenever they were about to commit a crime, they would steal a vehicle. They often drove the getaway cars just a short distance where someone was waiting for them in another car, and then they would burn the stolen car to destroy the evidence. And when they were aware the

FBI was getting close to one of their people, they had an extensive network in which to hide any fugitive. Their system was so elaborate, that getting away with the crimes was simple for them.

The information she obtained from his computer had also provided the FBI with a number of seemingly legitimate businesses that they had used to launder the dirty money. It also directed them to an old warehouse that was stocked full of tech 9 semi-automatic guns.

By the time they called her to testify, she already knew that what she had given them had made a big impact on the trial. She was finally pretty confident that Johnny Castilletti was going to be shut down. He surely would be found guilty and go to prison, and he might even get the death penalty. She walked to the stand slowly and with her head held high, placed her left hand on a bible and raised her right arm to the square. "Do you swear to tell the truth, the whole truth, and nothing but the truth, so help you God?" Without looking at Johnny, she responded, "I do." She knew he wanted her to look at him. He was sure if she did, his look would weasel its way into her head and scare her into backing away from her original claims that had been fully and carefully documented in her deposition. He didn't want her to testify under oath, but he still managed to keep his cool and didn't exhibit one iota of fear to the jurors and onlookers.

Near the end, she was asked if the person she was referring to in her testimony was in the courtroom and was then asked to point to him. She had avoided eye contact throughout the whole questioning process, but now she knew she had to look at him. She put her head down and said a quick prayer, then took a deep breath. As she raised her head, she caught a glimpse of the stars nestled in the corner of the red and white stripes on the American flag hanging restfully from the immense bronze stand to her right and suddenly got goose bumps. For the first time, she not only saw its beauty, but she felt it. This country was about justice and she needed to play her part.

The witness box was attached to the left of the massive dark mahogany judge's bench. As she looked across the bench and into the courtroom, her eyes rested first on the table where he was sitting and then to the handcuffed fists resting on the table. From there, her eyes moved to the seat behind the table where he was sitting. Slowly, very slowly, she lifted her eyes and found herself staring directly into his. They were black and dark and evil, matching perfectly the description she had given them of this cruel man. Without hesitation, she lifted her frail white hand, and pointing her finger at him said, "That's him." This time she didn't move her eyes away from him immediately. The anger she saw in his look was like a fire and she could feel the heat from where she was sitting, but it didn't burn her like it had before; instead, it engulfed her with warmth. The Lord had answered her prayer, had given her strength, and she felt with certainty that she had done the right thing. She just stared at him, and for a moment she thought she saw him shrink slightly in his chair. It was Johnny who looked away first this time.

"Thank you, Ms. Reyburn. You may step down."

It was over. She no longer had to worry about how it would go, or if she would say the right things, or if she would fall apart before she could say anything at all. She didn't have to wonder if they would misconstrue what she said and twist the meaning to benefit their case. She didn't have to agonize about holding up under the pressure. She had done well and after all these months, her part was finished.

After the closing arguments from both sides, the judge gave the jury some final instructions before sending them off to deliberate. There was some speculation that it could take quite some time for them to reach a verdict. They had been sequestered since the first day of the trial and, of course, would continue to be. Juries are rarely sequestered, but sometimes, especially in federal cases, it's deemed necessary. They can be sequestered for a number of reasons. Patricia had read up on it and discovered that The American Judicature Society lists the reasons as: 1) preventing exposure of the jurors to prejudicial publicity; 2) minimizing pressure from non-jurors for a particular verdict; 3) ensuring juror safety from harassment, threats, or actual violence; or 4) promoting a perception of fairness because of assurance of no outside influence. In this case, every single category supported the sequestering of the jurors. Maybe the thought of going home would speed up their decisions, but everyone knew this case was too important to rush.

After three long agonizing days, the jury came back with a guilty verdict on 36 counts. In the sentencing phase, Johnny was given the death penalty. Patricia felt an unexpected twinge of sadness, but it was short-lived. Mostly she was relieved.

That night she slept better than she had for over a year. She had a wonderful dream where she was lying in a meadow of wildflowers. They surrounded her in their loveliness. Bright red Poppies dotted the background, while royal purple New England Asters, cloaked her body like a blanket, warming her very soul. The white Queen Anne's Lace surrounded her face like a veil. She reached over and picked some and could smell the carrot fragrance emanating from the bruised roots. Bachelor Buttons were intertwined throughout the others, giving a pop of cornflower blue to the field. Many flowers she didn't recognize by name, but each one lent itself to the beauty of the landscape. Yellows, reds, blues, violets gave this dream the most gorgeous scenery she had ever seen. Who said you don't dream in color? The best part of all was she could see herself smiling and it felt good. She was left to sleep as long as she could that next morning. Everyone acquainted with the case knew she needed it. She didn't wake up until 11:00 a.m. She couldn't remember when or if she had ever slept that late. She wasn't accustomed to it and never had been, but she awoke feeling refreshed and happy. She smiled and felt hungry. It was going to be a great day— the beginning of the rest of her life.

That day, she pretended her life would resume its normalcy after a short time. Deep down, she knew it really wouldn't. She was well aware that she would have to stay in witness protection for a long time—years, actually, but it was fun to imagine herself hugging her mom and dad again. She wanted to make believe, albeit for just awhile. It felt good.

Later that day, Agent Gaines stopped by assuring her of her safety as long as she stuck to the plan, but he also told her that an appeal would be forthcoming. In the recesses of her mind, she knew that would happen, but hadn't allowed the thought to surface until he said it out loud. "We have to be diligent and careful until that time comes," he warned her. "They will want to find you now more than ever before."

So her fantasy was over. Her bubble had burst. She was back to living in fear and seclusion. She was sick to her stomach again and was sorry she had eaten that morning. Was life really worth living? She decided it was, at least for the time being, if only to keep more people from getting hurt by the Castilletti clan. It was better to sacrifice herself, just one lonely person, than to have countless more lives destroyed.

That evening, she got into her pajamas and slipped her tired body under the covers to one more night of sleeplessness. It simply wasn't in the cards for her beautiful meadow dreams to last. Instead, she was back to the gruesome nightmares.

CHAPTER 24

February 2009
"Departure of a Friend" (Heather & Celeste)

"But friendship is precious, not only in the shade, but in the sunshine of life, and thanks to a benevolent arrangement the greater part of life is sunshine."

Thomas Jefferson

————————•————————

I t had become somewhat of a ritual with Celeste and Heather since 2003 when they had their first girls' day out on the beach. For five and a half years they made it a habit to hang out whenever they had a day off together. Where had the time gone? It was only natural that they had become soul mates as they shared their most intimate feelings, both happy and sad, on the shores of this beach.

The warm, soft sand that had accumulated and been deposited by the continuous tides every day for thousands of years made a perfect mattress to lie on. As they spread their blankets and closed their eyes, they found it easy to drift off into an unharried world, free from troubles, or at least a world where troubles could be shared with a good friend and worked out. The sound of the waves appeared to rush up and grab their troubles and quickly swoosh them back into the ocean where they would be lost forever.

Sharing their concerns with each other seemed to divide their burdens in half, as each good friend seemed to shoulder some of the weight of the other. On the other hand, sharing their dreams and their joys seemed to multiply their source of enjoyment.

Yes, they truly had become lifelong friends and nothing would ever change that. But because they had relied on each other for the past few years, Heather was finding it difficult to figure out the best way to tell Celeste her news. The only thing she knew for sure was that the beach was the best place to do it.

They picked their usual spot and got settled in, just lying there in silence for the first few minutes, with nothing but the sound of the seagulls squawking above them. But it didn't take long for their conversation to start as each of them rambled on about their week, their work, their home, their spouse, the new store in the mall, what was for dinner and on and on. They were so comfortable in each other's company that Heather almost forgot she had to tell Celeste her news.

Then the perfect opportunity came. Celeste said, "Remember back when we first started coming here, and I was in such a state over Adam's job? I was so young and so emotional. It was a hard time for me, and I don't know what I would ever have done without you. Your friendship got me through a really rough time in my life. I'm glad the Castilletti gang assignment is over for Adam, and while he's had a number of other scary missions, none have terrified me like that one. I don't know, maybe I'm just older and more seasoned, but I still think that case was the worst. It seems so long ago, it's almost like a dream. "

This was the perfect segway to transport their conversation from the past to the present. "Yes, I remember those days well. I was so worried about you. I'm glad we're not back in that time and that you are doing well now. If things hadn't changed, I don't think I would be able to tell you what I have to today."

It took a few seconds for Celeste to comprehend that Heather had news for her, and that it might not be the kind of news she relished. As soon as it registered she asked, "What do you mean, Heather? What's going on?"

Heather paused for a minute and took a deep breath as she eyed the yellow lab running ahead of its owner barking ferociously at the waves crashing the shore. "Celeste, this is so hard for me to tell you. I've spent the past week going over it in my mind, but there is no easy way, so I'll just say it. Clark and I are moving back to Boulder."

"You're what?" she cried. "But why? When? How did this happen? Is something wrong?"

"No, everything is good. We've talked about it for quite some time, but never really acted on it. Clark's job is a great job, if you like working sixteen hours a day. But I got a call three weeks ago from Breck – you know my friend I told you about – the one whose husband died two and a half years ago? Well, she has been asking us for years now when we are coming home. Even before her husband died, she wanted us to come back, but Clark just couldn't see how he could leave his well-paying job when he didn't have anything to replace it. But she called and told us about a position that was opening up at the firm she works for and thought it sounded like an ideal fit for Clark. At first he laughed it off, but the more she talked, the more intrigued he became.

"So he sent his resume to them and within a few days they called. They wanted to meet him, and he made arrangements to fly out two days later. When he returned, he was beaming. Breck had been right; it seemed a perfect match. The CEO took him out to dinner that evening and invited Breck to join them. She raved about the firm and their benefits and seemed genuinely happy to be working there. Clark said she could have been their top sales person instead of in their Operations Division. She did a great job recruiting him.

"Then he went to see my family and went skiing with my brothers and by the time he got back, he was sold on the idea. He wants to get away from the stress, and he wants to spend more time with me. Who knows, maybe if we had more time together we could concentrate on getting pregnant, although I'm not holding my breath on that one anymore. Maybe after a year or so, we'll even try to adopt. Clark is warming up to that idea.

"Anyway, three days later, they made him an offer. It's not as much as he is making here, but the cost of living isn't as high either, and it's not a bad offer. The only thing left for him to do was to convince me. To tell you the truth, Celeste, it didn't take much convincing. I love it here in Florida, but Colorado is home. When I saw how happy it made Clark, and when I weighed all the options, I knew it was the right move. I think deep down we always knew we would end up back there. The only thing I've been dreading is leaving my sweet friend. I'll miss you more than you know."

Heather lifted her face and looked over at this great lady who had always given her so much support. A tear was running down her cheek and suddenly the smell of the salty ocean consumed her. No words were exchanged for a few minutes, but the tear said it all. It had all kinds of hidden messages in it. Finally the silence was broken when Celeste gathered her composure and without looking at Heather asked, "When are you leaving?"

"In two weeks."

That was a surprise. "Two weeks!" she screeched. "So soon?"

"Yes, he gave his notice a week ago. We've already started to pack some stuff up. They want him to start as soon as possible, but we negotiated enough time to find a place and get settled. We'll stay with Breck when we get there, but we'll be anxious to find a home."

Celeste finally looked at Heather. Her voice was a little shaky, but she asked, "Can I do anything to help?"

"Thanks, Celeste. You're always there to lend a hand, but we're planning on having a moving company do most of the work, so I think you're off the hook on this one," she said smiling. Then they wrapped their arms around each other and they both let the tears flow. It was how it should be; one sharing in the other's joy and one sharing in the other's sorrow. It was as always . . . both of them there for each other.

When they got that out of their systems, they sat and talked about everything in their past as if it were for the first time or maybe the last time. But they both knew the distance would not end their friendship. They stayed for three more hours and talked as usual—nonstop.

It was overcast and, of course it was February, a chilly sixty-eight degrees and they knew it was time to gather their stuff and head home, although neither of them wanted to. They knew this would be the last time for a girls' day at the beach and they would both miss it.

Celeste looked at the ocean and saw two small children skipping along the shore, letting out delighted squeals as the water rolled up onto their feet. They seemed to have no earthly clue the water was cold. They just laughed and played as the waves rushed to cover their tiny feet and then giggled as it receded, leaving more sand between their toes and indentations where their feet sunk in just a bit. Then they ran around in circles picking up everything that caught their eyes; small rocks, seashells, one even picked up an old stick and started making pictures in the sand with it. Everything fascinated them. Everything was a treasure to them. In that moment they were best buddies. They were all advocates for their cause, searching for their precious objects and sharing them with each other when they found a special one. She hoped she could capture this scene in her mind and never lose it. Friendship was the best treasure of all.

"Breck is lucky to have you for a friend. I'm happy for her and for you, Heather. I really am. I want the best for you and Clark. But you have to promise me that you won't forget me."

Heather laughed. "Like that will ever happen! You're stuck with me for life, kiddo." And they both knew that was true. Their bond was stronger than this separation. The miles could never destroy this type of friendship.

"Who knows? Maybe I can talk you and Adam into moving out there someday. You would love the gorgeous mountains, Celeste. We would even teach you and Adam to ski. It's totally different from the nice warm sunny beaches in Florida, but it's different in a good way."

Celeste couldn't imagine Adam every leaving the state, but she knew without a doubt that they would be making visits out there. Maybe winter vacations would be a fun diversion from the beaches. Learning to ski sounded like a fun goal.

As they walked to their car, they heard the white capped waves rushing to shore once more, but neither turned around. They just kept moving forward.

CHAPTER 25

November 2012
"The Mountains are Calling" (Adam & Celeste)

"The mountains are calling and I must go."

John Muir

———•———

C eleste was meeting Adam for lunch. They had already found a favorite eating spot in Boulder near Adam's work. They had moved out here just over three months ago, but the city was already starting to take on a familiar feel. It's funny how their lives had changed in the past year, when their options started being laid out before them like a puzzle. First the corners, then the side pieces formed the overall framework of what was to become a scene from their future. They were sure there were missing pieces that held some answers somewhere inside the mysterious puzzle box, and it was a challenge to make them all fit together. But one by one, sections started filling in, and when the final puzzle piece came into view, they knew it was time to complete the picture.

They had come out to Boulder last year for a vacation at the invitation of their good friends. When Heather and Celeste worked together in Florida both they and their husbands, had become best friends. Ever since Clark and Heather moved back to their home town, they had tried to talk them into coming out for a winter vacation, raving about the extraordinary ski resorts.

After considerable coaxing from Celeste, Adam finally gave in and they planned a vacation for a ski trip. She actually wasn't nearly as interested in skiing as she was in seeing her good friend, and she was sure Adam knew that, but it was actually on her bucket list and she convinced Adam that she had always wanted to give the sport a try. Since he had been several times when he was younger, he already knew he loved it, and while he pretended to be indulging her, he actually was quite excited about the trip.

It was so different from the beach life they were familiar with. They had often jointly questioned how Clark and Heather could possibly give up the great expanse of the majestic ocean with its white-capped waves that so effortlessly transported the soft, warm sand to the shores forming those incredible beaches. Exchanging that for freezing cold weather and a back-breaking snow shovel just hadn't seemed like a reasonable trade-off. They agreed they would never be able to get used to a change like that.

To their surprise, once the mechanical ski lift carried them to the top of the snowy mountain and they felt the crisp clean air on their faces, the first corner of the puzzle was already in place. Adam did remarkably well, even though it had been years since he had skied. He was obviously more advanced than Celeste as he carved out a path smoothly and effortlessly down the slopes. But Celeste took to it naturally, starting out with a quick lesson from Adam in snowplowing, and from there, quickly learning how to maintain control of her direction and speed by keeping both skis parallel to each other. While not as proficient as Adam, she immediately learned to love the slopes as her confidence in her ability to get to the bottom grew with each descent. The mountains had captured their hearts. Neither of them was disappointed and they both fell in love with the place.

"What's wrong with a little frostbite?" Adam had asked Celeste, then immediately answered his own question with, "It's nothing that a little warm loving in front of a cozy fireplace can't cure." They both laughed as he gave her a little squeeze, but didn't think too much more about it until they returned home to Florida.

Once they were home, they discovered how much they missed it. They started talking non-stop about the mountains, the skiing and their friends. One night Adam came home from work a little early with some take-out dinner in hand. "How about a little Chinese?" he said, holding up the sack full of little cartons. It was a rare treat to have him home early. Over the years, Celeste had become accustomed to his long hours. After his first assignment was over, she had settled into a more relaxed acceptance of his job. During the Patricia Reyburn case, she never thought that would be possible, but time had a way of making things less complicated. She was delighted to have him home early, and the aroma of the delicious food had already escaped into the room. "You get the plates, and I'll unwrap the chopsticks," Adam said with a grin. After a relaxing dinner, they climbed in bed early, turning on the TV for a bit, but not really watching. Once again they started in on what had become a familiar conversation about Colorado. "I've been thinking a lot about it and wanted to ask you what you would think about moving there," he asked.

Celeste seemed somewhat surprised, but not the shocked reaction Adam expected. "How could we do that?" she asked. "Your job and my job are here, and I do think we need to work." She laughed a little, but Adam caught the sparkle in her eyes when he mentioned it. There was no real protest, so he knew this could be a do-able thing.

"You know in April I'll be thirty-five years old. I can only be a U.S. Marshall until I'm thirty-six, so I have to start looking at other career options within the justice system. It seems like yesterday that I wanted the job so badly I could hardly stand it. It's been quite a ride, but I knew when I took the job it couldn't last forever – although back then, I didn't think it was possible for me to ever reach the ripe old age of 36. But now I figure I should start looking at what's available, and maybe this would be a good time to make a change. That is, of course, if you don't mind."

"What about my job?" she asked, without much concern in her voice. With no kids, I still want to work." Trying not to be so obvious, Celeste was secretly ecstatic with the idea.

"I've done a little research and I've been talking to Clark a bit, and he said they are in desperate need of nurses out there. It should be easy to find a job. I asked him if he would talk to Heather and get a feel for it, but he wanted to hold off until I talked to you so that he wouldn't get Heather's hopes up if you were opposed.

"You've talked to Clark?" She was genuinely surprised now. That's when she knew he was serious. "Why didn't you tell me you had been checking this out?"

"I wanted to make sure you would want to move before I said anything. I didn't want you to think I was a nutcase. But since we got back from our trip, the more we talked, the more I thought you would go along with it, so I thought it was time to find out for sure.

Don't get me wrong, though. I don't just want you to go along with it; I want you to want it as much as I do."

She was silent for a minute and when she looked up into his eyes, they glistened with a happiness he hadn't seen for awhile. "I want to Adam. I've thought about it more than I can tell you, but I put it in a secluded place in my mind, allowing it to be just a dream to refer to from time to time. I knew you had fun on our trip, but I never really thought you would consider moving. She threw her arms around his neck and laughed and cried at the same time.

"I'll tell you what; you call Heather yourself tomorrow, and I'll start getting serious about checking what's out there for me."

She looked at her watch. It was 9:45. It would be 7:45 there. "Tomorrow? Tomorrow, you say? I can't wait until tomorrow. I'm going to call her right now." She reached over him to the nightstand on his side of the bed, picked up the phone and dialed.

Adam just laughed as he felt an inner peace stirring inside. He was sure this would be a good thing for them. His thoughts carried him away to the things he would need to do, only vaguely hearing the excitement in her voice as she talked to Heather. The edges of the puzzle had formed around that corner piece.

The next day, Adam came home with a number of job openings he had printed out. It seemed there were several opportunities listing his qualifications. He talked to Celeste about each of them, but optimism was lacking in his voice and she detected it right away.

"What's wrong, Adam? Have you changed your mind, already?" She couldn't believe he could do this. Just last night his excitement had stirred a desire in her that she couldn't contain.

"No, I really want it, Honey. It's just this case we're on will be going on for months—maybe even a year. I'm dealing with some troubled youth, and I don't want to turn it over to just anyone. When I looked at who was available to take over, I just didn't feel comfortable. Those kids need someone who can understand them. Of course, they don't know who I am, they just think I'm one of them, in on their plans, sort of as a leader, but if I leave, it will be like starting over. We'll lose all the ground we've gained because it takes so much to gain their trust and get in on the inside. I want these kids to eventually understand what they are doing before the actually do it."

Her heart sank. She already knew she could get a job--Heather had assured her of that and had emailed her some job postings from her H.R. site. She had started making a to-do list, and another section of the puzzle had started filling in. Adam knew he could get something he would like in Colorado, so his section was filling in also. But now, it might all break apart. They needed those last few pieces and it might not happen. That night after Adam fell asleep, she lay there wide awake trying to bury the dream back into that remote spot in her mind. She wasn't unhappy here. She would be fine. They both would be fine. It's just that he had gotten her hopes up so high and then knocked them back down. It was like a roller coaster and she liked the anticipation of excitement at the top of the hill better than the slowing to a stop at the bottom.

A month later, Adam came home with a big smile on his face. He walked in the door and picked her up, swinging her around in a circle. She laughed and said, "Put me down!" not really caring if he did or didn't. "Just what are you so happy about?"

Adam's supervisor had been looking for a good replacement for him ever since Adam told him he wanted to move to the Colorado area. He knew it was only a matter of time. He was well aware of all his agents' birthdates and knew none of his guys would be with him as old men. When Adam got to work that morning, Bart told him he thought he had found someone he would like. Adam wasn't overly excited because he had told him that before. "It's different this time, Adam. I'm sure this guy will fit the bill."

Adam didn't put too much stock in it, but had not seen Bart show this much enthusiasm in a long time about any candidate, so he went out on his morning assignments, knowing that after lunch he had to be back to meet this *incredible prospect.*

He arrived back at the office at 1:15, knowing he had about forty-five minutes until the guy was supposed to arrive. To his surprise, when he walked into the office, Bart told him he was already there. "He's in the conference room, Adam. Good luck." Adam wasn't as excited as Bart. In fact he was a little disappointed and quite irritated that he had shown up so early. He hadn't even had a chance to go over his resume. He had planned to do that before the appointment. Adam knew Bart thought very highly of him and wasn't relishing the thought of losing him, but since he was so excited about this candidate, he figured there must be something special about him. Adam also knew Bart would do anything for him, including finding a replacement even at the expense of his own team, so he picked up his pace, walked to his desk to get the resume, and went to the conference room, deciding to make the best of a difficult situation.

He rounded the corner and opened the door. The man was sitting with his back to him, his head down, studying some papers in front of him. He walked to the other side of the conference table, then turned and held his hand out to shake. "Hi, Adam," came a familiar voice from his past.

Adam looked and tried to focus at the somewhat recognizable face and voice. He heard a slight chuckle coming from the chair across from him. He studied the features quizzically, then ever so slowly, it came to him. "Lightning!" he shouted. "What are you doing here?"

"Well, first of all, it's Steven now. Just plain old Steven Bolt, and I've come to take your job from you." He laughed as Adam walked over and gave him a big old bear hug.

They spent the afternoon together, learning about each other's lives the past ten years. Steven had been just a kid, almost sixteen years old when he last saw him ten years ago. Since then, he had gone back to school, then on to college. He got his degree in behavioral science and then his graduate degree in criminal justice, following in Adam's footsteps. After that he went back to the Palm Beach Juvenile Correctional Facility; this time as a counselor, not an inmate.

"I'm so proud of you," Adam said repeatedly. He just couldn't get over it. Steven had told him he could never have done it without him. He owed everything he had to Adam for setting an example and believing in him.

Then more reverently, almost hesitantly, he asked, "What became of your sister, Lightning?" It still felt comfortable to call him that. He was almost afraid to hear the answer. "Did you ever locate her? What was her name...Sara, wasn't it?"

Steven smiled, "Yes, Sara. She's a doll. I'm so proud of her. I searched and searched for her when I got out on my own. I didn't stop until I found her. She had resorted to a few minor legal violations in order to survive, but she never wanted to do anything wrong. She's a good girl. As soon as I found her, I took her in, working three jobs in order to support her, but I got us both into school, and we were determined to keep our grades up no matter how much I had to work. We made a pact to that effect. It involved long hard days, but I had to set an example for her like you did for me. She graduated from high school with honors, and I was so proud of her. She's going to college now, and I'm helping her with that. I owe so much to you, Adam. I've never forgotten how you took me in under your wings and how you understood me and believed in me. I swore to you I would make you proud, and I intended to keep the promise. I hope I have."

"Are you kidding? I can't begin to tell you how proud I am of you, Steven. You have made my day! Actually, my year!" He smiled. There's just one question, though. You think you're going to take my job, huh?

"Well, I'd sure like to." They both laughed. It was the perfect fit and Adam knew it. It all made sense. He couldn't wait to tell Celeste.

"Here we are," Adam said, steering Celeste's thoughts back to the present. He took her elbow and they turned up the pathway toward the front door of The Boulder Dushanbe Teahouse. The first time they had come here, it was for afternoon tea. They had stumbled on it quite by accident and when they excitedly told Heather and Clark about it later, they found out it was a favorite of the locals, including Clark and Heather. She told them a bit about its history which added even more to its appeal.

In 1987, the mayor of Boulder's new sister city Dushanbe, Tajikistan, decided to cement the relationship with a teahouse. More than 40 Tajik craftspeople carved and hand-painted the stunning ceiling, tables, stools, columns and exterior panels. Afternoon tea was offered from 3:00 p.m. to 5:00 p.m. daily, but reservations were required 24 hours in advance. Whenever Celeste knew ahead of time she was going to meet Adam, she made sure she called for reservations.

The teahouse offered more than 50 teas, but there was also a dining menu featuring various Far East and Central Asian items like Indian Samosas with Pineapple and Red Pepper Chutney or something like Mediterranean Pizza and Thai Coconut Curry. They had tried a number of menu items, but today they were each ordering their most favorite dish. Hers was Curry Chicken Wrap with roasted chicken breast, toasted walnuts, golden raisins, scallions, and celery accompanied by a mixed green salad. She had never tasted such a flavorful wrap in her life and she loved getting it there. Adam ordered his favorite, Hungarian Goulash with slow-braised beef in paprika, with tomato and spices, parmesan spatzle and sour cream.

It was nothing like their traditional beach fare, but this was fast becoming their new home.

CHAPTER 26

December 2012
"Sunshine Prevails" (Greg & Breck)

"Keep your face always toward the sunshine and the shadows will fall behind you."

Walt Whitman

———◆———

H is shower would have to be quick. Greg had worked late on an unexpected emergency, and he was supposed to pick Breck up in half an hour. He grabbed his cell phone and started to send her a text, but decided he wanted to hear her voice instead, so he pressed dial by her picture on his 'favorites' list. "Hi Gorgeous! It looks like you're going to be late to the party."

"And why is that?" she asked unable to suppress the smile on her face. The sound of his voice made her grin no matter what he said.

"Well, it looks like your date will be late picking you up."

"I hope he has a good excuse."

"He does . . . I do! You see, I was abducted by aliens this morning, and they took me to their mother spaceship. They were going to suck my brains out, but I didn't pass their tests, so they just decided to let me go. Can you imagine that? I mean the part about not passing their test?"

Breck couldn't help but laugh. He constantly amused her, but she wasn't going to let this one pass. "That doesn't sound like a very good excuse to me. If you're not good enough for the aliens, maybe I should take another look at the situation. I've probably been hoodwinked by your apparent charm. But I just might possibly be able to get another date even though it's the spur of the moment. "

"No, no, that's not necessary. But did I hear you say apparent charm? Nice! So you think I'm charming?" He heard a 'you're impossible' kind of sigh, quickly followed by an almost inaudible chuckle.

"Okay, so maybe that didn't really happen. I actually think I lost my mind on the way and it took me a half hour to find it. And then I made a quick stop at the Food Giant, and got stuck in the blood pressure monitor. Man that thing was tight. My arm was turning purple! When I finally got home, I made the mistake of answering the phone for a telephone survey and lost track of time . . . it was just such an interesting survey. Then I sat down for a minute and dozed off. I was dreaming about a basketball game, and it went into overtime. Speaking of time, my watch was set to Tokyo time. Do any of those sound like a good enough reason to wait for me?"

She was trying to process all his comical justifications so she could retaliate with a good counter, but she was laughing too hard to think straight. Finally she said, "You know, Greg, they all sound a little phony. I think you are just making excuses."

"Well I didn't want to tell you in case you would be jealous, but I had to audition for American Idol. I didn't pass their test either."

"I'm still not buying it."

"Well, do you know how long it takes to give a dollar to every Santa you see?"

"Okay, okay, that one will win you a reprieve. I'll be waiting patiently, but be ready to tell me the real reason when you get here."

"Your wish is my command. Now I have to go shower, so you'll want to be near me all night. I'll make it quick so I don't delay seeing you one minute longer than I have to."

She pushed END and the call disconnected. She smiled and sat down on the sofa. The fact was she had been ready for over a half an hour. She couldn't wait to see him. It was Friday night and they didn't have to worry about work tomorrow, so she knew they would be up very late. They had so much to talk about. They were together almost every day now, but it never seemed enough. Every time they parted, it only took her about five minutes before she started missing him. She smiled and closed her eyes, drifting off into her dream world. That seemed to be where she spent most of her time when they were apart – in her dream world.

She was surprised at how quickly he had made the decision to make a permanent move to Colorado and even more astonished at how fast he had found a job. The economy had been on a slippery downhill slope for a few years now, and there were a lot of people out of work. She knew he must have impressed them, but that was no surprise. She noticed in the relatively short time she had known him, he seemed to impress everyone. She knew he was smart and while there was a hiring freeze on most of the State Government jobs, there just so happened to be a critical need for someone who could deal with the labor relations in the Governor's office, so here he was – back in a job he knew well, but this time in her state. She was thrilled.

It hardly seemed possible that it was less than three months since they first met. It felt like she had known him for years. Not only did they have fun together, but they had a lot of the same interests. He had even signed up to volunteer at the Friends of the Hospital Sports Program that she participated in, and they had already gone to the activities together a couple of times. He loved sports, and it was obvious from the first time she saw him in a volunteer mode, he loved kids and they loved him. They had plans to go skiing with the group next week and both were looking forward to it. She loved the way he interacted with them, treating them as if they had no disabilities at all, which drew them to him immediately. It's what they needed and wanted—to be treated like anyone else, and once they got their confidence up, they really did play ball and ski like anyone else. Breck loved the fact that Greg found these kids as remarkable and inspiring as she did.

When they were together they spent time at museums, theaters, going for walks, climbing trails and even miniature golfing with a promise to hit the real courses in the summer.

One night about a month and a half ago, when they didn't feel like going anywhere at all, they found themselves cuddled closely together in the small four-foot beautifully crafted Cypress wood rollback swing on her porch, enjoying the magnitude of an incredible sunset. They didn't want the bitter cold to distract from the beauty of the sunset so they wrapped themselves tightly in thick, warm fleece blankets and glided back and forth in a rhythmic motion.

Nothing compared to its glory. The big orange and red fireball got bigger and bigger until the horizon was covered with a variety of colors. The shades of gold blended into shades of orange which in turn blended into reds that were nearly scarlet. The reds merged with purples, which turned to light lavender before fading into the blue sky. They all blended into one palate, creating an exquisite landscape in unique sky oils. The brighter the red and orange the ball got, the more intense was the pink that covered the clouds. The clear blue sky was suddenly streaked with gold, as though the reflection of the sun was a brush, attempting to paint everything in its sight. But the beauty of the sunset was way too short-lived. It battled as if in war, trying to keep the glorious shades of color dominant over the sky. But little by little nightfall crept along the edge of the horizon. With its enormous fingers covering and curling around everything in its way, forcing itself into cracks and fissures, until it finally drove the fiery ball down into a deep abyss below the earth and the darkness won the battle, eventually turning the entire sky black and ending the sun's struggle for power as it succumbed to the night. Little by little the stars peeked out, sparkling like sequins against the black night, projecting their light through tiny holes in the dark canvas and the moon and stars had their turn to shine, knowing full-well the sun would win the next battle at the crack of dawn. It was truly a scenic phenomenon, and it was theirs to share together.

When the blankets no longer kept the chill from penetrating to their bones, they went inside and warmed themselves in front of the fire, resting in each other's arms and talking deep into the night. That was the first night of intense discussions between both of them. At this point she was totally at ease divulging more about her feelings for Jeff.

In the first weeks, both of them had worried about asking too many questions about the other's past, which was natural since they were just getting to know each other. They were more inclined to just let the other one talk about their former relationships if and when they felt like it. Over the weeks, Breck had disclosed more than Greg had, but they both knew without saying, if this bond between them were to grow, they had to feel secure enough to ask when they had a question. Communication was paramount in any good relationship. For the most part, intense conversations had been avoided somewhat, touching on details only occasionally. But with the first small glimpse into each other's lives, they realized how natural and comfortable it was, and it didn't take long before they both *wanted* to share with each other. There was nothing awkward about it.

Breck told Greg in detail about Jeff's death starting with the guilt she felt for sending him out that night. Tears were shed as she described what it was like for her in the hospital, seeing him all hooked up to those monitors and the ache she felt through her entire soul when they told her he was dead. She told him how she thought she could never go on. The horror she felt was incredible when she realized she could never tell him how sorry she was or how much she loved him. She ached with loneliness when she wanted so badly to be held in his arms only to be faced with the abrupt reality that she would never feel the comfort of his arms around her again. She shared with him how she got past those first horrible months by serving others at the Children's Hospital. She explained how the Christmas gift tree tradition began the year he died and was responsible for the beginning of her road to recovery. Greg was touched and asked if he could go along with her to shop this year. Breck was delighted – mostly because she knew he was genuinely interested in the idea, and also because he wanted to share in her tradition. She felt his sincerity.

Greg knew he really wanted to be a part of her life. He asked her if she ever thought she could love anyone as much as she loved Jeff.

With her head hung, she took a minute to gather her thoughts before she responded, and in that moment of silence, Greg began to worry what her answer might be. Then she spoke without raising her head. "I loved Jeff. I loved him passionately. I still love him. But he's been gone for six years now, and I've finally come to the realization that his death was part of God's plan. I don't know how or why, but I do know it's not for me to question God's reasoning. I'm sure he is in a wonderful place and serving people. I'm also sure he keeps an eye on me and is encouraging me in countless ways that I can't explain to move on with my life. Sometimes I just feel him near. It's because of the kind of love he had for me that makes me want that in my life again." Her eyes lifted up slowly, staring directly into Greg's beautiful blue eyes, the flicker of the flames reflecting brightly in them. Quietly, almost in a whisper she said, "I'm already starting to have those feelings again, so I guess my answer is yes. I absolutely do think I will love someone that much again, and I understand now that I don't have to forget Jeff in order to move on with my life. I'm absolutely sure that he would not consider it a betrayal."

They stared at each other for a moment, then Greg lifted her chin a little higher with his finger tip and bent his head down to hers, kissing her ever so gently. She responded willingly, welcoming his tenderness. He held her for awhile with no words interrupting their thoughts. It was a comfortable feeling, and while it was incredibly easy to talk to each other, they didn't feel like they always had to be saying something. They were just as content to sit together in silence.

Greg didn't want to move or disturb the moment, but the fire was dying so he lifted his arm from around her shoulder, getting up to put a couple more logs on and poking it to intensify the flames.

He didn't want the fire to die, because he wasn't ready for the night to end. While he worked on the fire, Breck went into the kitchen to get some fresh hot chocolate. "One marshmallow or two?" she hollered.

"How about three? I want it to be as sweet as you!"

"That's impossible," she joked, as she dropped four marshmallows into the oversized mug and poured the fresh hot chocolate on top of them so they could start to melt.

"I knew as soon as I said that, it was a stupid thing to say." He called back to her. Nothing could be that sweet."

The fire was blazing now and he crawled back under the blanket on the floor, resting his back against the sofa. He picked up a picture frame sitting on the end table next to him and looked down at the happy couple. She looked astonishingly beautiful and the look on her face spoke of complete happiness. The guy looked back at him, and for a minute Greg thought he was telling him it was okay—he approved.

Breck walked back into the room and saw him holding the picture. She didn't say anything, but lowered the tray so he could take a mug. He put the picture back on the table and took the whole tray from her so that she could sit down beside him. She sat down next to him, pressing her hip against his. She took a mug and he sat the tray on the floor next to him.

"Do I see *four* marshmallows?" he quizzed with a cheerful smile.

"I want to make sure I sweeten you up," she smiled, knowing full-well she couldn't ask for a greater guy. She knew without a doubt that Jeff would approve.

"I'll give it my best shot, but I'm warning you, if this doesn't work, I'll be demanding five marshmallows next time." She smiled and her face lit up. He couldn't resist leaning over and kissing her again. Her response was warm and inviting. They stared into each other's eyes for a minute then simultaneously turned their heads toward the fire. She put her mug on the end table then rested her head on his shoulder and tucked her arm through his. She was almost ready to doze off when he spoke. "I want to talk about Parris."

She was surprised. "Are you sure? I don't want you to feel like you have to just because I've told you so much about Jeff. I want you to do it when you are ready."

"I've never been so ready to share this with anyone. I really want to tell you." He looked directly at the fire and after a short pause, he started talking.

And so the night slipped into the wee hours of the morning as they talked and talked and Greg poured out his heart and soul, this time leaving nothing out. Greg told her how unlike him it had been to fall for someone so quickly and especially before they had even met. He told her how he hadn't believed in getting serious until he had graduated and how, up until he met Parris, that had been easy. He simply had been focused and had not wanted any serious relationship until he was out of college.

"I was intrigued from the first moment I set eyes upon her. She was almost hypnotic. There was something simple and unassuming about her, yet beautiful in a special quiet way. I fell head over heels for her, and couldn't get enough of her, yet she was obviously not quite so in love with me since she never reciprocated. It was strange, though, I had this sense for some unknown reason that she felt something for me, but had to hold back, and I just couldn't understand it. She kept her distance as though she wanted to protect herself from getting hurt. Several times she almost let me into her world, but when she did, the next time I would see her, she would act like it had never happened.

"She rarely talked about herself, but one night on the beach she disclosed her story about her grandmother and how she had taken care of her. On that night, I loved her even more. I knew she needed someone to care for her because it was obvious no one ever had. I could tell she was trying to remain independent, you know, unattached to anyone, but I also could see through her exterior and my heart told me she wanted nothing more than to be close. But she was afraid of something, of that I am sure. I'm still sure of it. My biggest regret was she never felt close enough to tell me what it was. I would have done anything to help her.

Greg told Breck in detail about the times they spent together. He talked again about how Scott had stayed close and listened whenever he needed him, even though he knew Scott hadn't agreed with him. Then he told her in great detail about his last date with her at the opera, how much she had loved it, and then how she suddenly vanished after that. Breck could feel his hurt when he talked about it. She knew he had loved her with all his heart; maybe he still did.

"After she disappeared from my life so suddenly, I was desperate to find her. I went over and over in my mind everything she had ever told me, but there were few clues. I cursed myself for never insisting on taking her home. She always had a good excuse for meeting me, and something told me I shouldn't push her. Her standard answer was that it was more convenient. There always seemed to be a good reason for it, and I thought I was giving her the space she needed. I spent years looking for her. That was in October of 2003, and I tried until May of 2006 to find her; two and a half years. I wasted two and a half years of my life just searching. I looked everywhere I could think. I tried to find out where she lived, but to no avail. I tried to find her grandma, but I couldn't find any such person. It was so mysterious.

"I was absolutely convinced she needed me, so I never stopped trying, but her trail was well covered, and I never found a clue. My efforts were in vain. I felt like I was caught in this tangled web, and I couldn't get free. I was so distraught that I didn't see how I could go on. Even if she left me for someone else, or just didn't love me the way I thought, I had to see her and know she was okay; to find out her reasons. But it wasn't to be, and I couldn't find any closure.

"I went on like that for much too long. It was affecting my work, and I had no personal life at all. One day a buddy of mine at work, told me I had better get a grip on reality or I would be losing more than her."

"Look," he said, "she doesn't want to be found. It's been too long and it's time to let it go."

"Basically it's what Scott had been trying to tell me, but Scott was much gentler. Anyway, I knew he was right, but it was easier said than done. I made an effort to concentrate fully on work while I was there, and finally I was able to get back into it, which helped. I really loved my job and I couldn't afford to lose it. But my nights were miserable. I ached to see her, to find out what had happened, to know that she was okay.

"Over time, it got a little easier. I went out on a few dates, but it was never quite the same. I wondered about her for years. In fact, I still wonder about her."

Breck could feel the love Greg had for Parris, and she hurt for him. Although their circumstances were very different, it was easy for her to understand the ache in his heart that wouldn't leave, because she had experienced that same ache. It was like a dull throbbing pain that never quite left. But somehow, after several years, she had managed to get past it. She never forgot, but she found a way to manage the pain so that it wasn't so intense. But after listening to Greg, she wondered if he was really past it or if he was thinking about Parris when he looked into her eyes or when he kissed her.

"Greg," she asked, hesitantly. "Are you able to move forward now or is she still a part of your life that you can't give up? Will you ever be able to move forward? I don't mean to be pushing you, and I'll step back if you want."

He grabbed her in his arms and held her tightly, almost crushing her to him. "Breck," he said, "you are my lifeline. You are what made me realize I had been clinging to a memory that was over a long time ago. I knew as soon as I met you that there was something more for me. Something that had so much more capability of being what I want out of life than anything I have ever known before. I guess I didn't put it in the right words tonight, but I wanted you to know how that love had affected my life, but I also want you to know that it is in the past. I hold a tender spot in my heart for Parris because I really believe she was hurting over something, but I don't love her any more. It took meeting you for me to realize that. If she showed up on my doorstep today, I would be happy to know that she was okay, but I would not want to go back to that life. The fact is, Breck, I've fallen in love with you. It's a very different kind of love. It's so much more. It not only fills me with desire, but with a caring so deep that I hurt the moment I leave you each night. I want to be with you always. I know you may think it's too soon to say that, so I've been trying to hold off, but it's no use, I just have to let it out. I know beyond a shadow of a doubt that I love you in a way I've never loved anyone before, and I know that I want to be with you for the rest of my life. I didn't know when or if you would be ready to move past Jeff, but tonight after you told me how you felt, I realized it was time to tell you how I feel."

She finally pulled away from his crushing arms and looked up at him. Her cheeks were wet from the tears streaming down, but they were happy tears. She didn't say anything, just lifted her head up and kissed him with a passion she hadn't felt since Jeff. "I wanted to take it slow, but I don't know if we can," she said.

"Well, we'll have to talk about moving this relationship on a little quicker then. We'll have to start talking about some dates."

He didn't have to tell her what he meant. She already knew. It wasn't a formal proposal, but she sensed one would be coming soon. He was talking about a wedding date.

The doorbell rang and she quickly snapped out of her dream world. She knew it would be him at the door and the real world was even better. She was excited to go to the party on his arm. She wanted the whole world to know they were serious. They hadn't all been together since she met him in September, so some of them might be in for a surprise. Knowing how the word spread in this group, however, they probably already had an inkling.

She opened the door to his bright smile and felt warm all over. He wrapped his arms around her waist and picked her up so that her head was above his and she bent down to kiss him.

"I'm ready to show you off," he said.

"Well, I think they already know me," she answered. "You know I've known most of them longer than you have."

"Yea, but they probably don't know you are mine," he responded.

"Well, let's be off then."

CHAPTER 27

December 2012

"Announcements of Joy" (Scott & Samantha, Clark & Heather, Adam & Celeste, Greg & Breck)

"Everything is created from moment to moment, always new. Like fireworks, this universe is a celebration and you are the spectator contemplating the eternal Fourth of July of your absolute splendor."

Francis Lucille

❖

Scott went to answer the front door to end the incessant ringing. Someone was pushing the doorbell over and over like a kid does. He had a feeling he knew who it was. As the door opened, he saw Greg and Breck standing on the porch in a warm embrace, kissing. He was right. No one but Greg, would ring the bell quite so obnoxiously.

"Uh-hum," he cleared his throat to interrupt them. "Get in here so I don't have to let all this cold into the house."

"Well I thought it was rather warm, myself," Greg said as he and Breck stepped across the threshold into the house that was already filled with their friends.

As the door closed behind them, Breck gave Scott a quick hug then stepped away from him and started walking toward a table where the girls were chatting about the latest fashions, understanding it was a matter of courtesy to greet and mingle with the guests. It would be impolite to go to a party and not socialize. Greg walked in the opposite direction where the guys were in what appeared to be a zealous discussion about the woes of the NFL. They gave each other one last glance before they went their separate ways, communicating with their eyes that it would only be a matter of a few minutes before they could join each other again.

Before she got to the group, Breck noticed Samantha Edwards in the corner talking to Heather. It looked like the conversation was intense, and it was obvious they were whispering, but she felt as close to these two as anyone in the room, so she detoured slightly deciding to join them and scope out the nature of their discussion. If they stopped talking when she reached them, she would know it was a private conversation and would say her hellos, then join the other cluster of women.

Breck knew Scott had been seeing Samantha for some time now, but wasn't exactly sure how serious they were. She hoped he had finally found the *right one*, and it appeared he had by the look in his eyes whenever he mentioned her at work. Breck had become his office confidante on a number of subjects, and she was pretty sure she knew more about Samantha than most of their friends. She walked up to them and said hi. They jumped just slightly as they had not heard her approaching footsteps, but were relieved to see it was Breck.

"Hi, Breck. It's good to see you."

"Likewise," said Breck. "Am I disturbing you? You look deep in thought."

"Of course not. You just surprised us. We were so deep in conversation we weren't paying attention to anyone else. We were actually talking about Scott, and I'm sure you could add a lot since the two of you work together."

"Well, all I can say is, he's about the nicest guy I've ever known, and he's been an absolutely remarkable friend to Greg over the years. Greg doesn't have a bad thing to say about Scott, and neither do I. Can I ask if you are getting serious?" Then she quickly added, "You don't have to answer that if you don't want to, but I have to tell you I think you would both find each other to be a great catch."

She smiled. "Yes, I'm afraid it's beyond serious, but I promised I would let Scott give you the details."

Breck was delighted and so was Heather. They had been hoping for years that Scott would find someone to fulfill his dreams and complete his life. He was such a good guy and not so shabby in the looks department either. They couldn't understand why it had taken so long. "Maybe he just hadn't met the right one," Breck thought. She smiled and saw how Samantha's eyes lit up when they talked about Scott. Heather interrupted her thoughts suggesting they go try one of the scrumptious looking crab-stuffed mushrooms that seemed to be staring back at her from the buffet table.

The party was fun as always. Scott had a large comfortable living room with hardwood floors and space to dance. Breck watched as several couples took advantage of it, swooning to the soft music and falling in love once more.

The stuffed mushrooms were as good as they looked—maybe even better, but the appetizers were just the beginning. When they brought out the entrees, you could hear the ooo's and ahhh's as the crowd gravitated toward the aroma. The caterers walked from the kitchen with their large platters of steaming hot food, and the chatter intensified as attention was quickly drawn to the elaborate spread. The long table was set up so the guests could walk down either side, eliminating much of the usual party congestion. There was a good variety, making it difficult to choose, but there was more than plenty for everyone to try a bit of everything if they wanted. There was veal Marsala, breaded chicken, sausage and peppers, ziti in marinara sauce and for sides they served roasted potatoes, garlic green beans and coleslaw. The parties almost always rotated from house to house so that everyone took a turn, but everyone always loved it when it was at Scott's. He paid extra attention to all the details, and they always went home feeling more than satisfied. He really knew how to throw a party, and he had the space and the money to spare no expense.

People piled food on their plates and went to the various seats at the tables which had been set up around the room. Scott stood back and watched his guests admiring the food as they mounded it up on their plates. Being the perfect host and gentleman, he waited until everyone had gone through the line before he went through and got his own. Then he found his way to the seat next to Samantha that she had been saving for him. Also at his table were Greg and Breck, Clark and Heather and Adam and Celeste. It seemed like three or four conversations were going on simultaneously at their table. They stuffed the food into their mouths between sentences with little effort. Finally, Scott looked around and saw that pretty much everyone was through with their dinner, and it was almost time for the caterers to remove the platters and flank the table with a plethora of outrageously delicious desserts. He knew this was the moment he had been waiting for, so he stood up and clinked his fork on his glass several times until a hush filled the room and everyone's attention was immediately drawn to his table.

"I just wanted to say it's been a wonderful evening, having my best friends join me in my home for this party. But tonight it's more than just a party. Tonight is a celebration. I wanted you all to be the first to know, that I have asked this lovely lady sitting next to me to be my wife." He glanced at Samantha and as their eyes met, Breck knew instantly they were hopelessly in love. It was indeed a joyous time to celebrate. Everyone in the room was cheering them on as he bent over and kissed her.

"Hey, old man," Greg said, reaching for his hand then pulling him to his chest and patting him on the back with a manly hug. "I can't believe you didn't give me fair warning. I'm so happy for you...really happy, Scott," he said genuinely and sentimentally. Then on a lighter note, "And the really good thing is, she looks like she just might be able to handle you," he said, winking at Samantha.

"Thanks, buddy. I wanted to tell you, but you seemed so preoccupied these days. Have you got anything to tell me?"

"Well, yes, I was planning to tell everyone tonight, but now I don't want to steal your thunder."

"Nonsense. Let's make this a night for all of us to remember. Keep in mind it's a night for celebration."

Greg looked at Breck and she nodded. Before he could say anything, though, he heard another glass tinkling from this very table. It was Clark who was standing this time. He had the biggest grin they had ever seen. Clearing his throat, he said, "I want to make a celebratory announcement also. After many long years, I'm happy to say, well I mean I'm ecstatic to broadcast to the ends of the earth, that Heather and I are expecting our first baby in May. It's a girl!"

he shouted above the wha-hoos and cheers. "I just hope she becomes half the woman that Heather is. You know it would be pretty sad if she took after me." Everyone laughed as another round of applause erupted.

When the noise died down and the applause began to subside, Adam stood up and clanked his glass. Once again the attention was directed to their table. "Well, I haven't known most of you very long, but already we feel that this is where we belong, and we want to thank you for making us feel so welcome. We are pleased to be a part of your group and delighted to call you our friends, so we may as well share our good news with you also. Celeste and I have been trying to have a baby for a long time also. When we had been through every procedure possible and it looked like nothing else could be done, we realized there were a lot of children out there in need of a loving home, and we figured we could supply them with one, so we applied for adoption. Two days ago, we were approved, so it's just a matter of waiting now. They think it won't be too long, as we are near the top of the list." Heather immediately stood up and walked over to Celeste. They were both crying and saying how happy they were for each other. It truly was a night to remember.

Then another clink of a glass and this time it was finally Greg's turn. Someone across the room yelled, "Hey, what's with that table?" Everyone laughed.

"Well, I thought I was going to be the only one to stand here tonight and make an announcement, but it looks like I got trumped by everyone else at this table. Many of you know, and many of you don't know that for the past few years I have been living in the past, moaning about someone who would never be and not realizing until I met Breck that it had been over with Parris Roberts for years, but I was just too thick skulled to understand that. I had been hanging onto a dream that never really existed. I can't thank Scott enough for standing beside me through thick and thin and for introducing me to Breck. I know that you are all aware she has had some difficult times also, and we have both come to the magnificent realization that it's possible to love again. And that we do. We love each other more than either of us ever thought was feasible. I can't imagine a life without her and she tells me she feels the same, although I know I'm getting the better end of the deal. We're working on a date, but plan to get married soon – very soon. Believe me when I say, I can hardly wait." His voice softened as he continued, "I love this woman with all my heart and feel truly blessed to have her in my life. I don't intend to lose her." He choked up and Breck saw a tear escaping his eye, and it made her love this man even more.

Everyone cheered once more. Scott stood and asked if anyone else had any more fireworks to add to this celebration. "No, the rest of us sat at the wrong table," a voice cried out, as everyone laughed again.

"Well, then, let's have dessert. The caterers had cleared the table without anyone paying attention to them and had loaded it up with cheesecakes, an assortment of pies, and enormous plate-size cookies."

When the night was almost over, Scott and Greg stepped aside and talked for a bit. It was hard to tell if they were happier for themselves or their best friend. People started clearing up and collecting their coats, now ready to call an end to a wonderful evening. Once again, being the perfect host, Scott excused himself and went to tell everyone goodbye as they walked to the door. Everyone congratulated him and thanked him for the wonderful evening and delicious food, before stepping outside to brave the cold.

Adam had been watching Greg and waiting until he was alone. He liked Greg and wanted to get to know him better. He walked up to Greg and said, "That's great news, Greg. I'm really happy for you.
"

They gave each other a hug as if they had known each other for years and Greg said, "Likewise." He felt lucky that everyone had welcomed him into this close-knit circle and apparently Adam felt the same way. Although they both had friends who brought them together, they realized they were both the newbies in the crowd which seemed to shape an instant connection between them.

"Hey, Greg, Celeste and I have been talking and thought it might be fun to get together one of these nights.

Greg was touched by this gesture of friendship, and eagerly agreed. "Sure," he responded enthusiastically. "We would like that too. I know I can speak for Breck because she loves people and would welcome getting to know you better.

"Do you think we could get together for lunch one day this week?"

I could make it on Tuesday. Would that work for you? Do you want me to bring Breck?"

"No, Celeste can't come this week, but Tuesday would work great for me. We can chat and get better acquainted and maybe we could set up a time to go out with the girls on the weekend or do something next week. Can you meet me at 1:00 at The Boulder Dushanbe Teahouse?"

"Sounds good. I haven't been there before but have heard a lot about it. I'm anxious to try it."

"You won't be disappointed. I promise. It's become a favorite of mine and Celeste's. Adam reached for his coat and said, "Again . . . congratulations. I'll see you on Tuesday."

Greg and Breck were the last ones left, and they knew it was their time to go. He and Scott exchanged extended goodbyes and congratulations one more time, as did Breck and Samantha, then Greg put on his coat and helped Breck with hers, and they walked out the door into the cold night air. He wrapped his arm around her shoulder and they walked down the street to their parked car. "It was a lovely evening," she said.

"That it was." It's nice to see so many people's dreams coming to realization—especially ours.

"Are you tired or do you want to come over for a bit and look at some dates on our calendars?"

Greg couldn't have been happier. He was ready to get this thing rolling. The sooner the better. He smiled and gave her one quick peck on the cheek before he opened the car door and watched her slide into the front seat. "Let's do it," he said.

CHAPTER 28

December 2012

"The Truth Revealed" (Adam & Greg)

"Truth indeed rather alleviates than hurts, and will always bear up against falsehood, as oil does above water."

Miguel de Cervantes

———◆———

I t was 1:15 and Greg was waiting at The Boulder Dushanbe Teahouse. He had actually arrived ten minutes early and was now beginning to wonder if he had gotten the date or time wrong or if Adam had forgotten. But he wasn't disappointed at having some time alone to take in the atmosphere of this unique teahouse. He hadn't even had any food and already knew he loved the place.

In addition to the food selections, the menu pointed out some interesting facts, and he was fascinated as he read. The ceiling was carved and painted by hand in Tajikistan exactly as it had been done centuries ago, using absolutely no power tools. The patterns were intricately designed in a traditional Persian art form. There were twelve elaborately carved columns and no two were alike. He looked up from the menu and glanced around, wanting to take in the sights of what he was reading. How exquisite it was. He made a mental note to bring Breck here.

Back to the menu, he continued reading. Eight colorful ceramic panels graced the building's exterior and displayed patterns of a "Tree of Life." Each panel was sculpted in Tajikistan, then cut into smaller tiles, fired, and then carefully packed and sent to the USA. Once here, they were repositioned together by the original creator Victor Zabolotnikov, who was visiting and who helped with the construction. Greg had never heard of him and made another mental note to do some research on his work. It was breathtaking.

There was a pool in the center of the Teahouse surrounded by seven hammered copper sculptures created by artist Ivan Milosovich. The life sized sculptures were based on a twelfth century poem, "The Seven Beauties ."

In the middle ages, the number "SEVEN" was considered a sacred number. Both mythological and scientific beliefs of the day held that the world was divided into seven countries; there are seven planets; weeks are divided into seven days; and the spectrum is composed of seven colors.

In his youth, the hero of the poem saw portraits of the seven *daughters of the continents* in a luxurious palace and lost his heart to them. Later, when he became the Shah of Iran, he sent for the seven women and married them. He had a renowned architect build a palace with seven cupolas, each colored a different color with a corresponding planet. On the proper day of the week, he would dress himself in the appropriate color, and go to visit the wife that corresponded with the day. Each woman would relate to him a story from her native land and praise the attributes of her own color. Each of the tales was closely related to popular folklore and combined the scientific and philosophical views on the symbolic effects of the colors.

The poem inspires honesty, virtue and kindness, while denouncing arrogance, villainy, greediness and treachery. And so, the princesses' tales served not only to entertain the Shah, but to ponder life and consider the secrets of the universe and human nature.

There were stories about each of the seven beauties or princesses, and Greg was engrossed in reading when he sensed someone walking to his table and he looked up. It was Adam. "This is quite the place," Greg said as he stood and reached for a handshake. "I'll have to come again just to read more about the history."

"I know. I guess that's why Celeste and I have fallen in love with it. It has such a rich history of art and poetry and architecture all blended together. I'm glad you like it. Hey, I'm sorry I'm late. I got tied up in a meeting and couldn't break away."

"No problem," Greg said as they both sat down. "I've been enjoying it."

They placed their orders and conversation came easily. They discovered they had a lot in common and quickly realized they were going to become good friends. When their food arrived and they began eating, Adam asked casually, "So what school did you say you went to?"

"Florida Atlantic University in Boca Raton. Why?"

"Well, I worked down in that area, and I thought I overheard you saying that. I was just thinking what a small world it is. Here we are both transplants to the Denver area, coming from the same part of the country."

"Yeah, it took a move across country to meet each other when we could have met in our own backyards, but didn't." They both chuckled.

"Did I hear you say something about a girl named Parris Roberts?"

Now Greg looked surprised. He stopped in his tracks, putting his fork down slowly and looking directly at Adam wondering why he would remember her name or bring it up. "Yes," he answered cautiously. It's a girl I met at school. She caused me a lot of grief and worry, but it's over, and I'm glad to finally be able to move on. What made you remember her name?"

"Well, I thought it was an unusual name, and I guess it caught my attention. Don't know many people with a name like Parris."

Greg relaxed and agreed. Their conversation continued, but had pretty much moved in the direction of Florida. Without his noticing, Greg found himself opening up to Adam about his life there and the agony he had gone through. "I don't know what I would have done without Scott during those days."

"He seems like a really great guy. It was nice that he was there for you. It sounds like you were pretty stuck on this girl. Are you sure you are ready to move on with Breck?"

Greg paused for a minute. Not because he had to think about it, but because he wanted his words to come out in the right way. He didn't want to seem insensitive. "I'm madly in love with Breck, if that's what you're wondering. It's different than anything I have ever experienced, including with Parris. I knew at the time I loved Parris, but it was not in the same way I love Breck. I wanted Parris to feel the same for me as I did for her, and I really think she did, but she had such deep dark secrets, and I was never able to get her to move past them, so she never reciprocated my love. I agonized about her for years after her split to who knows where, wondering what could possibly have happened to her and searching for her for months. She didn't leave a single clue behind.

Since I moved out here and met Breck, I have finally been able to move on. I mean *really* move on. I can't explain it. My thoughts were so encompassed on Parris for such a long time, and I had made her the center of my world. Yet the memories of her were starting to slip, you know the little details, the way she said certain things, and I kept trying to recover and hold onto those memories. I was even having a hard time remembering what she looked like and feeling guilty over that. I wanted to hold onto something, so I just kept holding onto whatever memories I could muster. It wasn't until recently that I realized I was no longer in love with *her*, but rather with the *memory* of my love for her."

There was a long pause and both of them were in deep thought. "I wanted to hear that from you, Greg, before I decided whether or not to tell you."

That caught Greg's attention. "Tell me what?" he asked.

Now it was Adam who waited quite some time before responding, wanting to make sure he said the right thing.

Greg asked him again, "Tell me what, Adam?"

Adam looked up and studied Greg's face. He said, "Greg, I knew Parris Roberts."

Greg was stunned. "You knew her?" he almost choked the question out. "What do you mean you knew her? Do you know where she is or what happened to her?"

"I do. Let me start at the beginning. You'll have to be patient because I want to say this right. She was my very first assignment. The name you knew her by was not her real name. Her real name was Patricia Reyburn. It was the most horrendous assignment of my career and nearly cost me my marriage. She was in the witness protection program, so her name had to be changed. It's not uncommon for people in witness protection to use either their first name or their last name, simply because they tend to remember it better and avoid slipping. In Patricia's case, that was impossible because she was the key witness in such an enormous crime lord case and the mob leaders were no strangers to the ins and outs of the law. So my superiors chose to let her use her same initials and Patricia Reyburn officially became Parris Roberts.

Greg was stunned. He was trying to process the information and it wasn't easy. Absolutely nothing like this had crossed his mind . . . nothing even remotely close. He had gone over and over a million different scenarios of what could possibly have happened, but this surely wasn't one of them. He had a lot of questions, but didn't know where to start. So he blurted out, "I remember reading the trial took place, and he was found guilty, so is she still in witness protection somewhere?" Of course if he was thinking straight, he would know that Adam couldn't possibly tell him anything, even that they were one in the same person if she was still in witness protection. Normally he would have reasoned that out, but his mind was in no state to think anything through very clearly. All his thoughts were scattered and his mind was in a confused, thick haze. He was clearly disoriented.

"Greg, it was a dark time in my life too, but she was a wonderful woman, and looking back, I'm privileged to have known her. She was much stronger than she gave herself credit for, and her conviction to do the right thing was strong. The U.S. Marshals provide 24-hour protection to all witnesses while they are in a high-threat environment. It was a lot of pressure because they drummed into us that no witness security program participant who followed security guidelines had ever been harmed while under the active protection of the U.S. Marshals. I definitely did not want to be the first agent ever to be unable to fulfill my responsibility."

Adam went on telling Greg all about Johnny Castilletti and his family empire in great detail. He told him how Patricia had met him and become involved and also how she had escaped his hold. It was too much to comprehend, and he knew it would take time to absorb the whole story. Greg remembered following the Castilletti family trial in the newspapers. A big lump was stuck in his throat as he thought about Parris being involved in such a high-profile case. He could hardly swallow.

"It's no wonder she got sucked in by his money after having to work three jobs to save for school and spend all her spare time taking care of her ailing grandmother. With no parents, and all those responsibilities at such a young age, she must have been attracted to his lavish life-style. I think I can understand a little bit of how it all happened, but still, it's pretty hard to accept. I wonder what I would have done differently if I had known. Would I have tried to help her out of the situation or would I have walked away from her?"

"Greg." Adam could tell he was pretty shaken and having a hard time. He looked white and for a minute, Adam was concerned he might faint. "Greg, Patricia's parents didn't die and she didn't have a grandmother she had to take care of. That was part of her new identity. I must say, she did well to keep the story intact. Not only witnesses, but also their families have to be protected. Her parents were unable to know what had happened to her or ever communicate with her. It was the one thing that crushed her. She missed them so much and wanted badly to tell them how much she loved them, but she was well aware that if the mob ever identified Patricia as Parris, they wouldn't hesitate to try to coerce from her parents where she was hiding and possibly harm them in the process. Knowing Johnny Castilletti, he almost surely would have killed them to get the information. That's why they could never know. As far as Johnny knew, she had made the incredible escape of the century. He didn't have a clue that she had created a new life with a different name. He didn't know she was right there in Florida until the time of the trial, which was years after she had escaped from him. She knew very well that if he had known, he would have beaten her parents to get information, so she never faltered on that part of her identity cover up."

"So how did she live? Where did she live? Where did she work?" The questions were coming faster than they could be answered now.

Adam continued to take it slowly, explaining that witnesses receive financial assistance for housing, subsistence for their basic living expenses and medical care. He told Greg that sometimes even job training and employment assistance are provided and in Patricia's case, they helped her with her education, so she would be able to provide for herself after her life was no longer in jeopardy.

"I knew about you. We were all briefed that she had been seeing someone, but most of the time I was not on shift when she was with you, but I had seen her with you a few times. I knew you looked familiar when I first saw you and had been trying to place you, but that was years ago, and time tends to fade the memory."

"Tell me about it."

"None of us had any idea your relationship was that serious because she saw you rather sporadically, and we were all happy that she was finding some pleasure in life while going through this incredible trial. As long as she didn't let anything slip and remained true to her new identity, and as long as she stayed focused on the case, we were anxious to see her find a way in a world where no one would be familiar to her. Basically, she was alone at a terrible time in her life, and it was nice to see her find some enjoyment in her otherwise lonely life on occasion. We had done a background check on you and you were squeaky clean, so we didn't stop her from seeing you.

"She was getting worn down. We all could see it, and we all had feelings of guilt about it, but there was nothing we could do. The whole process was so long and drawn out. It took years from when she first came to us until it was all over, and we knew it was taking a toll on her."

Greg glanced at his watch and realized they had been talking for almost two hours. He no longer noticed the beauty of the restaurant. He just wanted to get out of there and take a breath of fresh air. All of a sudden he felt constricted and hot, and he thought he might get sick or faint or something. He could hardly breathe. He pushed his chair out from the table and was about to stand up when Adam reached across the table and put his hand on top of Greg's indicating he wasn't through. Greg knew there was more to the story, but he had to get out of there. He looked Adam in the eye and without saying anything, they both stood up together. The bill had been taken care of an hour ago, so they walked directly to the door.

It was cold outside, but after walking a short distance in silence, Greg felt renewed enough to continue the conversation. "Where is she, Adam?"

"Is this going to affect your relationship with Breck after hearing all this, Greg?" he asked, avoiding Adam's question.

Adam was pleased to see Greg smile for the first time in the last two hours. He didn't even pause before responding. "It was a long time ago and a lot has changed. I really loved Parris at the time. I'm sorry she had to go through so much, and I'm sorry I wasn't able to be more support to her, but I love Breck now. Even if I could be with Parris at this very moment, I wouldn't because I don't have those same feelings for her any more. I am glad to have the mysteries of the past resolved, to know it wasn't because of me that she was so unhappy, and that I was not the reason she left, but all I can do at this point is to wish her the very best. I am glad to know that all she did resulted in the Castilletti clan being eliminated from the crime world. At least something good came from her pain."

"Well, her pain is over now, Greg."

"She's okay, then? What happened after the conviction?"

They brushed a skiff of snow off a bench and sat down. Adam continued with the story. "I remember when the verdict was announced. She had a good night's sleep that night, and we were all happy to see the relief she felt. But just a week later it was time for the sentencing to come down. Patricia insisted that she go. She wanted to make sure she would be safe at least for awhile. As soon as they had a quick review of all thirty-eight counts and replied 'guilty' after each one, the judge declared the death sentence without any hesitation. Johnny, turned around in the courtroom and looked at Patricia with a glare that would frighten the most well-seasoned criminal, and she fainted straight away, collapsing to the floor before anyone could brace her fall. Johnny smirked knowing he got his point across, looking very pleased with himself. I'm sure he was confident that his high-priced attorneys would get him an appeal, and his plans to get even were already forming in his head."

"And ... ?" Adam asked.

"We, of course, rushed to Patricia's side." It occurred to him that he kept referring to her as Patricia, while Adam continued referring to her as Parris. "She was so frail and had a hard time coming back around. Even when she did, we kept her down and called for an ambulance. She needed to start concentrating on her health again now that it was over, and we intended to help her."

Greg was picturing the whole sordid scene in his head and could feel hot liquid tears flowing down his cold cheeks. It was like a liquid salt extract touching his lips and burning them. His heart ached for her.

"When we got her to the hospital, her vital signs were weak and after running a few tests, they decided to admit her. She had gone too long without eating or sleeping and had deprived her body of any nourishment that she needed to keep herself going. When we realized how sick she was, we also understood what a trooper she had been through all of this. Actually we all thought that before, but it really hit us when we saw her lying on that hospital bed.

"The next couple of days they rejuvenated her with IV drips, and she started getting a bit of color back into her face. She put on a good show and said she was ready to get out of this place, but she was still much too weak. On the fourth day, Agent Gaines and I went to visit her, flashing our badges to get past the guards outside her room. We were surprised to see her sitting up in bed. She greeted us with a warm smile and thanked us for putting up with her for all these years. She seemed to be at peace with herself and it was good to see."

"Sit down for a minute if you can," she gestured to a couple of chairs in her room.

We sat and went through the cursory questions asking how she was feeling and telling her she was looking great. We talked a little bit about the trial and told her what a great job she had done and how grateful we were that she had hung in there. She expressed to us how pleased she was that it was over and especially pleased with the outcome. At least now she was certain it had all been worth it. Up until that time she thought it was highly doubtful that anyone could ever convince a jury when his high-priced lawyers had all the bucks they needed to pay people to refute the evidence. She had repeatedly asked us why we were all going through this when she knew it would never have the desired outcome. But now there was calmness about her, and it was obvious she was at peace with herself.

"The doctors were here this morning," she continued, not looking at them now, but rather at her hands with her thumbs twisting around each other. "They came to give me the results of my tests and brought along a couple of specialists with them."

We both assumed the specialists must be psychiatrists because we knew she would need counseling to get through this.

"It was a surgeon and an oncologist," she said, still not looking up at them. "It seems that I have cancer."

We hardly knew what to say. It took us both by surprise. We had watched her change into this frail little figure and noticed her gaunt sunken-in cheeks. We knew she had a hard time keeping her food down and couldn't sleep because of the pain in her stomach, but we never thought it was anything more than the horrible stress she had been going through. She had all the symptoms; constant worrying, sense of loneliness, depression, aches and pains, diarrhea, nausea, eating problems and sleeping problems. I could go on and on, but the fact is we over-looked the possibility of it being anything else.

"Patricia, I'm so sorry, but cancer these days is very curable. We'll make sure you have the best of care and we'll have you back on your feet in no time. We'll talk to your doctors and see what we can do to help," Agent Gaines said.

Now she looked up at him and smiled. "You've become a good friend. I'm grateful that it was you who was assigned to this case. I probably wouldn't have made it with anyone else. But now, it looks like it's too late. I have stomach cancer and it's Stage IV. It's metastasized to my lungs and liver. It looks like it's terminal."

Agent Gaines was sick and told her there must be lots of new things out there they could try – maybe some clinical trials. He would search around for them himself. I could see he was upset with the news and knew they had formed a deep friendship over the many years even though that was frowned upon in his job. She had gone through so much and she didn't deserve this.

She proceeded to tell us that she had come to peace with it. In fact, she decided, it was the best thing that could have happened. She told us she knew she couldn't live forever as a fictitious person. She wanted to die as Patricia Reyburn, not Parris Roberts. She felt her life had really ended years ago, just not physically. "I don't want you to feel guilty or sad about this," she said. Maybe I got into this whole mess to serve a purpose. You know... putting an end to the atrocities Johnny had committed. I can look at it from another viewpoint now, and I can finally like myself. Maybe I didn't get involved because I was stupid or bad person, maybe I was sent to him because he had to be stopped, and I was the person to do it. Maybe you don't believe in such things, but I do. I finally understand, and I am okay with it. I want you to be okay with it too.

When we talked to her doctor later, he was even grimmer about any possible positive outcome than she had been. The chances were so slim, and while they might be able to extend her life a short while, the quality of her life would be incredibly painful, and she wouldn't be able to do much of anything. They had explained everything to her in detail, holding nothing back, and she had made the decision not to fill her remaining days with surgeries, chemo-therapy drugs, tests and increased pain. They told her time would be very short, and she chose to go back to her apartment and enjoy as much as possible the time she had left.

"Adam, I need to tell you that in the end she talked a little about you. As I replay her conversations in my mind now, I realize that she actually did love you, but knew it could never work out. She was afraid to ever get that close to anyone and mentioned often that when she started to, she would end it so that she wouldn't involve anyone she loved in this mess. I am sure now that she was talking about you.

"Her one request was that they let her see her parents one last time so she could explain everything to them and tell them how much she loved them and had missed them and how sorry she was. We agreed and arranged a clandestine meeting, as we still wanted to keep her identify a secret from any leftover mob members who could still make her parents' lives miserable or even kill them.

"Their reunion was highly guarded, and the love they all shared for each other was unmistakable. Forgiveness was easily given, which is what Patricia was seeking more than anything. It not only gave Patricia closure, but her parents as well.

"The time left was incredibly short; much shorter than we ex-pected. She died three weeks to the day after she saw her parents the first time. We actually arranged two more visits after that. Her mom wanted to care for her diligently, but we couldn't allow that. The risk was far too great and would put her parents in too much danger, but Patricia knew of her desire to take care of her and was grateful for the sign of a mother's unconditional love. She couldn't bare it if she were the cause of her parents being involved in some revenge plot. We had a nurse with her twenty-four hours a day to give her medications to ease the pain and to allow her to spend the time in her apartment and not at the hospital.

"Her obituary read *Patricia Reyburn* as she had wished, not the fictitious *Parris Roberts* that she had become in order to hide from the Castilletti gang. Her parents weren't at her side when she passed away, but they were there with her in spirit and that's why she died with a smile. Her last words were, 'I love you Mom and Dad.'"

Everything was out now. Greg knew the whole story. He was sobbing into his hands as they were cupped over his eyes. He needed some time to absorb it all. Adam reached over and put a comforting hand on his leg. Neither of them had noticed the cold, but now the awareness of its bitterness was suddenly cutting through them. Both shuddered wondering whether it was the cold winter air or the story causing them to tremble. Maybe it was a little of both.

"I wasn't sure whether I should tell you or not, but I thought it might be better to put some finality to your untold ending. I knew it would hurt, but my judgment told me it would be better in the long run. I couldn't have told you any of this if she were still alive because she would have been living a life in witness protection."

"I'm so glad you did, Adam. I really appreciate your honesty and your taking a whole afternoon out of your schedule for someone you hardly know. I know it will take some time for me to absorb all this, but I know you did the right thing. It's funny how I could ache so much for her, literally feeling the hurt she must have felt, yet feel joyous in her freedom. I did know her well enough to know she would never have been able to make it for an entire lifetime in that made-up world. I knew it was eating her up already, I just didn't know the cause of the real pain. I think she not only is free from physical pain now, but I believe she is happy in another world. I'm sure she has been forgiven and indeed hailed for her bravery. I think she is fine now . . . just fine, and I'm so grateful for that knowledge. My heart has been broken for so long, and just recently started to repair itself when I met Breck, but now it's as though you have performed an operation to finish the repair and I am totally free from pain."

CHAPTER 29

December 2012
"An Old Flame is Extinguished" (Greg & Breck)

"Absence diminishes mediocre passions and increases great ones, as the wind extinguishes candles and fans fires."

Francois de La Rochefoucauld

———◆———

"Can we postpone our shopping trip until tomorrow?" he asked the minute Breck's perky hello answered the other end of the line.

It startled her for a minute because he sounded so serious and never failed to greet every call with a kind of flattery of some sort. It didn't take a genius to know something was bothering him, and in a few short seconds, what seemed like a million possibilities flashed through her mind, number one being that maybe he had a change of heart. "Sure," she responded pleasantly. "What's up?"

"We need to talk."

Now she was really concerned. This did not sound like her Greg, this was some stranger she didn't know. A sick feeling came over her and her stomach started to churn. "Okay, do you want to come over here? I can whip up something for dinner."

"No don't worry about that. I don't want you to go to any trouble and besides, I want to spend the time talking. I'll just grab some Chinese on my way over. We can do our Christmas shopping tomorrow night, if that works for you. This is important, Breck."

That was a relief. If he was suggesting they just postpone their planned shopping outing until tomorrow night, it couldn't be about the two of them. Or could it? "Greg, is everything alright?"

"I've had a really rough day and just need to talk to you. I have a lot I need to tell you," he said quietly. "How about if I'm there at 6:00?"

"Okay," she answered just as quietly. "I'll see you at 6:00." The dial-tone sounded in her ear for several seconds after he hung up. She couldn't seem to put the phone down. She was baffled by their short conversation.

Greg arrived at 5:45 and she was just changing her clothes. She had only been home from work for a brief fifteen minutes and was expecting to have at least half an hour to freshen up. She knew it was him ringing the bell, and she quickly stepped into her jeans and threw on a sweatshirt. She hurried to the door and opened it just as she heard the second ring. The minute she opened the door, he grabbed her and pulled her into his arms holding her in a tight embrace. It was as if he were afraid to let go. Breck knew something was really troubling him, and the sooner he got it out, the better.

He handed her a brown paper bag filled with way too many Chinese take-out containers. It looked like he couldn't make up his mind, so he got one of everything. "I just got home, so I haven't had a chance to start a fire. Will you go start some magic in the fireplace and I'll get some plates?

He pulled her away from his hug, still holding onto her shoulders and looking directly into her eyes, just staring at her. He was silent for a moment, then shook his head in the affirmative and told her to hurry.

Breck went into the kitchen and reached for a couple of plates from the cupboard, grabbed some spoons for dishing out the food along with a roll of paper towels and a couple of forks. She felt nervous—almost panicky, as she placed the items on her gently-worn, well-loved Moorish style tray. She stalled, running her finger across the intricate pattern of the inlaid bone as she tried to imagine what was coming. She took a deep breath, trying to shake off the uneasiness she felt, then picked up the tray and walked into the living room.

The embers were already glowing and the first of the flames were leaping to nearby logs reproducing new flames and causing the warmth to penetrate the room. Greg was sitting on the couch waiting for her. She placed the tray down on the coffee table where the food boxes were waiting and sat down beside him.

He brushed a stray strand of hair that had fallen across her face and rubbed the back of his hand softly across her cheek. He stared into her eyes for a moment, then reached down and took her hand in his, feeling the softness of her skin cradled in his palm. Their faces turned toward the fire and they both stared at the flames in silence, neither of them reaching for a plate or food. She interrupted the hush and said, "Talk to me Greg. What's the matter?" She studied his face and saw his eyes start to water.

"I went to lunch with Adam today."

She had known he was going, but had forgotten. She wondered what that had to do with anything. "Oh, that's right," she responded. "How did it go?" She was trying to promote conversation.

Ordinarily that was the last thing she had to do with Greg since generally there was no lack of communication between them. The silence was not the usual comfortable silence they sometimes enjoyed, but rather, felt somewhat foreign and a bit awkward, and she was finding it difficult to know how to get him to open up. Whatever was on his mind was obviously really bothering him, and it had to be discussed. Still, nothing was said for a few more minutes. She tried to think of a good approach, but fear of the unknown kept interrupting every thought, interjecting worst-case scenarios through her mind in rapid flashes. She simply couldn't think rationally.

Then suddenly it was Greg who interrupted the quiet and started talking. She was grateful and a slight sigh of relief escaped from her. He started at the very beginning, and slowly repeated every detail of the exchange between him and Adam, as closely as he could remember, trying not to skip any element of the story. Breck didn't interrupt with a single question the entire time he was talking. She just let him tell the complete account. Once he started, she knew it was important not to disrupt the flow, and besides, there would be time for questions later. The whole thing was so bizarre, it almost seemed like fiction. When he finally stopped talking, he took a deep breath, exhaling slowly, and it was clear that he was finished. It had taken him two hours to get through it, and as she glanced at the table, it registered vaguely in the back of her mind that the food was still untouched, but neither of them seemed to care about that right now.

It was her turn now. It was hard to know what to say, but she loved this man so much and just wanted him to know she was there for him. "I'm so sorry, Greg. I know how much you loved her. Are you okay?" Then cautiously she asked, "Do you want us to take a break so you can sort out how you feel about us?" Almost dreading the answer she added, "Or do you already know?"

He got the message instantly and turned to her, grabbing her almost roughly and pressing her to him once again. "No, Breck. I don't want a break from you. I not only love you, but you are the one person I want to share everything with, and I needed to share this with someone. I'm having so many feelings simultaneously. First, I'm so very, very sad. Sad that Parris' life was so tormented by these horrible circumstances; sad that she was unable to tell me about it; sad that I was unable to help her; sad for her agony; sad for her illness and her death. But at the same time, I'm relieved that this nightmare is over for her. I can't make sense out of these feelings. They seem to conflict with each other. I feel a release of some sort, and I'm overwhelmed with the feeling of closure that has finally come to me. It feels like the weight of the world has been lifted from my shoulders, but should I be feeling that way after learning of her death? I guess there were still questions lingering in the back of my mind that were unresolved; not about love, but about what happened to her and wondering if someone had helped her in any way. All these different feelings caused me to feel a bit guilty. I keep wondering if I should feel more grief and less relief."

"Greg, are you sure you are going to be able to get past all this? Even if you don't want to take a break in our relationship, do you want to slow it down? Greg . . ?" Breck could hardly get the words out; they were almost choking her, but she knew the question had to be asked. "Greg, are you positive you don't still love her?" The fire was warm, yet shivers ran up and down her back. She was afraid to hear the answer.

"I have a special place in my heart for her. I always will. What's left in my heart is a special kind of love, but it's not a romantic love,

Breck. It's more like a friendship. I'm grieving for the loss of a friend, yet beyond the anguish, the relief I feel is indescribable. Although I've been experiencing so many different kinds of emotions, the one that is most prominent is relief. I feel a release from bonds that have been holding me way too long. I can't expect you to understand all my feelings, but I wanted to share them with you as best I could. As soon as I heard, it was as though I knew beyond a shadow of a doubt that the romantic love I had for her at one time was completely gone, and I knew you were the only person I love and want to be with for the rest of my life. I actually knew that before, but for some reason, this knowledge provided me a freedom that I had craved for such a long time."

She was crying now—tears of sadness for Parris and for Greg, but tears of joy for a future that she knew would complete her. She loved this man. She took his face in her hands, then wiped away a tear before it had a chance to work its way down his face. "I love you more than anything else in this world, Greg Williams."

"And I love you more than anything else in this universe, Breck Grayson." He kissed her softly on the lips, then on her forehead and made a circle of kisses around her whole face, until he ended up back on her lips, but this time with less tenderness and more passion.

April 2013

"Staying up all night is a waste of sleeping, and a waste of sleeping is a waste of dreaming, and dreaming is important because the more dreams you have, the better chance you have of one coming true."

Anonymous

———◆———

Greg looked around the room at all the friends he had come to know and love in such a short time. It seemed like they had been gathering together at these parties forever. Some of them actually had, even though he was relatively new to the group. Here they were all together once more at Scott's where it had all started, just last fall. It seemed like forever ago and yet it seemed like yesterday. Several different clusters had formed around the room and chatter from each group filled the space, but collectively it was indistinguishable. He studied each couple one at a time, reminiscing about what had been and contemplating what was yet to come.

He studied his childhood buddy, Scott, who had announced his engagement to Samantha Edwards in December and married her two months later in February. Samantha quickly and easily became a favorite with everyone in the group. She had a soft, quiet, humble demeanor and had that somewhat unique talent of listening to people most of the time rather than talking, which endeared her to everyone. She laughed and enjoyed these friends, but never felt the need to be the focus of their attentions. It was more important to her to stand back and let others take the lead, but she always listened and cared. There was no pretence about her. She was truly genuine, and everyone seemed to be drawn to her. Often when the group was gathered together, she could be seen standing outside the main circle of conversation with someone who had dragged her off to the side to tell her something that they needed to share with someone they could trust. And as she got to know these people, it became apparent to Samantha why Scott loved these friends so much. Likewise, they knew she was good for Scott. She made him happy and of course that made Greg happy. No friend had ever meant more to him, and he knew no one ever would. A friend as loyal as Scott comes along once in a lifetime.

His eyes followed the crowd around the room until they settled on Clark who was holding Heather's arm protectively. She was expecting their first little girl in a couple of weeks, and she looked enormous to Greg. He kept thinking she should be at home resting, but she seemed to be enjoying her time with her friends. Heather and Breck had an especially close relationship, and Greg watched as Breck caringly took a glass of punch over to her, using it as a disguise to check on her. Heather was usually the one to show concern for everyone else. Her sensitive nature lent itself to caring for others, but it was Breck's turn to wait on her for a change.

Adam and Celeste had become very close friends with Greg and Breck. They got together often for weekend date nights. While Adam would never be as close to him as he was to Scott, they had formed a special bond the day Adam told him about Parris. They shared something that had been an intimate part of both of their lives, and Greg would be forever grateful to him. Adam and Celeste had told them about their adoption plans last December, and to everyone's surprise, especially theirs, it would be sooner than they had anticipated. As they prepared for the blessed event, they thought they were ready until they learned that instead of a baby it was going to be two babies—twins! It didn't take them long to gear up for two though. Their two little boys were going to be born in May, shortly after Heather's due date. As soon as their birth mother met Adam and Celeste, she knew they were the right ones to adopt her children. She had interviewed an inordinate number of couples, but none had clicked with her like they had. Better yet, they didn't hesitate for a moment when they learned it was going to be twins. They were ecstatic. The birth mother was a fine young girl, who found herself in a predicament she had never anticipated she would be in, and she was unable to keep or care for her babies. She wanted her babies and loved them, that was obvious, Adam and Celeste had told everyone, but she was wise beyond her years and knew the best thing she could do for her babies was to find loving, caring parents, and she was so grateful to find Adam and Celeste. They had attended birthing classes and gone to all her doctor visits, and she genuinely appreciated their support. She even invited them to be present at the birth. Adam and Celeste were counting the days until they could become parents. They had already developed a deep love for these unborn infants. Greg knew they would make great parents.

He looked over his left shoulder and saw Breck walking toward him. His smile broadened as he saw his lovely wife. They had talked about a wedding date last December, and agreeing that they didn't want to wait, decided on January. They knew it was quick, but they couldn't see any reason to wait. They had a small wedding with a few close friends and family then went on a honeymoon to Bali. It was the best two weeks of their lives, but even better times were on the way. Now here they were ready for a new venture. She was already pregnant and looked more beautiful than ever. She radiated with that glow that people talk about and that other women covet. They still had four weeks to go until they would find out if they were going to have a son or daughter, but neither of them cared, they just wanted to be a family.

The evening was drawing to a close and the pregnant women needed to get home to their nice warm, comfy beds and put their feet up. It had been another great party, but they knew there would be many more in their future. Friends like this would last a lifetime. They imagined having future parties in the park on warm summer days where they could all take their children for play dates. Greg got Breck's coat, and they extended their thanks to Scott and Samantha along with their good nights to everyone else. There had been an unusually hard April snowfall, and Greg gripped her arm tightly as they went down the walk, protecting her from any possible mishaps. He wasn't about to let anything happen to her and their little one.

That night it didn't take Breck long to drift off to sleep. These days she fell asleep almost the second her head hit the pillow. Greg stared at her and thought about how lucky he was. She made him happier than he ever could have imagined. Every day he woke up feeling grateful to have her by his side.

He finally drifted off into what started out to be a somewhat restless sleep. A familiar dream began playing in his subconscious. Everything looked recognizable, and he was in a place he had remembered from a previous dream, years ago.

There was the white picket fence with children playing behind it on the grass in front of a nice home. Everyone was having fun, and he was there, playing with all of them. At first he couldn't make everyone out, but there were several children and several adults and somehow he knew which child was his own. As the haziness faded, the faces became clearer.

In one corner of the yard he could see Heather and Clark. Clark was handing a balloon to an adorable curly-headed little girl. Her hair was brown like Heather's, but she looked exactly like Clark. She smiled up at her daddy like he had given her a crown of jewels. He tied the bright red balloon around her wrist so it wouldn't fly off into the sky. As Heather turned around slightly, he could see she was pregnant again. It was another little girl. He didn't know how he knew this, but he did.

In the middle of the yard were two little boys, reaching out to try to tag the other one, each barely escaping the other's reach. They were Adam and Celeste's twins. It was amazing how much they looked like them—one like Celeste and the other like Adam. In every sense, they belonged to them. Adam and Celeste sat nearby watching them closely to make sure they didn't get too rough. They were still pretty young, but not too young to throw a punch if they didn't like how the touch tag game was going. Adam and Celeste were happy and content.

Sitting under the large oak tree, was an adorable little toddler, digging through a basket of balls, looking for just the right one. One by one the little boy pulled them out of the basket discarding them carelessly all over the lawn until he finally pulled out the small rubber football. Obviously it was his favorite. You couldn't mistake him for anyone else's child other than Greg's with those gorgeous blue eyes. Greg could see himself walking over to the tree and holding out his hands indicating he would play catch with the tiny boy who could throw the ball almost better than he could walk.

Over by the barbecue stood Samantha and Scott, who were apparently in charge of cooking the hot dogs and hamburgers for lunch. She glanced up at Scott and smiled as he reached over and rubbed her belly. She was pregnant with a girl, almost ready to deliver. Scott was the happiest he had ever been.

Greg was a little uncomfortable. He kept looking all around searching for something. Yes, something was missing from this dream, just as it had been the last time he was there. More characters had been filled in this time, but something was still missing.

He heard a noise and turned around just in time to see the eye-catching stark white Nantucket picket gate swinging open, then quickly closing as the contrasting black thumb latch automatically locked shut. A smile lit up his face as he saw Breck walking through it holding a platter of buns. Now the whole dream took a proper form, and he knew it was complete. The boundaries were marked by the white picket fence that surrounded the yard. Breck walked down the foot path toward him. Everyone was there who was supposed to be there this time. The reason he hadn't seen Parris the first time he had this dream, was because she didn't belong in this perfect picture. There had been a time and place for her in his life, but this wasn't it. That time and place so far in the past wasn't meant to be permanent, but the time and place in this dream was. He loved this woman he was looking at more than anything else in the world. Instinctively he knew it wouldn't be long before more little children filled this yard. This dream could end now. He was ready to start living it.

When he woke up, he was smiling and asked Breck if she wanted to know if they were going to have a son or a daughter. She looked at him quizzically, tilting her head and studying his face. Something inside her said, "He knows." She nodded her head, and as he looked at this beautiful woman, tears ran down his cheeks. He laid his hands on her slightly swollen belly and said, "We're going to have a son." It felt right to her and she accepted it without question.

"And guess what," he continued. She shrugged her shoulders. Scott and Samantha are soon going to be announcing Samantha's pregnancy. They are going to have a little girl."

They laughed and reached for each other. It was a happy day for them. It was a happy life. Gone were the days with the parties they had enjoyed for so long. They would happen occasionally, he was sure, but for the most part, they would now be replaced by children's play date parties.

The real-life dream behind the fence was about to begin.

Author's Notes

While the Palm Beach Juvenile Correctional Facility located in West Palm Beach, Florida is an actual youth facility and the description of the programs and the grounds is accurate according to the public information provided on their website, what went on inside between the counselors and the youth in this book is purely a figment of my imagination. Since the facility is recognized as a top-notch facility, I used my own thoughts as to how they might be treated to achieve maximum reformation of the youth, but I have absolutely no expertise in this matter, and I am not familiar with any actual cases.

All characters and scenes in the book are fictitious and are a result of my own imagination. Some places are real and some are not. Although much research was done in describing locations in the book, I acknowledge any errors of fact to be my own.